COCK AND BULL

WILL SELF is the author of many novels and books of non-fiction, including *How the Dead Live*, which was shortlisted for the Whitbread Novel of the Year 2002, *The Butt*, winner of the Bollinger Everyman Wodehouse Prize for Comic Fiction 2008, and, with Ralph Steadman, *Psychogeography* and *Psycho Too*. He lives in South London.

BY THE SAME AUTHOR

FICTION

The Quantity Theory of Insanity
My Idea of Fun
The Sweet Smell of Psychosis
Great Apes
Tough, Tough Toys for Tough, Tough Boys
How the Dead Live
Dorian
Dr Mukti and Other Tales of Woe
The Book of Dave
The Butt
Liver
Walking to Hollywood

NON-FICTION

Junk Mail
Sore Sites
Perfidious Man
Feeding Frenzy
Psychogeography (with Ralph Steadman)
Psycho Too (with Ralph Steadman)

COCK AND BULL

WILL SELF

BLOOMSBURY

LONDON · BERLIN · NEW YORK · SYDNEY

FT
Pbk

First published in Great Britain 1992
This paperback edition published 2011

Bloomsbury Publishing Plc, 50 Bedford Square, London WC1B 3DP

A CIP catalogue record for this book is available from the British Library

ISBN 9781408827413

10 9 8 7 6 5 4 3 2 1

Typeset by Hewer Text UK Ltd, Edinburgh
Printed in Great Britain by Clays Ltd, St Ives plc

www.will-self.com
www.bloomsbury.com/willself

Cock is for Cressida and Charles,
Bull is for William.

CONTENTS

COCK

A Novelette

I won't describe, that is, if I can help
Description; and I won't reflect, that is
If I can stave off thought, which as a whelp
Clings to its teat, sticks me through the abyss
Of this odd labyrinth; or as the kelp
Holds by the rock; or as a lover's kiss
Drains its first draught of lips. But as I said,
I won't philosophise and will be read.

Byron, *Don Juan*

1

The Prelude

CAROL HAD ALWAYS FELT at some level less of a woman when Dan was around. Not that she ever would have defined what she felt in these terms – and she certainly wouldn't have used this particular language. Carol had completed one third of the degree course in sociology at Llanstephan, a small, dull Welsh college. Her tertiary education was brief. She was exposed to enough of the student radicalism that was then in fashion to have been able to attach to her feelings of alienation from Dan neat tags of feminist jargon – but Carol was too insipid to shape her critique. So while men weren't necessarily stupid or chauvinistic, neither were they 'phallocentric' or 'empowered by the male phallic hegemony'. And women, on the other hand, they weren't depressed, oh no. And neither were they 'alienated'. Of them, never let it be said that their 'discourse was vitiated'.

Carol had spent long, sapphic nights at Llanstephan under the influence of a rotund lesbian called Beverley, who hailed from Leeds. Beverley lectured her on the jargon, attempting to move her from the casting couch to a speaking part in the cod philosophy. They grew tense on instant coffee and eventually fiddled sweatily with the toggles of each other's regulation bib 'n' braces.

But despite these relatively exotic experiences, Carol, the daughter of a desperately self-effacing woman and a dissatisfied autodidactic electrical engineer from Poole, was not impelled into an original lifestyle, or even inclined to complete her degree in order to counter the masculine cultural hegemony. Beverley's sour-cream flesh and probing digits failed to release whatever lode of sexual ecstasy Carol might have had locked within her narrow bosom − as did the blind−mole bumping of the seven or so penises that had truffled up her thin thighs since she started going in for that sort of thing.

This was left to Dan to achieve − by a fluke, entirely. And it was this fluke, combined with Carol's tendency always, always to take the line of least resistance, in all that she ever said, or did, or even thought, that gives this story its peculiar combination of cock and bull.

A pub-crawl down the snaking high street of a Warwickshire market town, this was the prelude to the chain of chance. In the manner of students the world over, Carol had departed from Llanstephan with two colleagues, one of whom she knew only vaguely. The vague one, in turn, had a still vaguer acquaintance with some design students at Stourbridge. A party was in the offing. The three Llanstephanites, Carol, a girl called Bea, and the boy, Alun, set off at dusk in a borrowed car and burrowed across Wales and then through night-time England in the narrow tunnel carved by the headlights.

The party turned out to be Dan's post-exam binge. Other boys, in the soul rebel uniform of tight dungarees and woolly caps, punched him on his upper arms. Carol noticed his sad, self-deprecating smile – folded in at the edges with a hospital corner – and wondered if he were quite as keen on the pub crawl as they were.

He was.

Atherstone had been selected as the crawl site, because it has the greatest number of pubs on a single street of any town in England (or Wales for that matter): twenty-two in all. The party from Stourbridge intended to start at one end and proceed to the other, downing a drink in every single pub along the way. It had been Dan's own idea.

The evening grew smokier and closer. Carol had started on gin, but soon, her head swimming, she switched to lager. At some crucial, undefined moment – finding herself staring, uncomprehendingly at the opening line of *Desiderata* ('Go placidly amidst the something or others . . .') – Carol realised that she had crossed over from being rather tipsy to being decidedly drunk.

The HND design boys clung to one another's shoulders. 'Come on, Eileen!' they shouted in parodic Geordie accents. They had prepared scorecards with the names of all the Atherstone pubs in one column and the other columns left blank for the names of the drinks, units of alcohol they represented and so forth. But by now they had given up on comparing each other's performances and instead were simply and uncompli-catedly drunk.

Carol looked at Alun and he looked at her. She realised how little he really knew these Stourbridge boys. The only real link was with Dan, whom Alun had been at school with for a couple of years in Cardiff, but they'd never really been *that* close. Carol rightly felt her own social position as even more teased out and attenuated than Alun's. But then Dan looked at Carol, and for some reason she saw some compassion in those hospital-corner creases and in his mousy forelock that pointed in the same direction – towards the floor.

They fucked on a thin foam mattress. With rasping predictability Dan entered her too early, she was tight and dry. And he came after three sandpapery strokes. But for some strange reason, some synaptic glitch, Carol came as well. Her orgasm crept up on her while she gazed in pained abstraction at an arty poster. It was the first orgasm she had ever had with a man inside her. Later, in a disoriented, boozy blackout, she squatted and peed on a pile of Dan's textbooks that lay in a corner of the room.

When she returned to the numb mattress and hun-kered into a foetal curl, she felt Dan's forelock brush between her shoulderblades, his neat mouth nuzzled her back flesh. She responded, millimetrically.

Dan and Carol were married a year or so later, and just about everyone who knew them reckoned that she had to be pregnant – but it wasn't so. It was that brief, ecstatic lancing and subsequently balmy wave that had wedded Carol to Dan, and despite the fact that the experience had not been repeated Carol still felt obscurely bonded to him. She felt certain that the feeling she had for his slight, slab-sided white body with its little brown moles was love. And his sandy hair which naturally fell into a twenties crop – the forelock arching over his sensitive brows – that too was lovable. And Carol also responded to Dan's deftness. Like many other design-oriented people Dan was good with his hands and made amusing little things out of paper and card. Their wedding invitation was in the form of a paper sculpture. On opening the card a church created itself; the little paper doors opened and disgorged a cut-out wedding party – it was terribly clever.

Carol dropped out of Llanstephan and went into digs near Stourbridge to be with Dan. She had never really got to grips with sociology anyway. It had been the only course for which she could fulfil the matriculation requirements, and Llanstephan had been the choice of the UCCA computer rather than her own. Carol's auto-didactic, electrical engineer father was disappointed, and made his displeasure felt in a rancorous wedding speech, full of twists of convoluted and pedantic irony that were lost entirely on Dan's family and guests, who, coming from more solid, middle-class homes, thought he was trying to be funny. Neither of them was religious – and the list was at Heal's.

Carol's mother was less disappointed. She knew Carol to be like herself, good when subjected to the influence of the same, but lazy and with no profound convictions. As Carol was also lithe, and pretty in the mean-featured English provincial way, it was best that she married young and was subjected to a steadying influence.

Carol was nineteen when she married Dan. Dan was twenty-one – with a year to go before completing his HND. After he had qualified, he managed to get a job with a consultancy in London that specialised in corporate identity. They moved from their one-room flat in Stourbridge to a two-bedroom maisonette in Muswell Hill, North London.

It was about this time that Carol realised that she felt less of a woman when Dan was around. That she hadn't articulated this feeling was really down to that strange loyalty engendered by their single, simple drunken coming-together. That she was unable to put it into more abstract and potentially empowering terms was due, as we have said, to Beverley's failed influence.

But in London Dan, exact in denim blouson and leather trousers, brought home fellow designers for supper or drinks. These creatures, with their padded kapok jackets and modular plastic accessories replete with winking LCDs, spoke a new language to Carol. As she learnt the vocabulary she began to understand that this world was one of potentially unambiguous satisfaction, sexual or otherwise.

And so Carol began to see Dan for what he was: slight, sour, effete, unsure of himself. She began to let it sink home that those three sudden strokes really had been nothing but a fluke.

2

Climbing on Board

D AN CALLED SEX 'climbing on board'. He'd picked the phrase up from an apple-cheeked German boy with whom he'd pulled potatoes from an East Anglian field during a short, wet summer. Now when he wanted his little bit of relief he would say to Carol over supper (which they ate sitting side by side like passengers on some endless marital branch line), 'Mind if I climb on board tonight?' or, 'How's about I climb on board later, darling?' Eventually Carol began to stare murderously at her oval platter whenever she heard the hated catchphrase. And once, as she sawed too vigorously at her M&S Chicken Kiev, a spurt of butter marinade shot from the ruptured fowl and fell, appropriately enough, like jism on Dan's tented crotch.

When he did climb on board Carol, the journey was inevitably brief and the transport was effected with little exertion by either party. The hospital corners of Dan's mouth would be tucked in a little more deeply, his breathing would flute and subside. In due course Carol would roll over to avoid the damp patch.

That Carol didn't revolt against this cramped and

pedestrian sex-life was largely a function of her pacific nature. With Dan packed off to work for the day, to add serifs to the uprights of characters forming acronyms, or remove them as the case may be, Carol found herself with lovely, indolent time on her hands. Like her foremothers, she would clean and categorise the wedding chattels from Heal's and the more recent acquisitions from Habitat and the Reject Shop. She would straighten up the maisonette. And then, perhaps, she would take a walk in the park, or a trip to the library to exchange books. For six months Carol learnt Spanish, but she gave it up when it became too difficult. She considered getting a dog or cat for companionship but she had never liked the way that they paraded their leathery genitals, so she settled for a caged cockateel instead. Something Carol was prepared to wait for was children. This acceptable catchall served to hide from Carol the extent to which nuzzling up against Dan had already, mysteriously, shrunk her womb. Whittled away at her capacity for selfless mothering. The way her marriage was developing she began to feel prepared to wait a very long time indeed.

After two years in London, Dan was promoted to head the typography team at work. This was very good going for a twenty-four-year-old. Coincidentally, he began to climb on board a lot less – and drink a lot more.

Dan was one of those people who change character when they drink. With Dan it was a comprehensive metamorphosis, as if he had forgotten his own self entirely and taken on a distinct new personal history. Of course a chronic sot, in his cups, has no memory beyond the previous two or three minutes of staggering and altercating. He is a short-lived thing, a May bug, born to live, grow, propagate and then succumb to the next spring shower – or, in Dan's case, the next shower of Lamot.

Dan was a blacking-out drunk, he was a falling-down drunk. He was the kind of drunk that knelt on dinner tables, canted forward from the waist, spewing some rubbish about a girl he had once loved in Leighton Buzzard. He was also the kind of drunk who would then vomit copiously in mid-peroration. And – wait for it – he was also the kind of drunk who never, ever, re-membered not to eat spaghetti bolognese or chicken tikka masala before he went on a binge. To put it in the modern idiom: he was a disaster area, albeit of slight proportions.

When Dan and Carol married they had both belonged to lower-middle-class sets at their respective colleges. Lower-middle-class in terms of what used to be called, in my days as an undergraduate, 'fastness'. I suppose that at more sophisticated institutions these children might have supped *drugs*. But as it was the boy students in these sets merely drank heavily and so did the girl students. Their consumption of alcohol was deemed a badge of matur-ity, of acceptance. So it was that in pullovers they grouped around curved, panelled bars, arms held aloft to form scenes of near-Canadian clubbability. Later, they would crash Mini Coopers into street furniture, or their hips into room furniture.

In spring and autumn Carol and Beverley had drunk pints of bitter in straight glasses; in summer they had chug-a-lugged Pilsner lager in bottles capped by fool's gold foil; in winter they had supped on a thick barley wine called 'Winter Warmer', which did just that. Carol had a good head for alcohol – in fact she had a spy's head for alcohol; for as she drank, her washed blue eyes grew flatter and beadier, giving an accurate, if tarnished re-flection of some pebbledashed saturnalia. That's what one felt, watching her: that as she drank, she was some-how accumulating evidence against those who got drunk. When Carol married Dan, some of the hearties that had seen them boozing together quipped that it was a case of an under-the-covers policewoman having finally cornered her suspect.

He paused. It was the first gap of any significance in his speech. For the first couple of minutes that he had been speaking, I had fretted. The storyteller had cornered me in the compartment shortly after he had boarded the train at Oxford. He was like some ersatz ancient mariner; and after a rapid-fire exchange of inanities re. weather, travel and so forth, he had teased out what was little more than a thread of conventional politeness on my part into a skein of spurious intimacy. Then he had used the train's lurch to a standstill in the orange

*evening of a rape-field as a pretext to 'tell me a story', i.e.
enfold me in this repellent tale.*

*It wasn't exactly that he had spoken all of the above in a
breathless hush, or as an onward galloping rant. It was rather
that, despite allowing his voice the full dramatic range and
cadence required to bring his, admittedly flat, characters to life,
he had then compressed this dramatic inflection into the smallest
of possible intervals.*

*As I say, I chafed under the tale, desperate to interrupt and
silence him. And then, when it became clear that he wouldn't
provide me with any polite opportunity, I succumbed to it.
When the man paused, I was thrown out completely and the
silence lay with the dust on the old, minute checkerboard of
British Rail plush.*

*But the pause did give me time properly to examine my
travelling companion, the creator of the bibulous Carol and her
saturated spouse. He was plump and his little hands formed a
fleshly cup – in direct alignment with his sagged, flannel crotch.
His nutty hair rose to form two birds' wings which swooped
across the pinkish tips of his ears. His face had the wire-biting-
into-Edam look of a man grown old with little physical exertion
and no physical danger save for the mineral drip, drip, drip of
sherry, Madeira and claret dissipation. From his grey flannel
trousers and tweed jacket, I took him to be a slightly faggoty,
fussy middle-aged don. Given his embarkation point and the
underlying snobbery of his characterisations, this didn't exactly
constitute a great feat of detection. Nor did it take the most acute
of social observers to tear away the moulded panels of his accent,
in order to reveal the very chassis of his diction. Which had*

14

perhaps been spot-welded by elocution lessons, some forty years before.

From where I sat I could watch the sun, which, in sinking, touched the edge of the Number Three cooling tower at Didcot Power Station. This rose up, over the rape, like some malevolent piece of statuary – an Easter Island god – in all its monumental bulk, evidence of some sterile and un-productive culture. The don sat in silence, his plump little arms folded.

I don't know why; I have no explanation for what I did next. I certainly had no liking for the don's story, but perhaps I felt like a disappointed cinemagoer – having paid for my ticket I'd be buggered if I was going to walk out of the film. If I couldn't have less, I would make do with more. You can see therefore, how the copula naturally insinuated itself, so:

'And . . .?' *I ventured after some time.*

'What!' *He started.*

'And – having cornered her suspect?' *What a fool! I wilfully goaded him. He thrashed at the cue, a small seal with a large fish.*

'Her suspect . . .? Oh yes, I'm sorry, I went into a kind of reverie just then, it comes upon me unexpectedly. Just as it did then – when I am in full flood . . .' *And he was off again, the train jerked into motion and the don and I were utterly alone, yellow-islanded by low wattage in the jolting darkness.*

'I don't know what it is,' *he continued. His little hands held either side of his head, as if they were contacts between which the current of thought leapt and fizzed.* 'A lapse, a fugue, a thought jamming and sparking like a severed high-tension cable between the two lobes . . .'

Dan, then . . . Dan had always drunk and always got drunk. It was just another of those things that in the beginning had made him endearing to Carol. He lost himself charmingly and entirely, like a Dervish in a whirl or a swami in a trance, and then he would recover himself the next morning at breakfast, pulling on his identity like a woolly.

'I really tied one on last night,' he'd say, mock-shamefaced, his deft fingers tucked away in the tops of his jeans pockets, his hair all tousled. 'What! Doncha remember what happened?' And whichever of Dan's floating crowd of mates had happened to be along on this particular crawl would recount its dénouement. 'You were standing by the rack, right on the bloody forecourt of the garage, man! And you'd grabbed one of those big two-litre cans of oil. You kept shouting . . .'

'Come over here and get greased . . . yeah, I know.' Dan would break in in tones of genuine remorse, the one acute phrase somehow surfacing out of the sewage morass that was his memory of the previous night.

To begin with, Carol not only tolerated, she even welcomed, the mates. 'Mates' who were elements of Dan's Stourbridge boozing set, now transplanted to London. Mates, who for convenience's sake we shall call: Gary, Barry, Gerry, Derry and Dave 1 (Dave 1 because Dave 2 comes later). On most evenings Carol counted them all out of the flat and, five or six hours later, counted them back in again. And in the morning, when Barry lay, his fat freckled forearms slapped down on the flower-patterned spare duvet, and raw, yellow callused feet sticking out over the end of the spare futon divan bed, Carol would wish him a cheerful 'good morning' and bring him a mug of tea. Then she would cook Barry (or Gary, Gerry, Derry, Dave 1 – she was quite fair) an enormous fry-up. Bacon, eggs and sausages with all the trimmings, including black pudding, for which they had all gained a taste in the Midlands. Some way through the breakfast ritual Dan would make the kind of appearance I have described above.

But then, somehow, Carol lost patience. Either that, or the character of Dan's boozing sessions with his mates changed. It was difficult to say which came first. Naturally, this very issue was the grist of the subsequent friction between them. Carol stopped Drinking (with a capital 'D') herself, and she stopped tolerating the Mates on the futon divan.

In the mornings she lay rigidly in bed while Dan, in the *en suite* bathroom, irrigated his head under the avocado faucet. The tepid water flowed over him and into the avocado bowl.

'We never fuck any more,' she said. And watched while Anne Diamond straightened her skirt on the television.

'Whozzat?'

'We never fuck any more. You've always got brewer's droop.' In moments of tight emotion Carol regressed to the tropes and figures of urban Poole, such as they were.

'Don't be vulgar,' said Dan, and he involuntarily hawked, as if to illustrate what was prohibited.

'You're always pissed.' She pursued him. 'We used to get tipsy and even pissed pissed for fun, to be sociable. We did it as a means . . . [and here perhaps *were* some of the meagre fruits of Llanstephan] . . . not as an end in itself.'

'I still drink to have fun,' was Dan's pathetic rejoinder. 'Why else would I drink?'

There, you have the measure of the man. And when she pressed him further, he said, 'I don't want to talk about it,' and left. Which, when Carol came to think about it, had always been his stock response when anything between them that smacked of emotion veered away from a treacly gooey-goo love sentimentality, or the good companionship of hail-fellow-well-met mates.

Not that Carol longed for the two of them to sit down opposite one another and dissect their relationship to-gether – as if it were a fish dinner. Everything in her own upbringing – and nature for that matter – cried out against such a course. This was not the Poole way. The Poole way with 'relationships' was a turgid misunder-standing, leading perhaps to an evening in the allotment shed shouting, or an extra valium. So Carol let it ride.

She got another caged bird, a mynah this time.

Beverley, who hadn't been in touch for over two years, arrived in Muswell Hill unannounced. Dan was out drinking with Gary. After an edgy evening watching a repeat of *Columbo*, Beverley had her way with Carol on a pile of Dan's work shirts, which were stacked on the half landing, freshly ironed and en route for storage.

This was quite different to Llanstephan nights. Beverley had brought a dildo with her, or a lingam, as she called it. She had been instructed in its use by a flat-faced Tamil woman who lived in Shrewsbury. It was a ghastly little knobkerry of ironwood. But despite that, with it inside her vagina Carol could feel a potential for pleasure in the internal contemplation of its ongoing rigidity; its failure to wilt, its determination to stay just as it was. If it wasn't for Beverley's horrible face, the schoolgirl myopia and cartoon curls (and that sour cream smell: was it sweat, or worse?), Carol could perhaps have unslipped the surly bonds of her meagre restraint and flown off into orgasmic orbit.

Carol's head thudded against the skirting board. The lingam thudded into her. Beverley's thumb thudded against Carol's perineum. Dan thudded on the door to the maisonette. 'Let us in, love,' he called, 'I've lost me key.'

He'd also lost Gary in the John Logie Baird on Fortune Green Road. However, in the Bald-Faced Stag in East Finchley, he had acquired Derek; a lapsed Methodist and fervent member of the British National Party. For good measure, by way of possessing a trinity of attributes, Derek was also a stinking piss artist.

As he came into the main room of the maisonette Derek took in the dangling strap of Beverley's bib 'n' braces with fanatic eyes, from under a dead straight fringe that must have framed a million commercial handjobs. He had them sussed. Later, when several more cans had been circulated he tangled with Beverley; calling her first a commie, then a Jew and only latterly a dikey cock-teaser. Carol thought she might have to call the constabulary, and feared for their lease. Dan slept throughout – but a man who sleeps with his head lying on a phone table can never really sleep with a clean conscience.

3

Frond

T HE MORNING AFTER the night when Dan tried to memorise STD codes by pressing his cheek hard against the booklet for eight hours, he woke up groaning. 'Gor . . .' he exclaimed to a sunfilled kitchen, 'I really tied one on last night.' There was no one to answer. Beverley and Derek had gone and Gary had never returned. Dan found Carol upstairs, watching TV-AM in bed. He cursed, seeing how the hands stood on the little clock in the corner of the screen, but he was interrupted in mid-curse. The lining of his stomach had been saturated like a sponge with alcohol, and then compressed beneath the waistband of his jeans for eight hours. He just made it to the bathroom. Carol blocked out the sound of his retching by humming, and affected not to notice when he came nuzzling back to her and slid his thin head up under the bedcovers. 'Jeez, I feel awful,' he said, 'just awful.' And then he fell asleep. Carol waited half an hour and then she called his work.

So began the era of the sick calls. With monstrous regularity, once, twice and even three times a week, Dan would fail to make it to work. From what snippets of information Carol could glean, Dan was no longer the blue-eyed boy at the design agency. They were only snippets because Dan was as unforthcoming about his work as he was his feelings. Carol knew better than to risk a direct question; that would just precipitate a re-tucking of those hospital corners and a bob-bob out the door by that by now lank and tired forelock.

Along with absenteeism came more drinking. Carol found suspect bottles of sticky liqueur and smoky aquavit in odd places: under the sink, in a hollow pouffe, behind a ventilation grille. But the novelty of unearthing Sambucca from the sock drawer, or Poire Guillaume from the pelmet, soon palled.

About this time, Dan's mother came on a visit. She was a formidable woman in late middle age. Dan had been the child of her latter, inferior marriage. Before Dan's father she had been married to a man who had made his fortune out of sherbet fountains. She was possessed of the pear-shaped figure that English women of a certain class and disposition inevitably acquire. And to go with it she had astonishing tubular legs, encased in nylon of a very particular caramel shade. The effect was one of kneelessness, tendonlessness – Dan's mother's legs, one felt, if cut into, would not bleed. They were somehow synthetic, plasticised.

She stayed for four nights. Night One: Carol cooked chilli con carne and they drank a bottle of Matéus Rosé. Night Two: Carol made shepherd's pie with the leftover mince and they drank an odd six-pack of Mackesons that Dan 'found' at the back of the fridge. Night Three: Carol made lamb chops and they drank a bottle of Valpolicella. Actually, it was a two-litre bottle that Dan had brought home especially, and he did most of the drinking. His mother didn't really seem to notice. On the fourth night Carol didn't bother to cook. Dan, maddened, shouted at her right in front of his mother, as if it were her presence that gave him the licence to behave in this appalling fashion. He stormed out of the maisonette and came back banging, crashing and ultimately puking at four a.m.

In the morning, before she left, Dan's mother took Carol to one side. She hadn't addressed Carol directly more than ten times during her entire stay.

'You remind me of myself as a young woman,' said Dan's mother. Carol looked into the uttermost denseness of her rigid coif. 'You're quiet, but you're not stupid.' Carol stared fixedly at a bad watercolour of Llanstephan that a be-scarfed admirer had once given her, willing Dan's mother not to say anything too intimate. Embarrassment wasn't an emotion that Carol was familiar with, but she did know when she should adopt a mien appropriate to someone receiving a back-handed compliment. Dan's mother went on. 'I see my son is becoming an alcoholic. It doesn't surprise me – it's in the family. My father died on a mental ward. He had been a celebrated high court judge. He had what they called a "wet brain".

'The day he died I went to visit him. He was terribly thin and his eyes glittered. He grabbed my wrist and said,

"D'ye see them?" "What?" said I. "The peacocks," he said. "They are beautiful with their radiant plumage, but why does matron let them run about the ward, it can't be hygienic." He died an hour later. My son is the same, although I cannot imagine that he is sufficiently grandiose to hallucinate peacocks. There's no reason for it, you see – it's hereditary. Try and hold out, my dear, if he asks for it I'll arrange for some help. But if things get too bad, my advice would be to leave him.'

And with that she left herself. Heading back to Burford with all sorts of goodies she had tracked down in the West End. Goodies she hadn't bothered to show Carol.

It was two nights after her departure that Carol masturbated for the first time. It is true that she had been thinking about masturbation, albeit in a rather woolly way, for some time. But she hadn't concretely imagined what it would be like, or indeed what she would have to do.

Dan was out with Derry. They had heard about some pub on the Pentonville Road where a man had been killed the preceding weekend: this was their macabre excuse for an unseasonal Oktoberfest. 'I shan't expect you,' said Carol, standing in her nightie and dressing-gown, unaware of cliché or irony. She retired to bed with a Jilly Cooper. In the book, a woman was wanked off with great expertise by a Venezuelan banker. Carol, who was no connoisseur, found the description exciting, and more importantly, technically illuminating. She put the book aside. Her hand crawled down under the covers to the crackling hem of her nightie, and lifted it. Her fingers flowed up the smooth runnel between her thighs. She cupped her vulva and then kneaded it a little. One finger slipped inside the puckered lips and sought out the damp pit of her vagina.

The access of power thrilled Carol to the tips of her carmined toenails. Of course she had been aware of the act, but the liberation from being climbed on board, or pummelled by Beverley's exhausting manipulations, was ecstatic. Carol orgasmed within seconds, one finger on the slick dewlap of her clitoris, another inside herself. The *News at Ten* theme tune drummed a counterpoint to her subsiding sighs.

This, then, was the pattern that they established: Dan went out drinking, and Carol, as soon as he was out of the way, treated herself to a really big wank. Over a period of some eight or ten weeks, she staged productions of a number of masturbatory playlets, all of her own devising. Her imagination wasn't that fertile, but we mustn't laugh at her legions of buck niggers, priapic and grinning; nor at her Latino playboys, who bore down on her riding foam-flecked polo ponies, and dismounted only to remount . . . Carol.

How those fingers flew! And how Carol discovered herself; every millimetre of damp erogenous site was mapped out. How peculiar that Dan, with his deft hands, had never bothered to discover *this* spot, had never chanced to trail his fingers *here*, or *there*.

One night Dan, Gary, Barry, Gerry, Derry and Dave 1 all took off for Ilford. Their goal was an enormous nightclub, famous for its 'caged' bar. This was mounted on concrete, enabling the young men and women who patronised it to reach fabulous levels of intoxication, and to indulge in commensurate behaviour without being able to trash, vandalise or *bemerde*. At dawn they were hosed down by thick-set men wearing dinner jackets.

In Barry's car on the way there, Dan was clearly troubled and more than usually silent. The others asked him what the problem was, but he wouldn't reply. So, in lieu of sympathy they offered him Jack Daniels.

At home meanwhile, behind drawn, patterned blinds, Carol was getting down to business. She undressed in the living room. She had discovered that the juxtaposition between her own nakedness and the room's bland formality really excited her. And furthermore, by moving around the room she could catch sight of herself in numerous mirrors and glass surfaces that had been vigorously Mr Sheened.

She undid her blouse and ran her hands over her nylon cones, seeking out the gap between breast and cuirass. She undid the buttons of her slacks and let them swish to the floor. She kicked herself free of them. *A Whiter Shade of Pale* oozed from the CD player, Carol's hand slid under the waistband of her pants . . .

★   ★   ★

'*Do you believe in horror?*' The direct question threw me out completely. I had been utterly absorbed, and, despite myself, a voyeuristic party to Carol's onanism. Now the don had broken off, without warning or explanation.

The train lurched and clattered over points, I could see the modern lines of Reading station swimming towards us out of the dusk. The don repeated his question: '*Do you believe in horror?*'

I summoned myself: 'Do you mean the occult? Beasts, demons, ghouls, table turning, that kind of thing?'

'Oh no, not that at all.' *The train juddered to a halt. People in nylon windcheaters and off-the-peg suits dis- and embarked. But even this profoundly workaday sight somehow failed to rupture the thickening atmosphere in the compartment.* 'Oh no, not outlandish horror. That's chickenfeed, mere persiflage. What I'm talking about here is *real* horror. The horror that shadows each and every aspect of the ordinary, just as surely as the darkness shadows that vending machine over there.' *He pointed at a vending machine that hung about in the shadows on the platform. A whistle rose and fell, the train jolted and moved off once more. The don shifted on his buttocks and leant forward, adopting a didactic, tutorial posture.* 'You know that poem of Roethke's, how does it go? "All the nausea of brown envelopes and mucilage, Desolation in hygienic public places . . ."'

'No, no, that's not *quite* it. But you know what I mean . . .' *His faced bulged at me, as synthetic as injection-moulded plastic.* 'That's the horror that interests me, the horror that we all feel, left alone in a living-room, in the mid-

afternoon, in the centre of a densely populated city . . .
that horror.

'There is that horror and its interaction with another
horror. The bloody horror of gynaecological fact. Modern horror films are all blood and the membranous stria
of bio-goo. But really they have simply rendered ex-
ternal what is at the very core of our dearest friends.
They have just turned inside out the sock of feminine
biology.

'So, while you wait for what is going to happen next,
prepare yourself for these two kinds of horror and unite
them in your mind. Then you will be able to calmly
assure yourself, that the muffled "bong" of that ultimately distressed spring, as you subside alongside Carol
on to one of the pieces of her suite, really *is* a reptilian
alien tentacle, lunging through the soft upholstery.'

Carol's hand travelled down, through her furze, doc-
tored to a socially acceptable flying vee. Her pinkies
scampered ahead to truffle in the gashed loam. But here,
where Carol had tactilely surveyed every pore, set the
theodolite of her hand on every mound, she found
something new. Her fingertips just skated over her
clitoris, tucked as it was under the hood formed by
her inner labia, like a tree growing in a gulley.

But en route to her vagina, in that place where there
should have been nothing but slippery anticipation, the

tipping deck before the sea, she found instead a tiny nodule, a little gristly frond of flesh.

Of course, had Carol troubled to wield her hand mirror as she had been instructed, had she placed it where Dan's mouth had so seldom been, she would have been in a position to establish the truth. She would have clocked immediately that the frond was an outgrowth of the spongiosum material surrounding her urethra – that somehow her vestibular bulb was being grossly flexed from within, pushing forth a miniature volcanic column of tissue, sinew, blood and vessel.

Now the body is an old peasant, it retains a vivid memory for felt (and imagined) injustice. Even more peasant-like is the body's tendency to retail little proverbs or sayings to its accompanying mind. A good example of this practice, so ubiquitous that it is scarcely ever remarked on, was prompted by Carol's discovery. Her finger probed. There was definitely something there, something that seemed quite large and embedded. Something that neither felt full of fluid, like a cyst; nor insensate like a wart or a callus. 'But,' said Carol's body to her mind, 'objects in the genitals, like those in the mouth, do appear to be so much larger than they really are.' And with this folksy assurance Carol let the gristly frond rest. One finger headed south to her vagina, another north to her clitoris. In due course, *A Whiter Shade of Pale* took on form and substance and became a *Rider on the Storm*; and when the rider had passed by Carol was left behind, naked and gooey, spent on the slip-on cover.

But that was not the last of the frond, oh no, far from it. For although the peasant body dismissed it in the short term as an accident, a filament of meat stuck between the teeth and swollen against the gum, it also retained a memory like an embarrassing polaroid taken at a hen party. And when Carol was relaxed and unsuspecting the following afternoon, her vile body thrust the photograph in front of her mind and threatened blackmail.

She was in Safeway at the time. She had asked a Muslim shelf-stacker where the bacon was kept. The shelf-stacker, whose uncle was a haj, and who believed that Allah struck down those who ate the flesh of the pig with cancer, did his best to give Carol the most obscure and misleading directions. As she turned away from where he knelt, pricing up tins of puréed tomato, the frond swelled up in her mind with such alacrity, that she became petrified, fearing that the awful little promontory might come bursting out of the tight armature of her jeans and elasticised underwear.

As soon as she found herself in a deserted aisle, Carol popped her fly buttons and her hand sought out the damp interior. Jesus! There it was, larger than ever! Was it just the sensitivity of her fingertips, or had the frond actually grown? Was it just her imagination, or could she, with her probing digit, actually feel some kind of structure to the frond; some internal viscosities of its own that suggested that it was not simply a raggle-taggle end of gristle, but something sensate?

The curious head of the Muslim shelf-stacker appeared around the end of the gondola. Carol withdrew her hand from her jeans and broke out in a sweat, just as if she had been discovered wanking next to the bouillon cubes.

Now, say you. You find a gristly frond growing in your vagina masturbating of an evening. What could be simpler than to make an appointment at the local health centre and in due course visit your doctor?

'What seems to be the problem?' says the doctor, a kindly middle-aged woman, the Friends of the Earth badge on her lapel winking at you in philanthropic conspiracy. You tell her. She asks you to take off your clothes and hop up on the examining table. Once there, she examines you with a care and dexterity that is in itself instantly reassuring. The examination completed, she provides you with a completely satisfying explanation of the frond: its origins, its form, its likely extent and duration. You leave the surgery with a prescription for various salves and unguents; there is no problem.

That's what you would will Carol to do, isn't it? But Carol's medical experiences hadn't been like that. Carol's mother was too inhibited ever to even say words like 'sanitary' and 'towel'. This left Carol to discover her own biology in the fullness of time. The fullness was reached in the showers at school, where Carol had the misfortune to start with a bang rather than a whimper; a thick and bloody discharge splashing over her wet shanks. Some of the other girls screamed, Carol was mortified. Her mother, fidgeting like a rat, fixed her up with 'STs' that evening.

At Llanstephan Beverley had been astonished by Carol's ignorance of her own biology. 'The female body is incredible,' she breathed at Carol, using her enthusiasm for it as a rope with which to pull herself closer. 'It is an ever-changing, self-regulating mechanism. A kind of chemical factory really. Totally unlike a man's body, which never changes, which is static and lifeless.'

That night in her blond-wood study bedroom, half wired still on instant coffee, Carol dreamt that she was an enormous chemical factory; like the ICI refinery near her parents' house in Dorset. Great twisted ganglia of pipes burst forth from her vagina, some of them emitting vast plumes of dry ice spume, others winking with warning lights protected by metal basketry. Her head was marooned far away on the esturine sand; her great buttocks were shoved up against the concrete causeway. Little men, wearing hard yellow hats and driving little yellow trucks, hovered around her anus and vagina. Carol awoke screaming.

Subsequently she was persuaded by Beverley to attend a well woman group, which met in the house of an active and sympathetic faculty member.

Here female undergraduates were encouraged to probe their breasts, their genitals, and even to worm their fingers upwards, towards their gonads. It was all designed to help them to appreciate the wonder of their own biology. Carol learned to palp for cancerous lumps, and to utilise a hand mirror in the search for cell dysplasia; so as to obviate the need for some man to perform the ritual humiliation of dilation and curettage.

Carol stuck it out for three sessions, but baulked after a demonstration of the application of a poultice of comfrey and live yoghurt to a large, inflamed pudenda. It wasn't that Carol felt that the poor girl was being hurt, exposed or humiliated (although she was all three). It was rather that some atavistic impulse led Carol to feel, suddenly but with absolute conviction, that such things were better left in the dark, where they belonged.

So, Carol had no sympathetic woman GP, friendly, and determined to adopt a holistic approach. Instead she had Dr Flaherty, the local doctor, with whom both she and Dan had registered as a matter of course within a month of moving to Muswell Hill.

Carol had been to see him once, on account of a dry heave of a cough. She judged that he was just the doctor for Dan as soon as she clapped eyes on him; poking his cropped and buffeted head around the door of the waiting room, ushering her through to his inner sanctum. For Flaherty was stinking. Stinking at three o'clock on a Tuesday afternoon. Stinking as if his whole body had been dipped in a mixture of cooking sherry and Rémy Martin. Flaherty was stinking, arsing, fucking drunk. Drunk, drunk.

He made a half-hearted attempt to persuade Carol that she needed a chest examination, but it was a feeble effort. As she left the surgery, clutching her prescription for linctus simplex, the ancient receptionist, clad in white like a nun, but with the withered face and beady eyes of a Neapolitan procuress, looked at Carol as if she were personally to blame for the distempered premises with their foetid odour.

Needless to say, Carol had not been back. But she did send Dan. It was after the occasion when he had gone missing for a full thirty-six hours. And Derry, by dint of working backwards from fuddled supposition to more lucid fact, had eventually discovered him, cuddling a bottle of Night Train, underneath Charing Cross railway bridge.

Dan returned from his consultation with Flaherty with two bits of information. Firstly Flaherty told him that what he had experienced was an alcoholic blackout, otherwise known as an instance of Korsakov's Syndrome. And secondly, Flaherty urged Dan not to worry. 'My dear boy,' wheezed the patchy and varicoloured old medic, 'you don't have a drink problem. No man has a drink problem until he drinks more than his doctor!' And then he filled the surgery with great gusts of evil, shit-smelling laughter.

Now medicine is the modern religion and doctors are our shamen, possessed of arcane knowledge and imbued with the necessary wisdom, and commensurate powers, to decoct the auguries and then to cast out the evil spirits that plague us, whether they be spirits that infest the body, or worse, spirits that infest the mind. But once one has abandoned the idea of seeking assistance from a doctor, one has instantly entered a twilight zone, a crepuscular territory, where the anatomy and its corruption through disease becomes fantastical and phantasmagoric.

Over the next forty-eight hours, Carol agonised over whether or not to see Flaherty; or to call Beverley and ask for advice; or to do nothing at all, in the hope that whatever the gristly frond was, it would just shrivel up, wither, collapse in on itself. In a word: just plain disappear. Leaving her genitals pristine, smooth, a delight to find and find again, just as she had been doing in the few short weeks since she had discovered the joy of wanking.

Carol would be ironing, or tucking in a bedcover, or making free with the Shake 'n' Vac, when the gristly frond would come teasing its way back into her mind. Her agitated claw, seemingly against its mistress's will, would once again make its exploratory journey. The frond would still be there. It could be her imagination, inflamed by anxiety, but each time her fingers prised her labia apart, the frond seemed a little larger, a little more gristly.

After forty-eight hours Carol, despite her insipid nature, was really quite upset. She resolved that in the morning she would either call Beverley, or make an appointment with Flaherty; one or the other – if not both. What swayed her and buried the issue for the foreseeable future (what a trite expression! How can a future be 'foreseeable', especially when you're growing some ghastly frond between your soft thighs), was a great life change that swept over both Carol and Dan. The herald of this life change was Dave 2, and its harbinger was Dan's mother.

Morning came, and a grey wash of light found Dan, his cheek thrust hard in the carpeted right-angle of the bottom stair. The vomit had got into his hair and down the round collar of his fashionable leather blouson. He cried over his Alpen. Those folded corners were turned into raw gutters, the better to funnel the salty stream into the Swiss cereal. Carol was not unsympathetic but she wasn't sympathetic either. She pulled the sides of her terrytowelling robe tighter around her slim shoulders, and idly noted that the TV-AM weatherman, an effete creature missing from the screen for these past two months, had now reappeared on BBC Breakfast Time, wearing a suit.

Dan blubbed as he dialled his mother. And then he blubbed to Carol that this would be the last time – the last time he would ask her to phone work on his behalf – and the last time that his behaviour would make it necessary.

'I'm stopping boozing, Carol,' he blubbed, and his deft fingers scouted and shaped the edge of the breakfast counter, as if it were some benchmark of sobriety, soon to be attained. 'I've asked Mum for help. I knew that she would know what to do. She's sending someone to see me this evening, someone called Dave. He's going to take me to a kind of meeting.'

All day Dan lurked around the house, propping his

pounding head against door jambs and patterned cushion covers. God, how his hangdog look infuriated Carol! Never before, not even in his cups, had Dan disgusted her as he disgusted her now. He was such a turn-off. And now he was giving in to his mother, accepting her estimation of him and seeking her help. This was weakness run rampant.

That afternoon Carol went to the pet-shop at the Quadrant. They had had a fresh delivery of cuttlefish. Carol brought back two pieces, one for the mynah and one for the cockateel. The cuttlefish was white, dry and light in her hand, like a bleached bone. She pushed it through the wire bars. The birds looked at her with their solo-eyed, insectoid stares. Dan came up behind her, she could feel his forelocked head nuzzling between her shoulderblades. She shrugged him off. In the kitchen, while she waited for the kettle to boil, she could hear Dan in the living-room, still blubbing.

4

Dave 2

D AVE 2'S REAL SURNAME was Hobbes, and his
parents still lived in Shepton Mallet. Had Dave
2 not had the great good fortune to be an alcoholic,
one feels that he might well have struggled for some
time to find his true vocation, that of religious
whipper-in; spiritual barker; moral double-glazing
salesman. For that was Dave 2. He was the man
on the door with a ready grin and a quip for the
wavering punter. He was a universal type. One could
imagine him in all times and at all places: wearing a
toga and explaining the fish symbol, or resplendent in
a round-collared tunic, Marxist catechism in hand,
drumming home the simplified fallacies of Dialectical
Materialism.

But given the particular historical moment within
which he found himself, Dave 2's chronic alcoholism
had provided him with a passport to Alcoholics Anonymous. The AA dogma was loosely based on Christian
principles, but there was a residual zeal for low church
liturgy and ritual that, in the hands of types like Dave
2, all too quickly fanned up into a witch-burning
Salemite passion. For, as William James so justly

remarked, the only known cure for dipsomania *is* religiomania.

And, at this juncture, the poofy old don paused again. He got out from his inside pocket one of those Mahawat cigarillos that were popular in the mid-seventies. He put it in his pink little mouth and lit it with a rolled-gold Dunhill lighter.

The props and the deft blocking that made up the whole performance were so in keeping with his soft countenance and the faggy invective that laced his tale that I became slightly uneasy . . . This sardonic, effete don with his amusing if mordant story . . . Damn it all, he had to be too good to be true.

The lights had gone out in the carriage, and we had ground to a halt again, while an Inter-City 125 whooshed past on the main line. The tip of the cigarillo glowed and dimmed in the close darkness. He cleared his throat with a click of firm sputum on palate, and continued.

Dave 2 was of that opinion himself. 'I'm fortunate to be what I call – and I hope you'll pardon my French, ladies – a pisshead. Yeah, I'm fortunate to be a pisshead. You want'er know why? Because it's brought me to a spiritual life: a life of the spirit. Oh, and why pisshead? Because sometimes I would get so drunk that I would piss all over myself. I was completely incontinent, totally, completely. So that's what I was – literally a pisshead.'

But being a pisshead had really been the least of it.

Indeed, given Dave 2's accounts of some of his more extreme intoxicated behaviour one might almost have said that had he *confined* himself to pissing on his own head, he would have been almost socially acceptable.

For, compared to Dave 2's lapses in memory and consequent losses of identity, Dan's escapades were mere awaydays. With Dave 2 we can see the compass of the whole Grand Tour.

Dave 2 had once had an alcoholic blackout that was so long that during it he had joined the army, gone through basic training and been dishonourably discharged, for, guess what, drunkenness.

And if you don't believe that this is possible, then spend an evening with Dave 2 and his cronies, because they know more about alcoholism in all its manifestations than an institute full of experts, and they are very keen to impart. So keen that a session with them is more tedious and introverted than being stuck on a desert island with a tour-load of constipated, bourgeois, middle-aged French women.

But of all this Dan and Carol were unaware. Instead, from the moment Dave 2 arrived at the maisonette in Melrose Mansions, both of them were captivated by his vitality, his immediacy; the way he seemed to smash into shards the very quiddity of a continuum in their lives that they had always assumed to be of the consistency of the toughest Tupperware.

'Bing-bong' went the door chimes at seven o'clock. Dave 2 stood in the vestibule, arms akimbo, jaw lanterned, a thatch of thick sandy hair tilted sideways on his head, so that one edge touched the collar of his army surplus fatigue jacket. This garment was Dave 2's trademark. He called it 'my uniform'. It was re-equipped for the campaign each and every day. One hip-dangling pocket was stuffed to overflowing with mock-gold flip-top boxes of Benson and Hedges Special Filter, and the other was usually stretched to its seams with some work or works of an improving or a spiritual nature. Books with titles like *Why Am I Afraid to Tell You Who I am?* or *Why Are You Afraid to Tell Me Who You Are?* and even the blunter and more comprehensive *Why Are We Afraid?*

Dave 2 then, lowering in the vestibule, under the neat certainty of the sconce, says to Carol, 'Dave, Dave Hobbes. I've come to pick up . . . Dan?' He said the name as if not quite sure, and an appealing glance seemed to come up at Carol from his yellow eyes. Seemed to, because it was a trick, an illusion. Dave 2 stood at least a foot taller than Carol, but constant abasements and attempts to achieve perfect humility had given him the ability to alter his height at will.

And Dave 2 saw a thinnish, blondish young woman, her flat hair trained behind lobeless ears. She had flawless skin, but it did have some kind of a waxy patina; and there was also an oddly collapsing aspect to her midriff, as if Carol were a card table in the process of being vertically folded for storage purposes. Dave 2 said later of this encounter and the first impressions he associated with it, 'It was obvious that she was ready for help, that she had reached her own personal Waterloo . . . She was all sort of faded and wrung out, weren't you?' And at this point he would turn to Carol, sitting next to him in the circle of chairs, radiant in white chemise, and she would radiantly smile her assent.

But when she opened the front door to Dave 2 this lay some weeks and several group meetings in the future. For the meantime, she just invited him in. Dan skulked off to get ready. He still had the adolescent awkwardness that makes a hash out of introductions. Dave 2, cosy with instant coffee and a fag in the kitchen said, 'He's awfully young, but if he's had enough, Carol m'dear, this could be the turning point for him.'

Dave 2 leaned across the breakfast counter and took Carol's forearm gently in between the thumb and forefinger of his huge, freckled right hand. This was a characteristic gesture of Dave 2's, and as usual, it came accompanied by a special, more spiritually intense, lowering of his burry West Country voice. 'You look all in, m'dear,' said Dave 2. 'I don't wonder that you haven't had a hell of a time coping with him.'

Carol tried not to shrug. She didn't want to do anything that might cause the grip of those fingers to tighten on her. She said, 'Oh, I don't know, it hasn't been too bad.' But Dave 2 wasn't taking 'not too bad' for an answer. This was a man who *firmly* believed that the word *fine*, as in 'I'm feeling fine', was really an acronym, spelling out Fucked-up, Insecure, Neurotic and

Emotional. Indeed, when Dan had become quite integrated into the St Simon's group, he was set to work by Dave 2, labouring, with a magic marker in his fine hands, to create a series of signs. In some, the acronym and its interpretation was written in sans serif characters, in others in serif script. It was all rather like what Dan did for a living anyway.

So, Dave 2 pressed on, undeterred: 'You say it hasn't been too bad, m'dear, but I can see that in here you're hurting.' Dave 2 removed the large hand from Carol's forearm and placed it in the vague area of his heart. His great chin filled up with dimples and his cheeks creased as his long face took on an expression that was obviously intended to betoken deep sympathy, or even empathy . . . yes empathy, for Dave 2, unchallenged by Carol, followed on: 'I can identify with your hurt, Carol. I've felt as you have – utterly indifferent to the fate of someone I once thought I loved. Utterly indifferent. Now that's what this awful disease can do to us, my love . . .' That was clever. Even Carol couldn't help but be jarred, and appalled, by the accuracy of Dave 2's probing spiritual diagnosis. In that moment of shared feeling Dave 2 hooked his nail under the scab of Carol's indifference and prised it up, exposing an area of pain. Of course Dave 2 could hardly have been expected to know that her real and abiding anxiety was centred not on Dan, nor even on the fact of her marriage, but entirely on the gristly frond that lay in wait at the very juncture of her thighs.

Instant coffee downed and a thin and wispy Dan buckled into his fashionable leather blouson, there was but token resistance on Carol's part to the suggestion that she accompany Dave 2 and his charge to St Simon's, and while they attended the Alcoholics Anonymous meeting she should attend an adjacent and highly congruent meeting for the relatives of alcoholics.

The atmosphere of the Al Anon meeting was a revelation to Carol. Here was the intimacy and sense of shared purpose that she had been exposed to when attempting to raise her consciousness with Beverley at Llanstephan, but united with a social veneer and sense of organisation that reminded her more of her father's allotment society.

She was shocked by the candour of these very English people in macs and cardigans who described in a matter-of-fact, if confessional, manner, episodes of the most disgusting drunkenness, domestic violence and sexual abuse.

A long, sad lady in a fawn suit recounted in a breathless rush the frenzied assaults that her husband, a bibulous and failed salesman, had made on her several orifices with various hard and vitreous objects, beer bottles and the like.

A middle-aged educationalist, intellectual with thinning hair and tortoiseshell bifocals, did his best to describe, plainly and directly, the obsessive dossier he had felt compelled to compile of the vomitings, douchings, colonic purges and gratuitous sexual acts that his sixteen-year-old daughter had engaged in, while he stood by madly impotent on two counts.

Not that evening, nor the next, but the one after that, did Carol feel relaxed enough to offer her own version, pallid and softcore by comparison, of Dan's pukings, *his* muttered obscene eructations and occasional beery gropings. The outrage may have been slight, but Carol's description of her own pallid indifference, and anemone-like withdrawal from Dan's distress, was wholly authentic. And when she had finished speaking, or 'sharing' as the group called their version of bearing witness to the Truth, she looked up from the linoleum to see the equine visage of Dave 2, who had joined the group from next door, and who was now looking at her with an expression of undiluted sympathy, compounded by admiration and something that might have been, but wasn't, love.

Over that week both Dan and Carol attended six of their respective meetings. And both of them felt the ideology of Alcoholics Anonymous swimming in to form a structure for their lives. There was something so reassuring about these twin groups of quite ordinary people gathered in circles of S-framed, khaki-bottomed chairs, under the flickering neon of the church hall. The Al Anon group met in the room set aside for the Sunday school, and as Carol's ears were warmed by tales of casual bashing and buggery, her washed-out blue eyes roamed over the walls, where a collage alphabet had been created by the children, and the curate had stuck up naive bible story pictures with red and gold sticky tape.

The drinking of instant coffee and the smoking of many, many cigarettes; the business of the group, concerned as it was with the treasury, the coffee rota and the sale of pamphlet literature; these were secure facts and routines that drew Carol in. As for the catharsis afforded by speaking of one's innermost hurts, fears and desires to a room full of strangers, Carol felt this too; albeit that her provision of the therapeutic goods was closely constrained by an unusual talent for compliance.

But this needn't surprise us. We know Carol to be like this. We have remarked before on her tendency always, always to take the line of least resistance. Why can't we let her have her Dralon confession in peace? After all, it might help her with that other, more intimate, more pressing problem.

While Carol was getting integrated, Dan, in a quiet and unspectacular way, was doing the same. From the day of Dave 2's advent and his first meeting at St Simon's, Dan had put down the alcohol. He found the admission that he was powerless over alcohol, the first and pre-eminent statement of the AA credo, easy to make. Since his student days at Stourbridge Dan had felt intensely that his conscious will was but an impotent, flopping marionette, inanimate until vivified – until sought out by the lager of Lamot. This WD40 of the soul would flood out of its can and form a thick, white cloud in Dan's narrow head. The cloud would over a number of hours resolve itself into a Genie, a giggling djinn that would manipulate the marionette-that-was-Dan, jerk him this way and that.

Dan, like Carol, found it hard to speak at the AA meetings. But unlike Carol, it wasn't because Dan had anything to hide. On the contrary, with Dan there was a niceness to the fit between his inarticulacy, his inhibition and his simplicity of mind, that is fortunately rare. Otherwise we would all be a great deal more bored than we are already. No, it was just that Dan had very little to say. But if catharsis was unnecessary, at least Dan now had access to the relief that came with learning that alcoholism was a disease. A disease with its own aetiology and pathology. A disease recognised by as august a body as the WHO. A disease prominently listed in the Observer's Guide . . . AA told him the disease was both chronic and incurable – that was the downside. The upside was that the symptoms of this disease could be entirely alleviated, given vigorous attendance at AA meetings and rigorous abstinence. Prior to this Good News Dan had feared that his mind, really as delicate and ductile as one of the paper sculptures he himself used to make, might have been on the verge of crumpling itself up into a little wadded ball of insanity.

Now Dan had friends, supportive friends. Dave 2 was so supportive that he would come home with Dan after the meeting to preach to him further. They would find Carol already at the flat – the Al Anon meeting started and finished a half hour in advance of the AA meeting – and the kettle on the boil. The three of them would then sit down around the breakfast counter to share the articles of Dave 2's faith. These he would pronounce with the kind of affectedly natural sincerity that is most typical of an Anglican priest at his worst.

The rubric of Dave 2's sermons was that of a kind of spiritual 'n' tell. He had a great number of quasi-devotional postcards and stickers that he liked to distribute to his new acolytes. An example of what was depicted on one of these would be: cuddly puppies in a wicker basket, the cutest dangling from the handle. Underneath there was a slogan in curly cursive script. It read, 'Faith isn't faith until it's all you're hanging on to.' Another showed kittens in a rumble-tumble bundle. The slogan read, 'What we need are lots of hugs!' Dave 2 also had A5-sized tablets of card laminated with plastic that carried the AA commandments (the Twelve Steps and the Twelve Traditions), or very important AA prayers: 'God grant me the serenity to accept the things I cannot change . . . etc . . . etc . . .' You know the type of thing. These he would slap down on the formica, as if they were the flesh that justified his burring, bleating homilies . . .

The don's voice trailed off again quite suddenly. The light in the little circular shade above his head had come on, and the nutty wings of hair that smoothed to his scalp were burnished and refulgent in the downlight. He stood, and in the tiny roomlet of the enclosed compartment, turned and paced from one door to the other. He stopped and looked at me, slope-shouldered, ecto-morphic. He was like a peardrop someone had dressed at Turnbull & Asser. His pate was framed by the gaudy surround of a retouched Highland photo, the proud stag poking its head from behind his ear.

The don looked at me and for the first time I saw something else in his eyes besides the usual facetiousness. A glimmer of hate? Or at any rate flat anger at felt or imagined hurt and insult. His clipped voice spat again: 'You're typing me, boy, aren't you? You're turning me into something that I'm not. An amusing character, an oddity, a type!'

Still facing me, he half crouched, half knelt in the space between the seats. He looked intently at my profile, as if trying to make up his mind about something, and then, apparently satisfied, he straightened up. He sat down opposite me again and recommenced his narrative in the same rapid, even tones. This more than anything else shocked me. There was some-thing so utterly pat and performative about everything that he did. It gave me the chilling feeling that I was not the first unwitting listener to be pinioned by the don. Nor was I the first audience for this tawdry cast. There was that and there was the compartment itself. I couldn't place my finger on it but somehow the decor was changing, as surely as if ghostly but efficient stagehands were playing their part. The scene was shifting more exactly to accommodate the don . . . But as if to forestall my examining this impression more clearly, he went on.

Suffice to say that Dave 2 became a fixture in the flat, an adept of the idiosyncratic toilet-roll holder, a hunter after Marvel and condensed milk for late-night brews.

5

It

THERE ARE THOSE people in the world whose lives really are as flat as those of characters in a slight fiction. You know the kind of thing: bound in light blue cloth and picked up for 25p from a cardboard box outside a charity shop. When you get on the bus and start to read a few pages you are struck immediately by the leaden feel of the characterisations. You chuck it to one side and with it go Dan and Carol – and Dave 2 for that matter.

Gary, Barry, Gerry, Derry and Dave 1 had never supplied any depth to Dan's life; no interconnectedness, no grout with which to edge the smooth, square featurelessness of Dan's identity. His mother dominated him in the manner of a Roman emperor. She might send a legion to pacify him from time to time but mostly she preferred to rule him through a provincial governor, a psychological satrap she had established in his very sense of self. And Carol? Well, we know about her. Dave 2's cards started to appear on the corkboard, next to joky parodic postcards from Camden Lock.

Carol and Dan's life was thus *exactly* like a work of literature: thin and pulped into existence. They floated *in vacuo*, cut off from parents, isolated from one another. Since there was no other conduit to direct them into the corpuscular circulation of society, while the current was on they flew like filings towards the healing magnet.

Each evening at their respective meetings Carol and Dave blossomed and then they raced home to receive a little Potterton-side sermon from Dave 2, who would depart punctually at 11.10 pm to get the last 114 bus heading north into the fastness of Friern Barnet, where he had a little quasi-serviced flatlet.

They hardly had time to nauseate one another. Padding passers-by in the alcove by the bathroom, bath-robed like Rock Hudson and Doris Day, their lips were sealed. I could almost say that Carol didn't have time to examine the gristly frond. I could almost say that, and I know that in a way, despite your enquiring fucking mind, you'd rather like me to do that, *n'est ce pas*? But you would also know I was lying, wooden d'jew? Of course Carol had time, no, took time to check out that little priser. Because that's what it was, a little priser. At odd moments she could feel it prising her apart below; sitting in the group listening to someone share, or else standing at the library counter, crotch bumping against the veneer slab, which, peeling away from its restraining rivet, clacked mournfully.

And how could we forget pissing and shitting? We mustn't forget those. Sometimes *I* feel that my body is nothing but one enormous, snaking bowel, stuffed full of ordure and but thinly covered with skin. Nietzsche, you know, suffered agonies on the toilet. In *Ecce Homo* he damns the Germans for their beer and sausage, bum-concretising cuisine. Like Gogol, another neuro-neuter, he roamed the cities of Northern Italy, seeking digestive relief in huge antacid bowls of pasta.

I digress. On the toilet then, Carol's usual sense of micturation was muted, she felt the stream somehow tramelled – funnelled externally. Looking down she would catch sight of a bead of flesh and set into it a bead of urine. Then Carol's fingers would brush and freeze as if skewered, on confirming the testimony of her eyes: it was *still there*. And now poking forward, out from the lips. She could hardly bear to encompass it with shaking thumb and forefinger. She could see herself, outlined in avocado, framed in the half-length mirror over the sink. Legs akimbo, underclothes like twisted fan belts between her splayed shanks, she sweated and twisted on her plastic horseshoe of a torture throne.

But grasp it she did. And feeling the, by now, wormlet of flesh and gristle between her fingers did something to her. On the one hand it hardened an awful bone of knowledge, a hard white femur or tibia torn from a pirate flag and shoved through her life, cutting her out from the herd, along with her secret. (Although it can be said with certainty that, as yet, Carol did not view this secret as having any greater import or connotation of the bizarre than an adulterous liaison or a dumped foetus.) But on the other hand, or *in* the other hand, the wormlet was there. It was, as it were, accomplished. And when, clothes still half off herself, she shiveringly, retchingly pulled it out and held it hard against the edge of a perspex six-inch ruler, the memory of capturing her brother Steven doing the same with his willy, some fifteen years before, came to her involuntarily. It wasn't an inference that she could slap aside. The wormlet was clearly not that strange after all, it was something that she had had an acquaintance with before, albeit in quite a different context.

'Monday, 9.45 am. Length: 7mm. Appearance: that of an extended clitoris, sac-like but containing an interior twistle of nerve-ending-packed gristle. Remarks: sort of a second fun button really.

'Tuesday, 11.45 am. Length: 8.5mm. Appearance: as yesterday but more distended still, clearly poking out from the *labia minora* now. The wormlet seems to quest for the light, just as the clitoris above retreats under its fleshy hood. Remarks: the increment in length of 1.5mm is not altogether credible. With such small increments we doubt the accuracy of the Oxford Geometry Kit six-inch perspex ruler.

'Wednesday, 3.30 pm. (In the library toilet, hence the brevity of this entry) Length: 10mm. Appearance: repulsive, it has a little eye. Remarks: I feel sick, very sick.'

Such might have been the entries if Carol had troubled to keep a written log detailing all the steps of its development. Of course she did no such thing. But strange to relate, within the context of her relationship with *it*, it was as if she had kept a matter-of-fact account.

Moreover this strand of Carol's character, the matter-of-fact, pragmatic, practical qualities – qualities one primary-school teacher had once reported that she possessed, but which, to my knowledge at least, she had never before exhibited – began to come to the fore in other ways as well.

Dan was set to work to build a cabinet for the CD/video module. Carol went off on the Thursday morning after her first Al Anon meeting and purchased the required rivet gun and composite wood slabbing from a DIY superstore in Wood Green. Work was scheduled to commence on Saturday morning. On the same trip to Wood Green Carol did something else she had been meaning to do for a while. She signed up for a course of driving lessons.

But Saturday came and as Dan outlined the shape of the cabinet on a sheet of tracing paper with a special pencil, Carol gibbered and cowered upstairs on her bed. A TV interview with Julio Iglesias's father, a prominent Spanish gynaecologist, was the trigger point that set her off. She inadvertently opened her fly buttons and took *it* out. 'Jesus Christ! I did that. I took *it* out!' Awareness screamed. She retched and up came All Bran, an irregular and unscheduled appearance for this most regulatory of breakfast cereals. Carol staggered off the bed to find the security of the carpet. *It* was rasped against the thick denim of her jeans by the move, and imperceptibly – thank God, because personally I don't think she could have taken much more at this stage – hardened.

Despite her so recent distress, Carol was nonetheless

totally unresponsive to yet another nuzzling interception from Dan, as she crossed the living room en route for the kitchen. And she continued to keep his nose to the grindstone for the rest of the day. For, the separate compartments of Carol's mind, which had always been strung out along a lurching, ill-lit corridor, had now begun to detach themselves from one another altogether. They were much like this compartment we are sitting in now. It is part of the train, yes, but we cannot access any other part of the train from it. And in that sense I suppose it isn't part of the train at all . . .

The don interleaved his plump little fingers and basketed a flannel knee as if well pleased with this piece of sophistry. Somehow I had failed to notice the pre-war rolling stock when I boarded the train. But what he said was true. The compartment was self-contained, with no access to the rest of the train. It belonged to an earlier age. An age when sexual assault was collectively believed to be something undertaken solely by those without the wherewithal to buy a train ticket. I wanted to discuss this oddity, this example of British Rail underfunding with the don, but he was off again.

. . . Carol had always been subject to a time delay between emotional event and emotional response. And therein, of course, lay the essence of her neurosis. But however attenuated, the connection did always exist, and, if you like, her failure adequately to explain why such and such an event might make her cry, while another might make her angry, was a guarantee of her real stability.

The proof of this assertion is in what began to happen to her next. With increased detachment came increased awareness. Carol flitted in the darkness along the gravelly grading, peeking into the lighted compartments of her mind. In one she saw herself at an Al Anon meeting, sharing; in another she was retching over *it*; in a third she listened attentively to Dave 2 and in a fourth she was turning away from Dan. The Carol in the darkness, the ghost, as it were, *ex machina*, smiled and passed on.

Carol was also getting more aggressive. When a plasterer set aside his hawk and praised her svelte figure – in demotic terms – as she passed along Fortune Green Road, she turned back and spat at him, 'Shove it up your fucking arsehole,' and walked on happy. Dan didn't notice the change, in part simply because he was used to her. Habit is such a great canceller-out of any reflective thought and Dan was nothing if not a creature of habit – and anyway it had never really been Carol that he was married to, but a simulacrum of her, spun from his own fantastic mental projections and the accident of his mother's indifference. ('She's just a little chit of a girl but frankly I don't think he could do much better.' This had been the Empress's response to the news of Dan and Carol's engagement.)

Anyway, Dan found himself sober in the clean, cold light of day, and remembered that once upon a time, before Barry, Gary, Derry, Gerry, Dave 1 and he had taken to regularly seeking out the lager of Lamot, they had gained much pleasure from squash, and all the mateyish towel-flicking, play-fighting and Lucozade-swigging that had accompanied it.

The first four days of sobriety had been sheer hell for Dan. He was so naive and ignorant that he had never known that you could have physical withdrawal symptoms from alcohol. The sweating, retching, and puking, together with the unsettling peripheral hallucinations, took him entirely by surprise. Carol reacted by exiling the sweating grub of his body to the futon divan. There he lay, storms of electrons coursing behind his narrow forehead. And as he tossed, he was subject to waking dreams in which odd sexual chimeras – women with testicles instead of eyes and men with vaginal ears – stood about, unconcerned, in a delusional lounge bar.

On the fifth day he rose from the futon and went to work. Apart from an odd tingling around the tips of his fingers and toes – as if he were a quadra-amputee, afflicted with the ghost memory of limbs long gone – he felt nothing. Not even a bat's squeak of a craving for alcohol beset Dan. He had handed over his will and his life to a power greater than himself. According to the AA credo the power did not have to be God, it could be any force greater than one's self, provided that it was benign and transcendent rather than phenomenal and temporal. Unfortunately, although Dan did try awfully hard not to personify his higher power, occasionally, being a vengeful God, it would manifest itself; appearing in Dan's mind's eye in the form of a heavyset middle-aged woman eating Battenburg cake, a woman not unlike Dan's mother.

Another week came and went at Melrose Mansions. *It* grew. Carol and Dan continued on their divergent courses, meeting up only in the short period before their respective meetings; and then afterwards in order to harken once more unto Brother Dave.

Dave 2, it needs to be said, was playing his own very particular game. For Dave 2 was a parasite of the emotions. Dave 2 could gain no direct pleasure from any intimate relationship, but rather, like some honey-sucking bird with an obscenely elongated bill, he gained an intense and even sweetly erotic pleasure from sucking out the juice from the private parts of other people's entanglements. And so, to this end, he encouraged each half of any given couple to regard him as their supreme and absolute confidant. When this ideal situation was achieved, Dave 2 attained his own strange nirvana.

But with Carol and Dan, things were proving a little tough. Sure, both of them were willing to confide in Dave 2, but the nature of their confidences was entirely unsatisfying. Both of them were vague about their resentments, hurts and passions. And the precise detail, the who, where, why, what and when, was altogether missing. It was this hot intimacy that Dave 2 desired more than anything else, so, like a spymaster, Dave 2 determined to employ an agent, and to that end he waited behind at St Simon's on the tenth day after Carol's induction and introduced her to Geena.

Geena was a fellow recovering alcoholic, a stringy old hippy thing in black lycra that smelt of patchouli long past its sell-by date. Geena was an old-time accomplice of Dave 2's, similarly sexually dormant, and addicted to the delights of what we may call – to coin a neologism – psycho-empathetic voyeurism, or PEV for short.

Geena came lurching up to Carol, rocking hard on her preposterous heels. Carol was helping to dispense handleless mugs of instant coffee to the Al Anon group members. Carol was struck immediately by the strange way that Geena's belly bulged out at the sides, as if she had a circular cushion rammed up her stretchy top. Struck by this and struck also by Geena's defiantly ethnic hairstyle. All of her thick black locks had been gathered up into a single plume on top of her head and garlanded there with skeins of fake amber beads. Geena's face was unremarkable to begin with; her flywhisk hair-do made it wholly unmemorable.

'Hi, I'm Geena,' said Geena, before Dave 2 had even had an opportunity to introduce them. 'The old pisshead here has told me about you. I insisted that he introduce us, I keep birds too.'

This was three arrows straight into the bull. Carol did

like her birds and she could be flattered as much as the next. But Geena's real stroke had been to ridicule Dave 2. Carol had begun to develop some profound doubts about Dave 2, after the first flush of her conversion had started to fade. And although the ridicule was clearly not intended to be pejorative in this context, Carol thought she could definitely sense some lurking malice.

Carol didn't need much urging to accompany Geena back to her flat off the Harrow Road. It was a long way but Geena had a car. Carol was doubly pleased because riding in the car gave her a good pretext for discussing her favourite thing of the moment – driving. Ever since Carol had started her driving lessons she had developed an unreasonable interest in everything to do with the road. She had already had two lessons and they had gone off more than satisfactorily. The instructor was feeling so relaxed towards the end of the second lesson, that he lifted his feet aside from the dual-control pedals and let her go solo on Green Lanes. 'You're a natural,' he told Carol. And only 80 per cent of the compliment sprang from his fuzzy desire to go where *it* was.

Geena and Carol talked about driving all the way down to the Harrow Road. Once there, they talked about Carol and a little bit about Geena. Geena clutched at her hosed and knobbly knees, and bent forward. She was flanked by low tables covered with ratty bibelots. Incense mouldered in a corner. Geena's face folded itself into a listening ear and Carol felt compelled to give her at least a version of the truth . . . about her and Dan that is, certainly not about *it*.

But the version was no better than what Dave 2 had already. And as an exercise in PEV Geena had to concede to herself that the interrogation had proved a failure. For the essence of PEV is to create in its practitioners' minds pictures of the most intimate aspects of their subjects' lives. A seasoned PEVist gets off, not on secretly watching sexual intercourse, but simply on *knowing* that it is taking place. But Carol's info brought Dave 2 and Geena no closer to this devoutly desired consummation. Instead, when either of them tried to form a mental image of Dan and Carol's intimate life, it remained as woodenly two-dimensional as an animated cartoon.

Returning home, Carol found Dan in the kitchen, looking flushed. He was sitting reading the local advertiser. After a game of squash with Derry, en route from work to St Simon's, Dan was feeling pleasantly tingly.

Dave 2 had been compelled to retire early for the evening. It was the first night since they had 'come into recovery' that he had neglected Dan and Carol. Dan had wondered whether this wasn't the beginning of the end of Dave 2's concern for him, but at the very end of the evening Dave 2 had come across to Dan and given him a really big hug. Dan went home with a new glow. Dave 2's hug had somehow unlocked a wave of sensual memories for Dan. Memories of entwinings, limb stretchings, sighs and lubricious sounds. Dan's sexual recall was so pathetically confused that it was difficult for him to judge whether these were genuine memories, or merely memories of witnessing actors, working at sex for the requisite Equity minimum fee. If you wanted to be clever and allusive you might say that Dave 2's hug was Dan's madeleine.

'That's your style, isn't it. Being clever and allusive, but what does this really amount to save for trying to get one over on good, ordinary, straightforward people? Trying to get one over with your slimy little mind and insinuating your snaky little cock into them while they're not looking! Pushing it up their trouser legs while they're strap-dangling on the train! Or while talking to them at a party flipping it up 'n' under their skirts! You're an incubus, that's what you are; a night creeper, a ravager, a rapist. Yes, that's right – a rapist! . . . You fuck! You fucking fuck . . . Oh gaa!'

The hate had been injected into the don's voice like dye into water. The aftertone hung there in the dusty compartment, puffing into dense billows of aggression. I sat stunned. Too stunned to pull myself away from his protuberant gaze and twitching lip, too stunned to say anything.

It was clear that the don was changing before my eyes, and along with this change came an alteration in the nature of his tale. It was becoming clear to me that the tale itself had no autonomous existence, that it was simply a direct expression of

63

the don's nature. And if any further confirmation of this hypothesis were required it was amply supplied within seconds, when the don, instead of leaping from his seat and throttling me, or metamorphosing into someone else altogether, resumed the story in the same rapid but even tones with which he had begun. Insulting me directly was no fun for him – or so I thought. He wanted me to suffer alongside Dan and Carol.

The rest of the evening Dan spent sacked down in the living-room watching a repeat of *Doogie Howser MD*. He ate some of the new poly-flavoured crisps: wiener schnitzel with red cabbage. Upstairs Carol did the same. He came to his twin bed at about eleven-thirty. He kissed Carol on the cheek and said 'night love'. They simultaneously snuggled down and clicked off their respective bedside lamps; just like synchronised sleepers.

But sometime during the night they lost this unconscious harmony. Carol, who had taken to sleeping with legs slightly apart, lying three-quarters on one side, felt a deft hand slide across the top of her thigh, towards *it*. Dan's lethargic voice, fat-bellied with desire, whispered in her ear: 'Is it all right if I climb on board?'

6

How One Becomes What One Is

C AROL STIFFENED. No, not quite right, bit of an unfortunate choice of words that, it would be better to say that she froze. Indeed she went so crisply hard that she might have been freeze-dried. What to do? Dan's hand, was it headed towards Carol? Or towards *it*?

It would have been entirely in character for Carol to shrug Dan off at this point. She knew the balloon of his erection to be so diffident that it was easily punctured. There was nothing whatsoever compelling about Dan's lust. Maybe she would have given him some explanation, but it would have been just as typical for her to simply turn aside. You'd like that, wooden d'jew? You'd like Carol to turn aside. I don't think you really want to confront this particular *mise en scène*. I doubt your capacity for genuine PEV. I doubt your ability to endure the trufflings and mufflings beneath the patterned cover. Tough.

Some access of *jouissance* made Carol not turn aside. Made her in fact welcome Dan's questing hand with her own and guide it towards her nipple . . . He lapped hungrily at her ear, as if sufficient stimulus might cause it to lactate. He nuzzled and snuffled, little bleatings issued from his lips. His silky thigh slid on top of hers; his free hand went to her shoulder, and like a sailor hooking his way up on to a mast, Dan swung on board with amazing facility.

But had it not always been thus? Cast your mind back to the prologue . . . And can you recall those three sandpapery thrusts that accidentally coaxed our Carol into tremulous orgasm; into the most *petit* of *petit morts*? Carol had no choice, comfort alone dictated that she open her legs. She did this and despite Dan's lower abdomen pressing into her groin, felt *it* pull free from its housing and this time perceptibly harden. Mercifully this ghastly sensation – full of bloody meaning – was at least eclipsed by Dan's sudden entry.

Now came the acid test. And as his mouth galumphed once more on to her wet neck, and Carol turned aside to look at the glass of dusty water on the bedside table, she knew that her fate might well be decided. Would he feel *it*? Would he notice? Could he avoid *it* pressing into his pubis? A little knotty thing, a baby brother snuggling up against its older sibling.

No, he didn't. And is it any surprise? After all Dan had never troubled to examine Carol's cuntal area with any kind of attention. He knew nothing of her true shape. For Dan this America, this New Found Land, had always remained *terra incognita*. Beneath the hairy diadem that did Carol adorn, Dan knew there was a hole . . . but he knew of little else besides. His thrusts had always been into an insensate void. The sensation he received from intercourse had always been mechanical and piston-like. Three thrusts and come; four thrusts a bogey; and five thrusts just about par for the course – and the hole.

This is exactly the handicap that Dan achieved on this particular round, to persist with our facile and demeaning golfing metaphor. And then he disembarked – again with great ease – and cushioned his slightly sodden muff and softening frond against her upper thigh. A few whispered tendernesses, in gratitude for the relieving milking, and he was gone, back to his own single.

Carol lay in the darkness. The digital alarm clock glowed and so did she. More than that – she exulted. Yes, exulted, although she was unable fully to acknowledge the source, or even the content of her feelings. For Carol it was enough that she had escaped detection . . . But really . . . absolutely *entre nous* I think it was because when *it* stiffened and Dan made his febrile stab at her, Carol thrust back. Yes! Lifted her hips a little from the mattress, using the tension of the springs to ease up and – not feel him sliding inside her oiled sheath, no. Quite the opposite. It was *she*, Carol, who thrust up inside him, just for one insidious instant. Gone just as soon as it was – oh, so barely, but nonetheless nakedly – acknowledged.

> ' "Morning stirs the feet and hands
> (Nausicaa and Polypheme)
> Gesture of orang-outang
> Rises from the sheets in steam
> This withered root of knots of hair

Slitted below and gashed out with eyes
This oval O cropped out with teeth
The sickle motion from the thighs . . .''

'You see, my memory for quotation improves as I progress,' *said the don, addressing me personally, directly and not simply as a unitary audience.* 'Eliot, isn't it? Hate his stuff. Uptight he was, a frozen puritan bumhole. Scared of cunt, wouldn't you say? But whose vagina was *dentata* in this context? Or to place the question in a more modern idiom: who was zooming who? Fucking kike Eliot. Not a lot of people know that, but you would, wooden d'jew?'

The very next day Carol went for her third driving lesson. Two days later for her fourth. At the end of the following week her instructor, a Turkish Cypriot, rasped his thumbnail along his moustache and confirmed what she already suspected. 'Youse know, pretty lady, youse can take your test now I think.' Carol felt exultation again, but not that dangerous thrusting exultation we touched on before; this was a more workaday sensation. It was combined for Carol with an acute awareness of a solid and mechanical species of causation in the world, of the form: push button A and B *will* happen.

Now of course it would be absurd to suggest that Carol had not been aware of this in the past, but her apprehension of her own impact upon this stratum of the world had never before been so nakedly and enjoyably intuitive. Driving in the school's Mini Metro; cutting an onion; completing a transaction in a shop, Carol felt empowered by all these simple acts, she felt her status as a potentially effective agent being pushed and moulded into shape by everything she did.

However, along with this came a velcro wrenching as the little hooks of Carol's will began to pull away from the little restraining loops of Carol's conscience. And alone, naked from the waist down, she began to dance in front of the mirror. At first she just stood, lowered her jeans, or raised her skirt and struck a few attitudes, almost unconsciously. But it felt so good to acknowledge *it*, to see *it* now that *its* purpose was starting to be revealed, that soon she advanced to a proper terpsichorean promenade.

It was now large enough to waggle a little if she shifted from one foot to the other in a sort of soft-shoe shuffle; and indeed one waggle led to another, *its* tension increasing with each waggle.

Carol stood in front of the full-length mirror that formed the cupboard door, regarding *its* incongruity: peeking out from her hair-bedraggled lips, devoid of the pouch that perhaps ought to accompany it. She sat down on the edge of the bed and the fingers of both her hands toyed with it. *It* was at least three, or even five centimetres long. A pinky-brown roll of flesh could be pulled back from its tip to reveal a little mushroom, in the centre of which was a dry eye. It was, Carol decided, a penis.

★   ★   ★

'To be a woman with a penis in our society – it isn't an overwhelming distinction, is it? Well is it?' *The don was testy, I was clearly a pupil.*

'No, I suppose not.'

'You suppose not. Why do you "suppose not"?' *The train clattered through a small station. I had a glimpse of an ornamental flowerbed; a fat porter; a swinging sign, and then darkness again.*

'Well, I suppose the increasing emancipation of women throughout this century has meant that they have – albeit in a rather metaphorical way – acquired some of the characteristics of men.'

'Some of the sexual characteristics?' *The nasty edge was entering his voice again.*

'Perhaps.' *I tried to sound non-committal in a way that might please him, a facetious way. But he came back at me hard.*

'I think you're being trite. That's a mistake that young men always make with these issues. At times their entire overview of the sexual landscape seems merely an attempt to blot out the gynaecological *Massif Central*. It's a metaphorical penis that you're talking about. I'm talking about a fucking literal penis, shit-for-brains, and "fucking" is very definitely the operative word here, because I'm talking about a cock that can fuck. I'm talking about a firm, springy, blood-filled sponge, with an enpurpled, engorged dome shooting spunk at you, shooting life at you: bullets of jism! God what a noble sight! I so, so, prefer the company of men, don't you? I said don't you?'

'Oh, absolutely.'

'Non-erotic male bonding, that's the thing isn't it; what our Ocker cousins call "mateyness".'

'Yes, yes, it's true.'

'The more non-erotic the better, wouldn't you say?' *And he accompanied this latest decoy of an assertion masquerading as a question with another sinister little wiggle that started at his fundament and ran all the way up his spine to his nut-brown hair. The irony was that as his physical presence became more and more androgynous, so his voice increased in both timbre and depth.*

'Yes,' *I said,* 'the more non-erotic the better.'

'Quite so. We cannot abide those pillow-biting, fudge-packing, shirt-tail-lifting irons, now can we, my precious?'

'Indeed not.'

'Good.' *He slapped his thighs with a rifle's crack and then said:* 'Well, if you're ready, then I'll resume.'

Carol found that she was beginning to prefer the company of her fellow endowed. She would step into pubs and sup pints at the bar. Or else eat lunch in a greasy spoon, craning over her sarnie to admire the airbrushed pudenda of that day's page 3 automaton. Naturally she didn't feel inclined to make a direct claim to common gender with the other patrons. She quite sensibly realised that the majority of men might not know how to respond to someone who could frig with one hand whilst tossing with the other. I do so like the rich, Anglo-Saxon vocabulary of our smut talk, don't you?

Anyway, that's beside the point, because Carol didn't consider herself to be male. She'd never been conspicuously genderful anyway. Babytalk left her cold, witness Dan's attempts to wallow with her in sympathetic semolina. Carol knew that her penis didn't make her a man but it did free her a little bit more from being anything else, it did unslip those surly bonds and surly girly locks.

To the underwear emporium then and don't spare the big-knobbed horses! Carol chose a small boutique on the high road, where she could be assured of a male shop assistant. She then thrilled to the conspiratorial talk of just how Dan might dangle. Carol didn't even have to dissemble that much because Dan's dear little waist was almost as neat as her own.

The next day she had a proper costume for her boudoir theatricals. This way and that she posed and pirouetted, but the shame was that she couldn't even fill the smallest of filleted pouches in the slinkiest of men's Italian briefs.

She pulled back the elastic of the waistband and fiddled with the newest member. By clenching and unclenching her buttocks she could get an internal, muscular handle on the development of what must surely be new peeing muscles. Carol was quite lucidly aware that soon she would be able to produce the most spectacular effects whilst micturating. Naturally the concept itself was inchoate but she did have a presentiment of that most trivial and yet enjoyable of exclusively male pastimes. Namely: directed peeing. But on the other front? Well, things didn't seem quite well-developed enough to be effectual . . . but maybe not.

Dan meanwhile endeavoured to persevere. Back on the fast track once more, on his way to heading the corporate design group at the agency, he thwacked balls with Barry on a regular basis. And in the evenings, he repaired to St Simon's with Dave 2. He also went by bus to meetings further afield. Dave 2 accompanied him on some of these trips, anxious to hear the words of alternative suburban seers, but mostly Dan went alone.

Dan realised that Dave 2 was gently encouraging him to gain his own position in AA, to become a member of the Fellowship in his own right. Dan was certain because Dave 2 had said as much. 'M'dear Dan,' he burred, 'I feel like a father to you, and perhaps that's a little too close a relationship for us, as recovering alcoholics, to have. We need to let go of one another. You need to find your own feet, find your own sponsor, just as I did.' Here Dave 2 was referring to the practice of AA whereby those members with a greater experience of sobriety entered into bipartisan therapeutic relationships with their junior, pisshead colleagues.

Dan acquiesced to this gentle parting. He had no choice, being such a doormat. But in his sensitive heart, even when Dave 2 was only away from him for an evening, he felt abandoned.

'Now don't you go feeling sympathetic for Dave 2. Don't embrace the fallacy of imagining that I have in some way misjudged or misread Dave 2. That I have spun you a line. Either intentionally or otherwise. There is no hidden hand in this tail; there is no lurking, shadowy narrator. What I tell you – that is the truth. *Allah Akbar*, you understand? I am a man of God. I speak the truth – God's truth. " 'There is no God but God."' *The don pronounced these Islamic phrases with the lilting cadence of a Sahel évolué. Then he reverted to the type I have to concede that I had defined for him and asked his pupil,* 'Why does this seem tautologous?' *But he ran on and answered his own question.* 'If we consider the Islamic notion of history we see a process of social evolution analogous to the Hegelian concept of the World Spirit. However, whereas for Hegel the *deus* was very much *ex*, for the Muslim the World Spirit and the World are the same thing. Thus we see a cosmological loop: that as the cock of progress thrusts through social form and change, it is at one and the same time taking itself from behind.'

No, no. Listen to the truth: Dave 2 had already got his freckled hooks into another scene which he judged to be

74

far, far juicier than Dan and Carol's marriage. A young girl of only nineteen years had precociously sought out so much of the lager of Lamot that she found herself at St Simon's with plenty of entertaining incidents to recount. She was banged up within weeks by an occasional group member, a Welsh ex-steel worker of dwarvish proportions but peculiar prettiness. There was a lot of brouhaha surrounding this scene, and convocations in coffee bars as the group divided into warring factions, each accusing the other of therapeutic as well as moral crimes. Dave 2 was in his element, hearing versions from one and all. These he held on to, as if they were long threads, trailing from barely stitched emotional wounds. Dave 2 waited – waited to tug.

And Carol? Our dear little Carol, still attending Al Anon meetings, but mercifully freed from the attentions of the PEV crew, Dave 2 and Geena? Who can say? Who can mark the precise point where bad very definitely turned to worse? And who can get inside a mind that, vacillating to begin with, now found itself under the pressure of a strong and secret desire? I say 'secret' but really you would have to say that it was more than that. What she felt was, well, inexpressible. But guess what she *did* next.

Well, Carol was entirely certain now of her mastery over Dan's mind, but she still felt that his body might present a few problems. So she too sought once more the lager of Lamot.

7

The Lager of Lamot

T HERE IS A CERTAIN kind of off-licence, which although always absolutely and spotlessly clean, is nonetheless ever saturated with coils of cigarette smoke that hang around the interior, as stiff and desiccated as dried dog turds. In such establishments the proprietor is invariably to be found behind the cash register, ram-rod straight, fag fuming in face, and perhaps the corpse of its predecessor still smoking in the tin ashtray on the counter.

These offie proprietors are more often than not cardigan wearers, hair slickers, Fellows of the Ancient Antediluvian Order of Buffalos. They are men of a certain gravitas, usually with a half-hunter for any occasion that promises to be waistcoated. Years of Remembrance Sunday parades have left these men with a straight bearing; on the other hand, years of envy and resentment have almost certainly rounded their shoulders. Latterly, years of Lamot tend to have exploded mines of capillaries across their faces, faces that are frequently tensed up like clenched fists with aching disapproval.

You always take these men for the Proprietor – they look so proprietorial. Indeed that is their aim. They want you to forget the name of the chain above the shopfront and make the profound mistake of enquiring after business.

A selection of unfortunate entrées might be:

1. 'How's business?'
2. 'Business slow?'
3. 'Business not so good at the moment?'
4. 'Quiet?'

And so on. The fag never leaves the mouth, the hand stays on the counter. The mouth opens and out comes a flat, weary litany of dissatisfaction.

Such an off-licence was Dan and Carol's local. The manager, a Mr Wiggins, and his wife, also called Carol (let's call her 'Ur-Carol' to distinguish her from Our Carol), were always firm allies in Dan's fight to consume.

Ted Wiggins would even step down from the dais of his cash register to hold the door open so that Dan or Carol could stagger through, laden with characteristic blue and silver canisters that contained their favourite brew. More often than not, Gary, Barry, Gerry, Derry or Dave 1 would accompany Dan to Wiggins's off-licence; and on these occasions half bottles of Dewars or White Horse might be purchased.

In addition to the normal range, the Wigginses also had a large selection of the cheaper bevvies on the market. These were products specially packaged – indeed branded – for alcoholics: syrupy beers, brewed in the vast steel vats of the East Midlands; re-labelled Philippino cooking sherries; toxically war-damaged

Yugoslavian Riesling and various other sweet wines from sour places.

This sector of the sanitised emporium was Ur-Carol's concern; indeed her domain. Ted was on his dais, Ur-Carol behind an unpainted, but spotless, plywood door. Whenever anyone strayed into that part of the off-licence, Ur-Carol would emerge from the door, looking for all the world like the plastic dog on the collecting box Ted kept by the till, going after its 2p offering. Shabby alcoholics, no matter how dirty, ravaged or potentially violent, she barred with absolute firmness: 'Get out! You're barred from these premises,' she would shrill. 'If I see you around this area again I'll call the police, now bugger off!' It always seemed likely that she might add to this: 'This is a respectable neighbourhood.' She was that sort of a woman.

But in truth, no part of London is entirely respectable. And even here, high on a hill, among the Edwardian villas with their snot-coloured masonry and their monkey puzzle trees, came filtering gyppos, tinkers, tramps and worse. Unspeakable travelling men wearing two donkey jackets and boots lashed in place with nylon towrope. Young men reared on morning glory seeds and regular inhalations of EvoStick, who had managed to reach maturity with huge lacunae in their minds. They parked their moribund buses and leper wagons on a piece of waste ground by the abandoned railway line and sought out the lager of Lamot. They were barred.

But on the other hand anyone who looked even

superficially respectable to Ur-Carol was welcomed with folded arms and remorseless chatter which issued forth in a flat drone from between yellow dentures.

Dan had long since joined Ur-Carol's temple of low-rent sedation. Many times she had thought to herself how much she liked a young man who had diverse tastes, for Dan would drink anything, he would go all the way from Château Haut Brion to Emu Export and back again. So it was that after three whole days had passed without seeing him, Ur-Carol went so far as to voice concern:

'Father,' she said, 'that nice young designer boy hasn't been in for a while.' (She always addressed Ted Wiggins as 'Father', although in truth, the only creature they had ever managed to nurture was a yapping Yorkshire terrier that frequently bemerded the spotless linoleum.) Wiggins grunted non-committally. Like so many of his co-cardigan wearers Ted Wiggins couldn't have given a dollop of trappist's toss fluid for Dan, but he *would* have given a whole gross of packets of tortilla chips to shag the arse off his young and slim wife.

Carol could do that to a man. As I have said before she had the kind of cramped, mean, English provincial prettiness that could encourage even a buffalo as long in the tooth as Ted Wiggins to dare imagine that he might place his scrawny shanks inside her scrawny shanks.

But Ur-Carol's concern at the disappearance of Dan and her namesake was far more straightforward still. In an area where fading gentility segued with the new health consciousness, the Dans of this world were easily her best customers. Give Ur-Carol an alcoholic in a pac-a-mac, a Gannex raincoat, even a herringbone crombie, and she'd be happy for months. She was like an old junkie, or a withered procuress, coaxing on these sherry-drinking widows and wine-supping travel-agency clerks. Dan had been her most promising protégé.

After about a fortnight, Carol passed the off-licence, seemingly by chance, and was snagged in by Ted Wiggins. 'Haven't seen you in ages,' he shouted at her through the half open, sticker-laden door, so anxious was he to detain this vision in a *Mail on Sunday* Readers' Offer raincoat. She came in, slightly, and explained what had happened. Ur-Carol emerged from behind her plywood door and, advancing as far as the circular niblets merchandising display in the centre of the shop – the outermost limit of her fiefdom – she tut-tutted as Carol told them both that Dan had become a member of Alcoholics Anonymous.

Ur-Carol knew all about AA. But she regarded it purely as a competitor, paying no heed at all to its dogma. As far as Ur-Carol was concerned, AA grabbed away thirsty throats, throats that needed and deserved to be slaked.

So Ur-Carol kept her thin lips zipped up and our Carol went away. But Ur-Carol knew that they would both be back. She twisted the copper bracelet around her lolly-stick wrist and willed it.

So it was no wonder that Carol chose the Wigginses' off-licence as the logical place to seek out the lager of Lamot. Just going there, walking along Fortune Green Road to the head of the parade of shops leading to the Quadrant, was second nature to her after living in Muswell Hill for two years. And when she got to the boozers' bureau it was the same as ever, occupying the very prong position, with glass frontage extending down both boulevards.

On this occasion, as Carol entered through the door on one side of the shop, her namesake exited from the other in hot pursuit of one of the mutant waste boys. 'You're barred!' screeched the harridan. 'Don't come back here again, if I even see you in the neighbourhood I'll call the police!' The mutant boy staggered on the pavement and regarded her with a fuzzy expression, which resolved itself within seconds into a visage of brutal irresponsibility. Ur-Carol had caught him off guard and hustled him out the door. He now managed to compose himself and with great deliberation his hand went to his fly.

Carol meanwhile stood alongside Ted Wiggins. Both of them were transfixed, viewing the action framed by the plate glass window as if it were being projected from behind them and they had paid to see it.

Although only newly accustomed to casually leaning side-on to a counter and hooking a hand into her jeans' pocket, Carol had graduated with commendable speed to using her fingers as an instrument with which to stroke, tug and generally hang on to her penis.

Men like to do that, don't they? They like to hang on. It's like genital thumb-sucking. Stroking the old todge in its 65% cotton housing doesn't really produce a sexual feeling, it's more like keeping the sensual rev counter at a steady 10,000 revs. But somehow or other, Ted Wiggins sensed Carol's arousal, an arousal that crept up the dial as the convoy man confronting Ur-Carol Wiggins pulled out his pride – a queer thing with a shaft as long and shiny as the ferrule of an alpenstock – and steamily pissed on the autumn pavement.

Wiggins used the distraction. Forever after he couldn't say exactly *why* he did it. All right, he'd been known to grope the odd woman, servitors or foreigners usually, but he didn't consider himself to be a molester in the proper sense, just an enthusiast. But perhaps he despaired. Despaired on realising that he would never provoke a sexual response from Carol, that he wasn't even as much of a turn-on as this perverse spectacle. And anyway, since the spectacle was afforded courtesy of the enterprise he commanded, perhaps he concluded that he too was entitled to a share of the dividend.

He stepped down from his dais and sidled up behind Carol. Outside, there was no dénouement in sight. Far from being intimidated or repulsed by the spluttering spout, Ur-Carol was pouring on more invective. The bemused wild man staggered and righted himself under her verbal strafing, but not before an arc of toxic pee had flown across both the shop window and his own trousers.

From behind Ted Wiggins gently inserted his hand between the warm denim tubes that sheathed Carol's upper thighs. He froze, in his mind's eye seeing the bench passing sentence, and then reached up and grabbed at Carol's penis . . .

Wiggins had intended to lurch into her at the same time and then claim that it was an accident – that he had cannoned into her out of desperation to reach the unfolding action in the street. But what happened next was determined entirely by Carol and her quickening reflexes. Sensing her penis under threat, Carol grabbed a bottle of Emva Cream that one of the fuddled pac-a-mac brigade had left on the counter, and, whirling round, she dealt Ted Wiggins a glancing blow on the side of the head. Such was the force of the blow that the follow-through took the bottle on to the steel casing of the sacred cash register, where it gloriously shattered.

You might have thought that this explosive and sticky incident would have sent Carol scampering out of the door of the shop, while Wiggins was still lying dazed on the lino, scampi fries rustling down about his ears. But no. Carol felt an access of phlegm so palpable that she almost harrumphed – and stood her ground. The shattering bottle, clearly audible outside, had given the wild man the opportunity to wrench himself away and head off, skittering and batting against parked cars, towards Ally Pally. Ur-Carol shot back inside the shop.

'What the fuck's going on?' she exclaimed, seeing her brilliant(ined) husband felled.

'He just tripped right over the counter trying to get to you . . .' explained Carol, trying desperately to inject a note of shock into what she was saying. They both stood and stared at Wiggins as, slowly, he struggled to his knees and shook his head like an old sheepdog.

The two Carols met each other's level stares over the collapsed spine of the tedious vintner, and there was great complicity in that eye contact – which meant that Carol's version of events was logged and not disputed by any of the parties involved. Not disputed at the time, that is.

'Oooergh. Fuck,' said Wiggins – he was clearly fine. During the Second War an entire case of Klim had fallen on his head while he was posted to guard a NAAFI storage dump at Acton. Ted Wiggins had barely stopped smoking for thirty seconds: the Wigginses were a thick-skulled breed.

When he was recovered enough to stand, Ur-Carol sent him off with an anaemic shopgirl from next door to get the wound dressed at the Whittington. Ur-Carol would, of course, have gone herself, but she had to mind the shop.

It's lucky that Ur-Carol did stick around, because once Ted was gone she made one of the great sales of her life. Carol flitted across the linoleum checkerboard from one glass side of the shop to the other, hands dipping down and diving up to reach out bottles and cans. On the wide counter – which was still being mopped and doused with Flash to eliminate the sweet smell of Carol's violent success – she ranked them in an orderly phalanx: first the Pilsners, Czechoslovakian, German, Austrian and the domestically brewed varieties; then the esoterica: Elephant from Denmark, Wildebeeste from the Republic of South Africa, Simpatico and Sol from down Mexico way; some Nigerian Gulder, a few high-waisted silvery cans of Japanese Sapporo; Carol even picked out a four-pack of a very obscure beer called Black Mambo, brewed in Mauretania, which no one, to Ur-Carol's knowledge, had ever bought before. On top of the esoterica Carol piled a squat pyramid of products whose branding aimed them at that tight sector of society between early adopters, ethnic minorities and rank piss-artists. The beers in this section were sickly sweet and double strength, they had names like 'Radical Stout' and 'Safe Haven'. Carol knew that Dan was a particular fan of one called 'Premier Class'. This came in a burnished copper can with a baroque coat of arms emblazoned right the way round the can. Below this was the motto of the English royal house: 'Honi soit qui mal y pense'. Before you think it, let me trouble to reassure you that the irony of this was lost entirely on its brewer.

After the esoterica and the poor people's liquid sedatives, Carol moved back to more familiar ground – taking a swing through that fictitious Asgard that must provide the provenance for the nomenclature so beloved by the East Midlands breweries' marketing men. From this branding zone Carol pulled out green cans of Odin, fiery orange cans of Wotan, the iridescent mauve bottles of Brunnhilde Brew, a plastic demijohn of Loki Lager and – naturally – plenty of the lager of Lamot.

The total bill came to over £100. Ur-Carol rang it up on the till; the automatic printer chattered and extruded the long frog's tongue of receipt. Carol took a taxi home.

8

The Icing Gun

S AFE IN THE FLAT, Carol changed out of her sherry-
stained jeans and set out to hide the beer. She didn't
want just to conceal it – that would have been easy
enough, for during the week Dan never paid any
attention to anything but the superficial. No, Carol
wanted all the beer to be out of sight, but effortlessly
accessible. She hid the beer so that she could lean out
from any vantage point in the flat and instantly access any
one of the bewildering variety of alcoholic beverages she
had purchased. This she achieved with a rare artistry.

The beer was hidden, the flat was clean. Carol looked
at the electric clock in the kitchen – she had two hours
before Dan would be back from work. She took some
steaks from the freezer and set them to thaw on the top
of the cooker. She put on the kettle and sat down on one
of the varnished pine benches that ran along the wall of
the kitchen. She scrutinised the cork board with its
coating of PCs, secular and devotional. But now neither
kind meant anything to her. The silent flat felt pres-
surised to Carol, as if, on this quiet autumn afternoon, it
were about to be lowered into the Marianas Trench – a
bathysphere for living.

Carol's flatfish hand skated down on to the lap of her dress. She regarded it as it lay there – for some reason it looked ludicrously arbitrary to her, as if it were just one of a number of possible wrist attachments that she could pull off and slot in at will. The electric clock buzzed subsonically. The hand slid down the schüss of material and plucked at the hem . . .

The train clattered across a small bridge and slowed again. I sort of thought that this might be an opportunity to take my leave of the don. I didn't mind the idea of waiting at some sleepy station for the next train. I had no stomach for the don's idea of horror and I felt he was giving his sordid little tale unnecessary airs by quoting Roethke. It was true – I knew that I had no thirst for the dénouement. I wished Dan and Carol dead, lifeless, decon-structed – or better still never constructed in the first place. I stood up for the first time since he had begun to talk and immediately felt much better. I was tall and he was short. And now, standing over him, I could see that he was going bald.

My standing up also ruptured the thickening atmosphere in the compartment. While seated I had felt intimidated and sucked in. I had become half convinced that the don was mad. I had expected some kind of an outburst when I stood up – that he might immediately get nasty – but he stayed silent. The train coasted to a halt. The window was half open anyway . . . I reached out into the warm pollen of the night and found the handle. I was on the point of stepping down from the compart-

88

ment when a railwayman appeared beneath me at the side of the track. He was holding a signalling lantern in his hand with both red and green lights illuminated.

'I wouldn't get down here if I were you, sorr . . .' *He had a burry West Country accent and an equine visage. The log of his head was surmounted by a Saturn's ring aureole of ginger hair. He looked up at me with sincere, dutiful eyes and went on.* 'The train's only halted to take on water – you'll be off again directly, as soon as we've got steam up.' *Before I had time to analyse these anachronisms a hand tugged at the back of my jacket.*

'Come on! Sit down! I want to tell you the rest of this story.'

I complied. The railwayman shut the door, I heard a whistle rise and fall, the train moved off once more through the close darkness. There was an internal shift inside me. It felt like something had given way, some membranous lining had ruptured. I shook my head from side to side, vigorously, and felt the tips of my hair flick against my cheeks and brow. But even as I fell back on to the plush and allowed the golden snowfall of retinal flecks to subside, I knew that it hadn't worked. I was still in the carriage, the don was still opposite.

'Don't try it,' *he said. The mutant was reading my mind.* 'You, boy, you're a literary train-spotter. No less and no more. But you've fallen off the platform you see. Your anorak is torn and dirty, your trainers are scuffed and you've lost your notebook. You're stumbling across the tracks at Clapham Junction – which as you know is the widest narrative interchange in Europe. If you don't watch it some purely local story, some commuting tale, will mow you down, cleave you in two, finally separate your dialogue from your characterisation. So-don't-try-it.'

'Try what?'

'Try and downgrade me in this fashion. It's unseemly, it's cheap. My reality shouldn't be tipped into a plastic laundry basket and flogged off in this manner. I reserve my right to centrality – to be the pro- as well as the an-tagonist.' *The don's voice picked up speed with the train. He was managing – once again – to marginalise me.*

' "It is better to travel hopefully than to arrive." Wooden d'jew agree with that – wooden d'jew? I certainly think so. And what that quotation tells us about the value of expectation can be applied to all areas of our life, can't it? I also think that the quotation . . . who is it, by the way? I simply cannot remember . . . tells us something about the value of good narrative, don't you? It points the way towards the positive values of storytelling. Naturally a story requires a coda, but this should not overwhelm the body of the tail. In truth I faintly despise the oblique and distorting innovations of the modern . . . don't you? I like something to be straightforward. I like a story to tell me no more or no less than the storyteller intends. I don't go looking for hidden meanings, I don't try and pick away at the surface of things, pretending to find some "psycho-logical" sub-structure that really I have placed there myself, by dint of sleight-of-mind. I like to call a spade a spade . . . Or a coon, or a nigger, or a buck-fucking Mandingo slamming his great engorged purple shaft into the bleeding, wrenching, splitting arse crack of some poor, pretty, pure white flower of a girl. Some soft thing, just past her first communion, all her clothes and underwear scented by a fucking lavender cushion. Christ, it makes me sick! Ga!' *I could see he was physically biting back the cud of his nausea.*

'So, anyway, stick with us for the end of the story, now won't you, my sweet? Won't you, my precious jewelkin? Pleaseums?' *His aged baby-face creased up with a sickly grin and then relaxed once more into dolly automatism.* 'Goody gumdrops!'

Carol's hand then, plucking once more at the hem, and then lifting up the whole bell of the dress bottom, scrunging it up to her waist, whilst she remained seated on the bench. Her fleshy tights sandwiched her blouse and underwear as if they were thick fungal petals in a transparent press. Carol took down the tights – freed them. She was wearing a neat pair of Y-fronts, they tented over her pubis, but still there was no satisfying sac dangling below. At any rate, this is what Carol thought, catching sight of herself, from the waist down, in the sheeny glass door of the music centre cabinet that Dan built.

Carol moved about the rooms, swivel-hipped, legs swinging out to each side, buttocks centred. She leaned against the doorjamb and tried punching a few imaginary upper arms with easy bonhomie. From outside the maisonette came the sound of the heavy wheeled canisters that contained the detritus of Melrose Mansions being shifted on to the garbage truck. Carol froze. Perhaps, she thought, perhaps I should go and show myself to them? After all, I have nothing to feel ashamed of, it's not my fault. And anyway they might find me attractive . . . I bet all of them have dreamed of finding a woman like me, a woman with just that little bit extra . . . to make them feel truly at home.

The Y-fronts fell down to her ankles and Carol stood as Nature intended her. She took her penis in her hand. It was small, brown-pinkly insignificant. She looked at it and thought What's all the fuss? But then it began to swell, to pump itself up, to inflate. And what a magnificent sight that was! For it didn't lift itself up in any ungainly fashion, there was nothing mechanical in its sudden growth, nothing wooden. Rather, like a flower opening in a stop-action film, the penis grew all at once, every part of it moving together, in concert, in harmony. It unfolded, spread itself to the sun. Lifted up its slim, supple length so that its smooth skin covering became taut, velvety. And as the head appeared, pulsing and bobbing, with a tear of semen in its slashed eye, Carol felt a surge of exultation. She clenched her buttocks and leaned back on her heels.

Some people say that the penis is an ugly thing, one of God's creative afterthoughts. They draw comparisons between its dangling extraneousness and the neat, fitted design of the female snatch. A pox on such pundits with their envious carpings. We know all about their pendulous labia, their cetacean clitorises and Moby Dick odours! Oh, Carol's penis, I could write an ode to it. The penis anyway is such a powerful thing, a solid rod packed with the fluids of life . . .

'Hold up! I sense something, my laddie. I sense that as I describe the glories of the newest member you are thinking along different lines . . . that you are placing different interpretations on what I am saying. Is this not so, my friend? My little cottager . . . Well educated are we?'

I demurred frantically.

'Good, because I hope for your sake that you aren't regarding Carol's penis as anything but what it is. I hope you aren't deriving any signifiers or symbols from Carol's penis. I hope you aren't undertaking some convoluted analysis of this story in your sick sheeny mind. And you know when I refer to "sheeny" I'm not talking about glass, don't you, my sweet? Only a faggot would do such a thing – and he would prettily lisp "it takes one to know one". Not so. Sometimes you don't even know who it is, right up to the moment when you feel the hot head

93

batter against your dry sphincter . . . or so people tell me . . .'

Carol ran her fingers along the obsidian rod. She is back standing in her tiled, fantasy courtyard. A fountain plays in a stone basin, all around are fluted columns. From somewhere comes the faint sound of a flamenco guitar, lightly strummed. From behind one of the columns, lightly stepping on heeled boots, comes a slim, elegant figure in short black jacket and tight trousers. He is handsome beyond belief, with thoroughbred features. He takes Carol by the arm and leads her to a divan upholstered with the finest of Persian kelims. And there he strips both himself and her, all the while running his fine, tapering hands over her smooth body, lingering over her penis, her clitoris, her nipples, her vagina.

Carol was really wanking by now. One hand pushing the skin of her penis back and forth, the other inside her cunt. The daydream divan corresponded to the divan bed in the living room. And it was here that the hidalgo started to fuck her, moving rapidly on from sinuous insertions to a seemingly infinite series of great whooshing strokes, each of which seemed to teeter on the brink, like a roller coaster at the very apex of its run, before sweeping in to fan up her fanny flames. Ooh! Ooh-ooh. That's ni-ice, isn't it? But I'll tell you, my little keikel, something funny was happening in Carol's little keikel.

94

Now of course she canted and moved her hips, and lying as she was, tipped back on the warm upholstery of the Habitat divan, she used its loofahesque action to enhance her pleasure. But this was something more than a thrusting back as she was thrust into (although that in itself was one of the innovations Carol had made alongside the joy of wanking). No, no. The worm turned. The cylinder was becoming the piston. And as she felt the sweet stirrings of orgasm in the deep pit of her loins Carol realised that she was *fucking* as well as being *fucked*, that she was inside the hidalgo, just as surely as he was inside her.

She came with great cracking thermofaxed plashes of jism. They shot out from Carol's third eye and fell, on the cushion covers, on the carpet, on Carol's smooth and hairless thighs. She dipped a carmine fingernail into the viscous mother-of-pearl fluid and brought it to her lips. Mmm! *Di-vine*. Salty and yet sweet and a texture unachievable by the finest and most famous of sauciers. Carol was transported.

She lay for a moment or two, replete, beautifully relaxed, her mind clear and even emptier than usual – then she mopped herself up matter-of-factly with a wad of toilet paper. She put on her Y-fronts, tights and skirt; straightened one or two things in the room, and sat down to wait for her husband to get home.

★   ★   ★

'Henry James only had half a cock. Not a lot of people know that. The poor man lost it chasing after a fire engine, trying to help out as an amateur fire fighter in his native Boston. He tripped and fell beneath the horses' hooves, only to emerge white and half unmanned. They carried him home to his exceptional family on a board. His brother William looked at poor Henry. He focused on the bloody patch that coated Henry's breeches, and challenged God, whomsoever he might be, to make his brother whole again. He was praying for all of us you see, he knew his brother. He knew that all we could look forward to was a series of thick, turgid novels; penis substitutes. Since poor Henters couldn't fuck anybody else, he resolved to fuck us all up with his serpentine sentences . . . uncoiling inside our minds like ever-lengthening weenies.

'Henry James and Mikhail Bakunin, that's the other great nineteenth-century non-cocksman that springs and then comes to mind. Bakunin at the barricades of 1848, rapier in hand. Bakunin at the inaugural meeting of the First International, striking the board and severing the working movement for all eternity; whilst all the time it wasn't a proud manhood that bumped for emphasis against the wooden lectern – but nothing at all. *"Die Lust der Zerstörung ist zugleiche eine schaffende Lust!"* Now there, there, dear, of course it is. And you know there's a pun there somewhere, but I'll be buggered if I'll grope for it . . . drink?'

I don't know where it came from but there was a small

leather-covered hipflask in his outstretched hand. His face
puckered up with bogus encouragement, he pushed the flask
at me again, willing me to take it, a card forced from a pack of
one. I did take it and raised it to my lips. The drink tasted of
vegetation, chlorophyll, it had the texture of semolina, or semen.
I tried not to gag as I swallowed, and handed him back the flask.

'Different, isn't it? It's called kava, by the way. The
Fijians make it by knouting some root or other. Its effect
is mildly psychotropic rather than sedative. They find it
helps them to perform certain feats, like walking across
hot coals and putting hooks through their penises. We
might disparage such activities as idiotic – or even more
idiotically, reverence them. But see how you feel in half
an hour or so, perhaps you'll surprise yourself.

'Bakunin didn't surprise himself much in that department. It was rumoured that the absent organ had been
hacked off by a playmate brother in a garden fight, but
nothing was ever proven. Imagine it, living out your life
as something much less than a man, you'd be the
opposite of Carol, but your sac would be worse than
unsatisfactory. It would be, tee-hee, the ultimate redundancy. With just a furry space where *it* ought to be.
You'd become a veritable teddy bear and intercourse
would be just that, or at best a frantic nuzzling. Frankly I
think it's all those stinking skin-cutters – Henry and
Mikey – deserved, for them it was just a little late visit by
the Möhel. I can imagine them, you know, sitting in hell
together; Bakunin in his beard and James with his shiny
pate. They are hanged men, joke men, upside-down

men. They have a table in the fungal horror of the Styxside café. Giant spermatozoa like antediluvian dragonflies whirr around their ears, they're being forced to eat Spanish fly by the handful, under the watchful eye of my old friend Goering – perhaps Chatterley would consent to join them, or Piers Gaveston *de temps en temps*. I'm a mine of penile facts, you know, a very deep shaft indeed, perhaps you'd like to hear more of my esoterica, no? *Dommage.*'

The don faltered. He allowed his voice to drop a half tone to a more companionable and relaxed pitch. A odd note of sympathy came in, which almost persuaded me that his earlier outbursts had been mere play acting: clever embellishments of his clever-clever story.

'There's this big thing about the progress of stories, isn't there, my lad? The writers say they never know what is going to come next. What will happen when the next sheet of foolscap is fed into the roller's maw. And of course this *is* like life. Life with its preposterously long odds against anything happening at all. And anyway *ex post facto* we will incontinently impose some tawdry motif on these senseless experiences and muddled ideas. All too often nowadays the motifs are crass – merely cinematic. Oiled, reflexive brain stems, plunging out from the face of some Levantine matinee idler. But that being said, inspiration is what we must call what Carol did next.'

★   ★   ★

Carol itched with anticipation. There were three hours to kill. She stripped off and wanked several more times, until all her genitals were raw with rubbing, but it was still only 4.30 pm.

She mounted the stairs to their pastel bedroom and went through the walk-in cupboard where their clothes were hung, Dan's to the right, Carol's to the left – sinister that, isn't it? Carol changed her clothes once more, but on this occasion she substituted someone else's, and then quickly rifled the drawer where Dan kept his papers: passport, birth certificate and so forth.

About five that afternoon, Ur-Carol saw Dan walking along Fortune Green Road. She recognised the baseball cap he sometimes wore, his narrow shoulders, and the distinctive leather blouson jacket, with its rounded collar and fake epaulettes. She was sorry he didn't stop into the shop to say hello, she wouldn't have pressured him to buy anything, she just would have liked it if he could have borne to be a little chummy. She watched his slight form until it was almost out of sight, and saw him cut through the alley between two houses that ran down to the overgrown railway track where the mutant waste mob had their camp.

At about a quarter to six, Carol parked the yellow Ford Fiesta in the side street behind Melrose Mansions. It was a hire car and it smelt strongly of rubber floor mat.

She went up to the flat and changed yet again. And although she had intended this to be an automatic, brusque performance, she still became lodged in front of the mirror, admiring her own naked form. When she could see her penis she seemed to fall into a kind of reverie, a waking dream. It was in direct contrast to how she felt when she was clothed. For now she acted with more decisiveness and sense of purpose than she had ever known before, but to what end she had no idea. Out of this mire thrust Carol's touchstone – and touch it she did, often and with increasing deliberation. It was about three inches long now when flaccid, but it was a good 'n' thick dick. And when erect it more than doubled in length, although it did not increase significantly in girth.

What now impressed Carol most about her penis was not its size or turgid potential – but its versatility. It was like New Zealand Lamb. When it was flaccid Carol could bend it effortlessly this way and that. As long as she didn't wrench at it, or allow her pointed nails to dig into it, she could twist it into a bewildering variety of shapes: a zeppelin, a ball, a manta ray, a nose, a horn. She even tucked it away completely between her clenched thighs, and stood looking at herself, rendered 100% womanly once again. But this made her shiver, and she happily let it spring back out again. When the penis was semi-erect she found that she could even fuck herself a little, turn her penis back on itself so that she was able to tuck its head inside of her vagina. But this was a children's game only, it was no kind of serious pleasure.

Like a middle-aged pop chanteuse, Carol punctuated her performance with her umpteenth costume change. This one was to be final. Carol knew she would take her bow and whatever encores were offered in this next outfit. And, as she dressed herself for the evening Carol allowed herself to become aware of the sharp contrast between the deliberation and efficiency of her actions and the vagueness and ambiguity of her ultimate intentions. Please, no psychobabble claptrap. There was no false bottom of self-deception set into the ground of Carol's consciousness. It was just that she quite simply couldn't see where all this was leading to. It was as if she were the lens of a camera; sharp foreground focus made necessarily for a muddied background, and vice versa. I always think life is a little like that, don't you? Rare is the individual who can retain the wider picture whilst concentrating on the detail. Very rare. So rare in fact that it can only be a stupid and ungrateful world, manipulated by covert conspiracies, that could possibly blacken or tarnish the reputation of such a man. And it would have to be a man, would it? You'd agree, wooden d'jew?

By the time Dan got back from work the focus was pulled to the middle distance and dinner was on.

'What's for dinner?' he said, clunking his trendy aluminium attaché case down on the floor.

'Oh, hello darling,' said Carol. She affected not to notice that he had come in, and hurried over from the stove to give him a fulsome kiss on his turned-down lips.

Dan noticed immediately that she was dressed up and wearing perfume. She had on a full-length apron, one of those ones that have a trompe l'oeil naked body printed on the front. But it couldn't conceal the stiletto heels, or the sheer stockings. And it was so uncharacteristic. Not that Carol had ever neglected her marital duties, as far as *nettoyage* and cuisine was concerned. She was far too well acculturated even to consider not getting Dan his evening meal, however much she despised him. But the sexy trimmings and the obvious affection, now that was a surprise.

'What's up?' asked Dan, sitting down to read the showbiz gossip in the *Standard* with a can of Coke from the fridge.

'It's our third anniversary, dummy,' replied Carol, moving from stove, to fridge, to work surface in the steps of a solo waltz. 'I thought we ought to celebrate.'

'Whaddya mean anniversary? We were married in April – it's now late September.'

'No, not that anniversary, dummy, the anniversary of the night we met, the anniversary of the first night we . . . you know.' Carol did her best to blush, but all it really amounted to was a beige tinge at the edges of her foundation.

'Oh, oh, that.' Dan was far better at it, he went puce to the roots.

And of course, as we know, Dan's macho bravado about sex, his 'climbing on board' and his former drunken rantings had all been show. In reality Dan was scared stiff of it. He feared that he didn't have what it took to satisfy a woman. Every time he had climbed on board Carol, penetrated her, and then wetly withered, he had lain, feeling her hips dig into him, conscious of his dwindling virility. His whole cock area was plunged in the sensual equivalent of muzzy darkness. He had tried to pull his cock into attention by tensing and relaxing his pubic and buttock muscles, but they seemed connected to nothing. With his mind attuned to the mechanical, Dan pictured the muscles as steel hawsers, that should have been linked up to the motive force for the great battering ram, but instead had been hacked away at, until their frayed ends pulled on nothing.

On occasion, although Carol had never seen fit to notice, Dan had leaked warm tears during this post-coital *tristesse*. He knew he ought to say something to Carol, to discuss frankly and openly the interface between his feelings and his penis. He had heard enough phone-in programmes to be familiar with the vocabulary, but he had never had the balls to do it. It was so much easier to sleep. And what if he could have got another erection? What would have come of it? Surely just another minute or so of pelvic bicycling on top of Carol's wan form . . . to be followed by more spent impotence.

And now that Dan was 'in recovery', as they said in Alcoholics Anonymous, his sexual feelings, if they can be dignified with that name, had taken a turn for the worse.

Dave 2 had told Dan that he could expect to find himself feeling intensely vulnerable, childlike and senti-mental, as the feelings he had repressed with alcohol came surging back. These would be the perfectly normal feelings he should have had in adolescence, but which he had prematurely knocked down and dragged out of his psyche, with the assistance of the lager of Lamot.

Dan's sexual feelings had never been anything but intensely vulnerable, childlike and sentimental. That fabled coupling when he had accidentally sandpaper-stroked Carol into orgasm had almost scared the life out of him. Drunk as he was, the moans and cries shocked him into the peculiar sensation that his triple thrust had hurt her, damaged her soft internality. This sensation summoned up as well an awareness of his little penis as a hard tool, a bludgeon, a corrector.

Dan recoiled from this; and this repulsion gives the lie to their true circumstance. You see, his relationship with Carol was a tragedy borne not of real circumstance necessarily, but of failure to communicate. What she could never have known was that after that night on the thin mattress in Stourbridge, Dan positively avoided the possibility of her orgasming; even that much reaction (and in truth Carol's orgasm had been a muted tea-break affair) assaulted his passivity.

And now he was in recovery, instead of resolving to 'talk through' his relationship with Carol, to 'openly and honestly' share his feelings with her, Dan was caught up on an almost continual basis in the most insipid of sexual fantasies. What he really wanted was to be gently wanked off, with a warm towel, by his female, emotionally inadequate counterpart. She wouldn't even have to take her clothes off to arouse him. To give Dan credit, he beamed this fantasy at all the women in the AA group (even the quasi–bag lady with her formaldehyde face), and sensing it, they ever so quietly drew away and avoided him.

It's lucky that Carol had taken the precaution of obtaining some cantharides; without them the evening might have been a dead loss. The man in the tight T-shirt in the shop where she had bought them had looked down the sides of his moustache at Carol. He rippled his pecs, as if he were about to start breast feeding her with testosterone and admonished her quite severely against giving him more than one. But looking at Dan again, from the vantage point of her own self-erecting scaffold, Carol was acutely aware of his flabby aura. While he went for a wash she crumbled two of the golden bugs into his Coke. They were funny little things, dry and desiccated, but golden red in colour, their wings and legs tightly folded into the body, as if they had arranged themselves on purpose for an eternal internment in some insectoid mausoleum. Instead, their heads, thoraxes and abdomens were pulverised by Carol's fingers. Dan came back from his wash and went on swigging the coke. He was thirsty, he had beaten balls with Barry after work.

They ate the steak, the sautéed potatoes and the green salad in silence. A candle burned down between them, timing their failure to communicate. Dan didn't so much as glance into Carol's (admittedly meagre) décolletage. Instead he read a copy of *Design Week*, paying more attention to the pictures than the words. Carol didn't mind, she was no conversationalist herself. She sat and masticated forty times before each swallow, and wondered what would happen next.

In truth she too was preoccupied, preoccupied by her penis. The afternoon's wanking had left her feeling bruised, numb. But now the blood started to beat up again. Carol was wearing quite tight satin knickers, but even so she could feel her pole stirring, attempting to tent the restraining fabric. On more than one occasion, as she was cooking the dinner, Carol had to turn away, lest Dan see something he shouldn't. And even when the todger wasn't seeking the light, Carol was visited by shocked intimations of its very furled quietude. But that's what it's like when you've got a John Thomas, isn't it? I mean to say that there are times when, even as a career-man, one double-takes on its very existence. They go so quiet don't they, curled up in their little cotton burrow, that one forgets them – and then remembers, what a revelation! A continual revelation, a never-ending story!

Carol had over-salted the potatoes and over-salted the salad dressing. She got her result towards the end of the meal. Dan looked up from his magazine and flicked back his forelock: 'Blimey I'm thirsty,' he said, 'I could really use another Coke.'

'Sorry love,' Carol replied. 'That was the last one.' And then entirely innocently, just as if it were an odd afterthought, she said, 'How about a beer?'

Dan stared at her. And then stared at her again. It was that quiet in the kitchenette that you could have heard a cock crow a mile off.

'You know I can't have a beer, Carol. And you know why.' His voice wasn't rancorous, and that was a good sign, rather it was weary.

'Yeah, yeah, sorry, I was forgetting, just for a moment. Anyway I thought just the one . . . perhaps it wouldn't matter?'

Ohhh . . . She was oh so clever, wasn't she? She knew how to twist the knife and no mistaking. She couldn't fail to be aware of the *real* dynamics of Dan's alcoholism, now could she? She had after all had the opportunity to study him at closer quarters for a very long time. She knew that Dan had no power of his own; she knew that he invested his decision-making faculty in whomever was near to him, whomever asserted themselves in a way that was vaguely congruent with what he wanted. How else to explain the close friendships with the undistinguished Barry, Gary, Gerry, Derry and Dave 1, or the speed with which he bonded with the likes of Derek the tosser, or for that matter Dave 2?

From the off, whenever she was within range, Carol had taken full responsibility for Dan's fundamental actions. He had abrogated it without even noticing. It wasn't that Carol was a trusted satrap of the Empress of Burford, she had after all yet to be invested with the sacred Peter Jones charge card. It was just that she was there . . . and as long as *she wanted* him to have a beer, well then . . .

'Well . . . I would like one . . . but what could I say to the Group at St Simons? What would I say to Dave 2? They . . . they . . . have faith in me.'

'Yes, but I have faith in you as well, Dan, and I think a single beer now and then won't matter too much. After all, they're always saying that you only put down alcohol one day at a time; this is our special anniversary' – on 'special' Carol essayed a coquettish *moue* – 'it can be one day when you pick it up.'

See how easily she smashed down the little ideological rockery that Dave 2 had erected in Dan's front-garden-sized intellect? It just goes to show the infinite malleability of the human spirit. Of course the salt helped, banking up the thirst Dan had acquired beating balls with Barry, and so did the Spanish Fly, which now started to beat up prickly flames in Dan's little crotch.

Carol plunked a distinctive can of Lamot in front of Dan. It was icecold and filmed with special-effect condensation. She produced one for herself as well. They drank them down, and then two more besides.

They moved to the living-room and Dan put on his requiem: Dire Straits. They slow danced a little before starting to tackle the rest of the eclectic collection Carol had assembled. Dan had a bottle of Gulder, then two or three of Pils. He was drunk by now. Carol, mindful of her role, was pacing them both carefully. She was tipping away three quarters of each of her beers into the yucca. She knew Dan was probably good for at least five or six more before he became useless, but the cantharides might be a random factor . . .

As he got drunker, the sense of sweet and directionless guilt made Dan maudlin and sentimental. In his cups he dampened Carol's shoulder with his tears of gratitude and self-pity. She uncorked a blue bottle of thick, sweet beer, brewed by a tiny, closed Walloon order. He gulped it down. The Spanish fly was holding him upright. He was surprised through his stupor to feel his thin dick stretch itself and yawn for some kind of action. He would have been very surprised if he had known that Carol was feeling exactly the same thing.

Under the solo-stares of the mynah and the cockateel *A Whiter Shade of Pale* seeped out from the music cabinet that Dan built. Carol slipped one white shoulder out of her little black dress. Dan slobbered on it but she managed not to wince. His hand went to her nipple – chinese burnt her pallid aureole – and then lurched to her crotch. How fortunate that she had tucked her penis back under her perineum, for even though the buckled bend stuck out a half inch from her vagina, his conditioned nerves, sedated at the periphery, would never notice. Nor did they; his hands flopped around on her like dying fish, seeking insufficient moisture, moisture with which to breathe.

His breath fluted in her ear, so laden and yeasty that she could imagine a host of micro-organisms streaming in and on to her brain. She was glad when the fingers swooped down once more and started to scrabble at her back and buttocks, as if Dan were struggling to remove the cellophane from some large product.

But lest we forget . . . Carol's hands with their carmine nails were voyaging as well. Carol's hands sought out the pressure points and tremulous gullies of Dan's body. They fanned down his narrow sides and swooped over his meagre hips, his boyish bum cheeks. They moved back up to his face, still soft with adolescent down. Carol had never consciously thought about what was going to happen, she was just blithely following an instinct, but her hands knew. Like busy predators they circled and plotted, ducked down behind the cover of breast- or hip-bone, and then shot up to survey the epicene country. Carol's hands felt the submissiveness, the yielding quality of Dan's body. It was Carol's hands that went to the metal-edged wings of Dan's check collar, but it was Carol's flat and nasal voice that eventually said, 'Let's go upstairs.'

As he passed the low coffee-table, tugged by Carol towards the narrow stair, Dan reached out, his hand scrabbled for the plastic webbing that held the four familiar red-and-yellow cylinders. It was the last time he ever sought out the lager of Lamot.

In the bedroom she pirouetted, her dress twisting fully off her narrow shoulders. She whirled round and let her hands rub her breasts, her thighs, her pubis, with rough abrasive strokes; the way she wanted to be touched. She was so instantly and fully aroused that it was all that she could do to clutch her penis back, to stop it unfurling and declaring her strange sovereignty.

She slid the rag-rolled corner of her bedside table between the back of her thighs and nudged her perineum against the acrylic of the clock radio. Wedged there, trembling; with the two waves of arousal beating up inside her – the one a heavy swell, the other a fast gathering breaker – she watched while Dan, hobbled by his trousers, teetered in the act of undressing and fell sideways, slamming his head in to the venetian-blind-slatted cupboard door.

Seeing his ribbed body folded against the ribbed door, Carol was overtaken by a wave of strange tenderness and stranger possessiveness. She hopped up and lifted him by the shoulders, lifted him like a baby, his nether parts still begirt with bands of clothing, and threw him on to the bed.

The unfamiliar intoxication, the shock of the rounded back of his skull whacking into the wall, saved lucky Dan from feeling the sinister power of this lift 'n' chuck; this unconscious absorption by Carol of all the wrestling throws she had ever idly seen on *World of Sport*.

Carol was now the deft one: removing Dan's velcro-strapped bootees, denim bags and snug briefs before he could say 'knife'. Not that Dan was really capable of saying anything at this stage. His eyes had slipped out of gear, was it Carol he was looking at, or his mother? His head slid sideways, saliva and Lamot bubbled at the hospital corners. This evening, someone had made up Dan's mouth with a rubber sheet.

He barely noticed when she turned him over. But he did notice when she entered him. He couldn't fail to, her cock was such a big, hot, hard thing; and his anus, although causally lubricated, was still tight with self-repression, bunged up with the enduring legacy of auto-erotic toilet training. She pushed into him and rent his sphincter, tore a crack in one of its muscular segments.

But hold up! *Tolle*! How was it for *her*? Surely that's the important thing. Fuck him, he's a passive thing, an empty vessel, a field upon which the majestic battle may rage, but Carol? Well . . . Isn't she beautiful? She's taken the prudent and I would say *beautiful* step of putting her silken scrap on over her suspenders. So now she can rip it away and let her fantastic penis tremble, oscillate up, all girded and framed by the black straps and slick columns of her upper thighs.

How she promenaded around the end of the bed! Holding noble, rampant postures for full seconds! Tearing off her bra so her meagre dugs could hang free. But hist! They are no longer meagre dugs, barely domed, surmounted by a disappointing aureole. Now she feels beneath them the firm saucers of pectoral muscle, she lifts her arms aloft and charming duck eggs of bicep boing up.

Downstairs, the Riders on the Storm were moving through the tinkling rain, shifting up from a trot to a canter. Carol's eyes passed over the litter of pots and plastic sticks on her glass-topped dressing table, but stayed on Dan's neon-tinted hair gel. The carmine nails snaked down to get it . . .

. . . Dan felt the cold glob of viscous tackiness, rammed by the sharp fingers into his arse cleft. Carol covered him, her chest on his back for a moment, and then she reared up, sighted along his humped spine and oh, so tenderly guided her penis home.

She felt its shaftiness, its columnar construction, its vascular rigidity. She felt the tight rejection of Dan's restraining ring but pushed in despite and *because* of it. This was her moment, she sensed. Her confirmation of what she truly was . . . Crass isn't it? The idea that being able to fuck Dan, actually penetrate him somehow *made* Carol aggressive, made her a rapist . . . Crass, but true. Come on, let's face up to it, if you hand someone a loaded gun and present them with a target – the outline of a man – then they're going to shoot at it, aren't they? It would be nothing but naive to imagine any other course. Anyway it isn't a case so much of the tail wagging the dog, it's more that the dog is the tail and vice versa. And if you say any different then it can only be because you have nothing whatsoever between your legs, no gash, no tool, no nothing, just the smooth and puckered skin that seals off a wound after an operation.

We were stuck in a tunnel. I couldn't be absolutely sure but I suspected from the way he had begun to pant, and the way that his Mr Kipling voice had begun to flake and crumble, that the don was playing with himself.

★　　★　　★

Hrrumph! Later, by pushing home hard with the rectal thermometer, taking a variety of swabs and blood tests, the pathologist was able to make a specious pronouncement to the press. Dan, he said, had understood little of what was happening to him before he mercifully expired; his blood/alcohol level was too high, and anyway any one of the head injuries that were inflicted on him would have been sufficient to render him unconscious . . . Bollocks! Utter kak! In truth he *was* aware, and he felt *everything*. Each sandpapery thrust into him, abrading the sensitive blood vessels, each smack of his narrow head into the pine headboard, each concertina-ed groan from his thorax as it tried to swallow the abdomen that reared into his diaphragm. And there were many such strokes, many such smacks, for Carol was a young woman in her prime, and as we all know, young women of this particular type are very difficult to arouse sexually, but once they are aroused they are even harder to satisfy without the most vigorous of jouncings.

She would pause at the top of a stroke . . . and then come on again . . . harder each time. She had lost the sense of thrusting into him, lost the feeling in her newest member, lost any awareness of the aftershock as with each push his skull slammed into the woodwork. Instead the whole world . . . nay even the whole cosmos, had contracted into a pulsing clanking thing, a pulling apart and rattling together of chain links, the spasmodic eruption of a white grub from its fibrous pupa . . .

She came with a bang rather than a whimper, the

114

bummy numbness of her genitals squishing home for the last time into the bummy mush of Dan's derrière, her thin *poitrine*, dart-tip nipples questing for the target, thrust forward as if breasting the tape, and she subsided. Subsided and looked, and saw: Dan's dying stare, fawn-like, innocently stupid, as the grey giblets fell from his shattered skull and grey porridge began to stain the flower-patterned pillowcase.

Carol heaved herself off what had been Dan and looked round for a towel to wipe herself with. She was standing on the landing tying the belt of her robe when she heard the 'bing-bong' of the door chime. She footed down to the half-landing and peered over the banisters. The downstairs hall was dark, but from where she stood, backlit by the uplight in the vestibule, she could clearly make out the distinctive, lopsided silhou-ette of Dave 2.

Dan's bowels loosened when he died, and it may be small consolation, but he also had one of his sweet little piddling orgasms, nice that isn't it? As I've said, the pathologist was a stupid man with no real powers of deduction, but we have to be fair, what would you be able to divine from such stringy auguries? There were two types of semen in the anal cavity of the dead man . . . and one of them corresponded to his own . . . indeed one of the semen samples had to be his own.

★   ★   ★

'I know what you're thinking but I think I'll trouble you to wait, if you don't mind, if you would be so good.' *The don emphasised the 'so good' with the double click of a large switchblade which he had drawn from an inside pocket of his jacket. He turned it this way and that, as if trying to catch points of light on its long, shark's snout of a blade. Then, sighting at me along it he said,* 'There's nothing democratic about this situation, boy. But, nonetheless, should you tire of deliberations I shall be only too happy to introduce my version of the guillotine.' *He placed the knife on the seat, next to his plump thigh, as if it required no further acknowledgement. I sat silently and absorbed the awful realisation. For, when all is said and done, there is nothing worse under the sun than the revelation that you have been a fool.*

'It always amazes me that people don't always think of doing things like that when they see an icing gun, wooden d'jew agree? They are such conspicuously venal objects, like giant painted tin hypodermics, complete with a penile eye. They are entirely logical, perhaps even essential tools for the injection of one man's semen into another man's body. At any rate that's what Carol thought the minute she opened the second cutlery drawer and saw the icing gun lying alongside the Kitchen Devils and the tenderising mallet, hard against the forgotten fondue forks and the kebab skewers shaped like miniature sabres. I'm getting ahead of myself.'

★　　★　　★

Dave 2 wasn't fazed when the door swung open and Carol stood in front of him in her nightie and terry-towelling bathrobe.

'Oh hi, Dave,' she said.

'I've just come back from a convention up in Colchester,' said Dave 2, hefting a flight bag of devotional literature that he held in his left hand to point up the fact.

'Come in, come in. I'll just put the kettle on.'

Dave 2 settled himself at the breakfast bar while Carol pirouetted around making the coffee. Dave 2 explained that he had come to see Dan. There was to be a fundraising jumble sale at St Simon's the following weekend and Dave 2 wanted Dan to make the signs. 'I think he went to a meeting directly from work,' said Carol distractedly. She was crumbling the last of the three golden insects into Dave 2's mug of Gold Blend . . .

It was like taking candy from a baby. To begin with they just had a good old emotional confab. Dave 2 had never known Carol to be so open and honest. If only she had been like this before! She would have given Dave 2 and Geena such pleasure. Here she was, gently sobbing out the frustrations and coldness of her marriage to Dan. Dave 2 couldn't prevent himself from placing an avuncular arm about her thin shoulders. She nuzzled into the foetid greasiness of the cranny between the worn khaki collar of his jacket and the worn khaki skin of his throat. 'Oh Dave,' she sighed.

Something fizzed in Dave 2's denim crotch. His thick and stubby penis prickled with pins and needles. It was like milking a cow. They never shifted from sideways-on positions on the pine bench, they just grappled with one another's shoulders. Dave 2 was never quite sure what was happening to him and in the light of subsequent events this is hardly surprising. Subsequent events and of course his own personal history, which was full, as we have said, of the most remarkable gaps.

He never touched her cunt or cock. His ginger fingers just managed to tweak at her darting nipple as she man-oeuvred the little plastic beaker under his bubbling spiracle. He came before he was even half-erect, such was the effect of the aphrodisiac on a man whose sexual ideal was Jenny Agutter in *The Railway Children*. He felt Carol's cool hand expertly tugging at his cock and balls, tugging at them with an easy and intimate familiarity. There was plenty of semen, which was just as well because some of it missed the plastic beaker and spotted the lino. Carol missed it when she cleaned up later on. But that was O.K. because the team from Fortune Green Police Station (two lumpen detectives and a wall-eyed forensics expert) also missed it.

Swish, went the blade of the knife in the enclosed air of the compartment, swish and then swish again. The don was beginning to conduct his finale.

'There's no accounting for other people's minds, now, is there, Jew boy? Oops, I'm rather out in the open now, aren't I? I've rather told you what I know about you, haven't I? Still not to worry. You must understand that this is nothing personal, this little prejudice of mine, it's the race I object to, not the individual. However, you are right to suspect that there is some connection between my carefully considered opinion of the Hebrew people and this marvellous recital which your waxy ears, full of the cheesy gunk of the *shtetl*, have been so fortunate to hear. You should know how Dave 2 felt, you should know how Dan felt. You should know because that's the sort of thing you like to do to people, isn't it? Well, isn't it? Taking Christian children by night, children as young as six or seven, spiriting them away to your synagogues and there they are stripped naked, isn't that so? Drugged . . . won't you admit it? And all sort of things are shoved up them, aren't they? Cocks of course, shiny, domey, kikey cocks and other more sinister things; ceremonial candles, fists and menoras. Deny it if you will . . . will you?'

'No.'

'You won't deny it?

'Why should I?'

He was on me in an instant. And of course that plump exterior, soft and apparently futile, was just that: an exterior. He was wiry and strained with strength, his hand gripped my throat, he plunged a knee into my crotch, the knife point came hard into my throat, hard enough to prick and draw a little blood. My ability to resist it — the loathsome spider of spindly intent — skittered away. And it left my mind scrabbling for purchase on the smooth awfulness of the moment. And what could it come up

119

with? Nothing but the peasant advice of the body.

When someone holds a knife to your throat you have to hold very still, that's the most important thing: hold still. They might gash you from nerves or because they misinterpret the slightest of movements, so bear that in mind and hold still!

Close to mine the don's face was a mutating thing. It is part, I realise, of the failure of my mind, this collapse of the second order. And as if to bracket it, give it phenomenal backing so to speak, my eyesight is failing as well. My vision is no longer stereoscopic. Contour and shape change as I flick from oval screen to oval screen. The thin, etched wrinkles that I had noted earlier were revealed as a restraining net, holding amorphous features together, features that threatened to change into something else altogether.

So we can say with some certainty that Dave 2, milked, humiliated, his principles shattered, was led around the flat by his penis, like a dog on a lead. Carol got him to drink, the manipulative bitch, destroyed his five years of sobriety in an instant. She alternately mocked him and wanked him. And then, as he sat in his cups, surrounded by empty cans, his limp dick dangling, she bashed him hard on the back of the head with a meat tenderiser.

He shifted his weight so that he could lean partially against the window. The knife stayed at my throat, but his other hand strayed away from my gullet and towards his crotch.

What could be neater, eh? The thin young man, curled in the boot of the yellow hire car. They found him down by the abandoned railway track, you know . . . looking peaceful save for the jagged hole in his head. To begin with they grilled the deadbeat travellers, they delighted in it. But it didn't take long to identify Dan as the young man who had hired the car that afternoon; and after that things began to fall into place very quickly . . . They found Dave 2 in the flat, still unconscious . . . they found the semen in Dan's dead arsehole . . . they matched it . . . bingo! Ur-Carol came forward and told them that she had seen Dan, that afternoon, walking towards the travellers' camp.

Poor Dave 2. Clearly he was a victim of circumstance, but then perhaps . . . tee-hee, he should have practised a little more circumcision. We should all take care in that department, shouldn't we?

His hand groped to undo fasteners, to pull apart the flannel and cotton lips.

★　　★　　★

I believe that Dave 2 has done very well inside. He's even organised an AA group with the other Rule 43 prisoners. I think that shows tremendous good faith, don't you? Naturally he was horrified by what he had done, but in a way it wasn't really him was it? I mean he was in an alcoholic blackout, he can hardly be held responsible for his actions . . .

'But what about you?' *It was my first defiant croak since the assault started, my first stab at redemption. Could I hit him where it hurts? In his soft, didactic underbelly?* 'Are you responsible for your actions?'

'Oh entirely, completely, utterly. I'm right in there. I can transcend your "typing", your insinuations, even what you imply about what I like to do in the privacy, yes, the very sacred privacy of my own home.

'You must have realised that anyone who could undergo such a splendidly original and entire meta-morphosis would be well-placed for further theatricals.'

He pulled back from me and stood. He closed the switchblade, still smiling. 'I think further force,' *he said,* 'will be unnecessary.' *It may have been the kava, or just the shock – but it was true. I felt like milk going off, all my limbs were transmogrifying into useless globs of rennet, I could not have moved – even if I had wanted to.*

The don was moving about the carriage with dread efficiency. As he passed and re-passed me the open gash of his flies came again and again before my eyes. Was there one fly, or two?

He sat and unlaced his shoes. He looked at me almost quizzically – it was as if, in that moment, another engineer had taken over in the studio – for this voice had a new accent and a different timbre, as surely as if a new tape had been shoved home and played. His voice now was sweet and cloying, full of the sugary puke of togetherness.

'Some might say that it's of no importance how I feel about my sexuality.' *He shook his heel and a brogue fell to the floor. His socks were argyll.* 'After all I'm an odd mule, a procreative cul-de-sac, a genetic dead end.' *He stood, unbuttoned his flannels at the waist and stepped out of them. There was no surprise in the liverish sag of his pants.* 'As I said in my story, I've tried doing it to myself, but the results haven't been too good . . .' *He slipped out of his tweed jacket and hung it on the hook provided. He took off his tie, using one hand to loosen it from the knot, like a boy – or an inexperienced man. He flushed with the exertion; perhaps, also, he was little embarrassed to be undressing like this in public.* ' . . . Miscarriage after miscarriage, each of my bloody slunks seemed to provoke me to create another.' *But he pulled off his vest just like a woman, his arms crossing over his chest, his hands going to the hems at the front.*

And when he had slipped off his pants as well, unfastened his garters and removed both them and the tartan socks, when he stood before me, naked as the day he was born, I felt a deep compassion for the don, for Carol. For the truth was that he had none of the mean-featured prettiness he had ascribed to his fictional alter-ego. (I want you to understand that I only use the following term by way of deploying the full range of possible epithets to describe his looks, but, to be blunt): he was a dog. He was one of those women with the body of a middle-aged male sedentary. Flat white dishes of breast – piecrusts on the kitchen table – came to a head, sort of, with nipples that threatened to invert if you pressed upon them. His un-thighs, his bent shanks, they were a travesty of shapeliness. He sat again and parting his knees, brought me face to face with the heart of the matter. It was a huge, brown jewel lying on the velvety plush. It was gnarled and veined, for all the world the hacked-off stump of an old oak. It spilt from the burst slit of his vagina like a pile of grain from a slashed sack. It was strange for me to observe how the lips of his vagina had been altered by the transformation. The dermis had hardened, browned, so that it seamlessly merged with the root of the penis, like a packaged shirt and V-neck pullover combination.

And that was the strangest thing of all, what in retrospect struck me most about the time I spent with the don. This fact: that there was nothing particularly disquieting about his genitals, or at least there seemed nothing threatening about them. It struck me as natural to want to take them in my mouth, to feel the hard head beat against my palate as the thick shaft pulsed against my lips and my tongue at last sought out the don's soft core.

The don may have had a man's figure but his body felt like a woman's His back was soft, lacking, even in arousal, the rigor of a man's musculature. And his breath – when he raised me from my knees, pulled me away from his crotch and leant forward to kiss me — was full of the vanilla essence of childhood. It was innocent breath, kind breath, trusting, uncorrupted breath.

He kissed me and undressed me, and then he raped me.

He raped me. And it's an unusual thing to be able to say this, in this day and age and in this successfully plural society, but he defiled me as well. Defiled me insofar that as he raped me he screamed and ranted, gibbered and incanted the most awful mish-mash. A vile medley of all the loose accusations he had already laced his story with: against Jews, intellectuals, Modernists and the psychoanalytically inclined.

And for him, it was plain, this rape had a resolving character. In forcing himself into me I could sense that the don was forcing himself also back into the now.

'Not yet,' *he said, kissing me kindly, his tongue coming into my mouth with the easy familiarity of a boiled sweet.* 'Let me do that for you.' *And he had knelt in turn before me. He kissed his way into my clothing, running his tongue over seams and buttons and zipper. I felt madly aroused, tripped-out by urge. But when he had my penis, instead of kissing, licking and sucking — he bit. Bit hard and then used my condition, hobbled by garments, to turn the trumps, to repeat his Dan act. He flipped me over, so that he could bugger me.*

'Who - says - lightning - never - strikes - twice - in - the-same-place-eh!' *He used each thrust to push home the words. He had me now, no mistaking. I had wanted it, hadn't I, I had asked for it.* 'You fucking yiddo! You dirty kike! You nancy Jewboy! You purulent, disgusting queer! England not good enough for you? My values not good enough for you? The rigid assurance of my cock not good enough for you? Do-you-seek-to-rearrange-things?'

I thought he was going to rearrange me — but he didn't. I thought that I would end up like his first husband, but on this occasion he wasn't playing things quite so rough. He just stunned me, battered me about with ringing clouts around my ears. He slashed, scoured and stropped me with strokes of his switchblade across my back and shoulders. And when he was done he left me. The door of the compartment swung behind him on its giant hinges. The peculiarly spacious, cold, diesel smell of a major London terminus quickly displaced the closeness of the compartment, blowing out the last few hours.

I struggled to my hands and knees, hiccuping bile. I stood; pulling up my pants and trousers I lurched to the door. The platform was streaming with disembarking passengers. It seemed impossible that any of them hadn't looked in this direction, hadn't seen the don's departure.

I leant out of the door using the step as a foothold. And there he was, going strong. He was walking free with the tight, mincing gait that I would have prescribed for him, given the chance.

And did I go to the police? Did I spill the proverbial beans? I should say not, oh so gentle reader. Wood-jew? Instead I paid my 10p and took to the tiled exposure of the Temporary Toilet. In the short-let cubicle I scraped the drying semen from the insides of my thighs with hard paper, closer to manila than tissue. And then, standing splashing water on my numb face, I saw a prefiguration of the interview room in the functional anonymity, the uncaring facility of the public's convenience.

There would be a detective constable and his partner – family men with wholemeal concerns – whose faces would become sicklied o'er as I ran through the particulars of my liaison with the don. They would shake their jug heads as they listened to how the don seduced me, bamboozled me.

'Now quite honestly, sonny, dressed in this get-up. I mean to say what do you expect if you venture out into the fictional night alone, looking like you do, acting as you did? I'm not trying to talk you out of us going forward, there is the physical evidence after all, but I think you should be prepared for what people are going to say. Because I reckon that they will be forced to conclude that you were asking for it. You actually wanted someone to perform to you. In fact, I'll go further. I think you wanted to be an audience. Oh, I don't doubt that you feel bad about it now, you feel used. But really, luvvie – come on. This is what you get if you sit there like a prat, listening to a load of cock . . . and bull.'

BULL

A Farce

*I hate the dreadful hollow behind the little
    wood,
Its lips in the field above are dabbled with
    blood-red edges,
The red ribb'd ledges drip with a silent horror
    of blood,
And Echo there, whatever is ask'd her,
    answers 'Death'.*

Alfred, Lord Tennyson, *Maud*

1

Metamorphosis

B ULL, A LARGE and heavyset young man, awoke one morning to find that while he had slept he had acquired another primary sexual characteristic: to wit, a vagina.

The vagina was tucked into the soft, tendon-edged pit behind his left knee. It is quite conceivable that Bull wouldn't have noticed it for some time had it not been a habit of his lightly to explore all the nooks and crevices of his body prior to rising.

So, Bull, lying in frozen bicycling posture, the duvet wrapped around his crotch and lower abdomen like an inflated dhoti, felt his hand and his hand felt him. It traversed the hair-frosted pap-hummocks on his chest and swooped into his sternum, only to rise again, like a downhill skier, on to the glorious piste of his tummy.

What did Bull usually think of during this instrument check prior to the day's take-off? Very little. Very little indeed. Awake and upright, or even in bed but accompanied, Bull was a perplexed soul. His broad brow was often furrowed with concentration, but his thoughts were like aging, arthritic sportsmen. They shambled, lurched and feinted around one another, always on the verge of contact but never quite achieving it. The strain of this tended to push his coarse (but shapely) features into close and unsavoury proximity with one another. But in the net-strained light of a London spring morning Bull did not think. Instead he tried to roll himself back into the surf of sleep. Again and again he dived forward, aiming for the point at which the wave of oblivion broke on to the beach of his consciousness; only to find himself, still lying on the grainy mattress, with repose in lapping retreat beyond and below him.

Bull stirred himself and made ready to wank. He rolled over on to his broad white back. His big arms freed themselves from the folds of the duvet and went to work to remove the thing from the bed altogether. Eventually it joined the carpet. Bull's hands went next to his thighs and kneaded them; to his knees and cupped them; back up to his buttocks and hammered into them like wedges. The vagina, the malevolent reality-gashing interloper, chose that moment to prink and snag against the back of Bull's left hand.

And suddenly he was on his feet, his mind screaming at the incongruity of his eyes noticing the plaster gape and mortar trickle from the damp patch beneath the window, while he, while he, while he had this . . . this . . . thing *on his body*. Or was it *in his body*? He could not tell. He knew only this: that there was something in the vulnerable pit behind his knee. Something that might be a wound, perhaps inflicted by a dying bed-spring, but already partially healed; or it might be a bubo or a carbuncle, grown in the night with horrible speed.

Whatever it was, Bull felt he could not stand like this, sucking on the lino from one sweaty foot to the next, without touching it once again. The thing, whatever it was, was an itch that mustn't – but must – be scratched; and writ Brobdingnagian.

Bull touched it again, without being aware of having made the effort. But this time the touch turned into a feel. The thing was raised and roughly oval in shape. It was perhaps four inches long; extending from the very crease of the knee-back down to where Bull's calf bulged out. Bull could feel that the wound or infection was bifurcated and that its crevice was wrinkled and reassuringly dry. But now he was aware of it, the thing was clearly serious, because whatever movements he made – either squatting or crouching to feel the thing, or frantically twisting to try and actually see it – set off frantic waves of internal sensation. Awarenesses of partings and viscous rubbings, of something deep into his body, stuck *inside* his body and apparently broken off at the haft . . .

Bull, still naked, staggered to the full-length mirror that was shinily affixed to the rose-patterned wallpaper. He placed his back towards it and sighted over his shoulder and down. His eyes met the cyclopean squint of the vagina, but before he could examine it closely Bull vomited copiously. He brought up full half-pints of twice-fermented lager, in which all the alcohol had long since turned back to sugar. These fell the fathom from Bull's mouth to the lino and then pushed out across it, wave after wave, each one taking with it a little surf of hair, and lint, and dust.

I'm sick, thought Bull to himself. Really sick. I'm ill. I have a huge infection in the pit of my knee. I better go and see the doctor. If I'm vomiting the infection must be beginning to poison my blood.

He pulled on a pair of trousers and went along the corridor to the bathroom, where he undertook a sketchy version of his usual toilet. He gathered together a handful of fossilised J-Cloths that had been wadded in the u-bend of the sink's outflow pipe.

The floor mopped, Bull dressed. Despite the fact that he wasn't going to go directly into the office he still put on creased trousers, collared shirt, jacket and tie. He regretted not being able to wash more thoroughly, on account of the wound, but he had shaved his wide pink face with fierce precision.

Bull went back along the corridor to where the phone crouched on a fake Chippendale stoolette and dialled the group practice where his doctor worked.

'Grove Health Centre,' trilled the woman on the end of the line. She had the vocal automatism that comes to people whose job description might well read: 'ceaseless repetition'.

'Could I have the Andersen Practice?' asked Bull.

'Just putting you throu-ough . . .' The woman's voice was cut off abruptly by the ringing of an extension, but

Bull could still hear her taking other calls from the switchboard. She said 'Grove Health Centre', and 'Just putting you throu-ough' at least four more times before Bull's call was answered and he was retrieved from the static limbo.

'Andersen Practice,' said another woman with a marginally different voice.

'I need to see Dr Margoulies,' said Bull. 'Has he any appointments available today?'

'Ooh-er,' came warbling from the receiver, 'I don't think so, and he's off for a week tomorrow to a Learning Jamboree.'

'Whaddya mean?' Bull was getting querulous. 'Learning what, precisely?'

'It's a kind of a competition you see.' (The girl was 'being helpful'. She had taken to heart the circular issued by the Health Authority requesting all employees to view NHS patients as viable fee-paying customers; rather than as the work-shy alcoholics, hypochondriacs and torpid valium addicts that they so clearly were.) 'Teams of doctors from the various health centres in the Authority's area go and camp in a field near Wincanton where they have a series of inter-active competitions designed to increase their awareness of the new reforms.'

'And Dr Margoulies is actually going on one of these things?' Squatting by the telephone in the gloom of the corridor, Bull's hand had strayed once more down his thigh to the inappropriate quim site. Sensing a lip under the gaberdine of his trouser leg, his fingers froze and retreated.

'Oh yes, he's really looking forward to it . . . But hang on a minute. There's a cancellation here for 9.30. How quickly can you make it over here?'

'I can do it in twenty minutes.'

'What's your name please?'

'Bull.'

'And initial?'

' "J".'

Bull hung up and called into the office. He got an Australian temp who took the message that he would be late in without comment.

Bull double-locked the door to his flat. He paused on the walkway and surveyed the scene. Bull's flat was above a parade of shops on East Finchley High Road. The shop units were of thirties vintage, red-bricked and vigorously coped and mansarded with snowfall ridges of glutinous rendering. But while the front of the shopping parade had the congruence that comes with aspiration (the tenants' association still managed to stamp on attempts to introduce loud or flashing signs), the back of the parade betrayed the building's utility. The walkway to Bull's flat ran up a ramp that ill concealed a number of huge, three-wheeled canisters of domestic and commercial detritus. This was the entry point to the parade for the tradesmen's tradesmen, and one was out there already, erecting a tiny portable railing around the oblong entrance to a subterranean ductal zone.

Bull looked at the gas engineer, he looked at the red-brick Methodist church that rose above the suburban roofscape, he smelt the spring air. He felt an odd vulnerability this morning which he attributed to his wound or burn.

But Bull didn't let this govern him. After all, he was a man with an appointment to keep, always a potent motivator. Instead he got into his car, pulled out from behind the parade, and drove off towards Archway.

So let us leave Bull, our protagonist, already well on the road to his personal Thebes. Already imprisoned in a stereoscopic zone where a shift in angle is all that's required for free will to be seen as determined. Let us leave Bull enjoying his last Heraclitan morning before being buckled into the implosion of farce. And turn our attention up and over Highgate Hill, down to the grid of streets that surrounds the Grove Health Centre.

In a house in one of the adjacent streets Alan Margoulies's wife Naomi was making the baby's breakfast. 'Making' really only amounted to pouring warm, boiled water from the electric jug on to the heap of nutritious grey powder in the plastic bowl. But for some reason this slight action rang her head with the metallic vibration of something like despair.

The baby was strapped into her high chair with a ludicrously professional piece of webbing, all steel Uclips and ribbed orange nylon. Looking at the baby's chubby face, with its flattened cheeks and 'O'ing nostrils, Naomi suddenly saw it as a clever little homunculus, an alien presence.

The baby, on the other hand, regarded Naomi with frank and blissful wonderment. She was of an age (about fourteen months), when each new morning represents nothing so much as a triumph on the part of the Continuity Department. The baby was amazed to see roughly similar objects, of similar colours, occupying the same positions as yesterday. And more than that the baby was delighted (albeit perplexed) that the actors playing her parents seemed to have remembered, once again, the parts assigned to them.

'Come on, ba–aby,' said Naomi, approaching the high chair with Swiss cereal in one hand and two spoons in the other. She gave one teaspoon to the baby and plied the other herself. They made free with the Farex. Naomi had to stand in an awkward position to feed the baby, because her husband, the doctor, was occupying the whole of one end of the big, scrubbed, plain wood table that dominated the Margoulieses' kitchen. Naomi knew better than to disturb him. Alan often had filthy tempers in the morning. If provoked he might easily spiral into quite staggering flights of abusive fancy.

Naomi couldn't decide what to look at. For some reason she felt nauseous this morning; and the sight of the baby squidging and patty-caking the beige pulp was more than she could bear. But then, the aerial view of her husband was just as much of a turn-off. Alan Margoulies may have been universally acknowledged by all who knew or met him to be a charismatic and sexually attractive man. But from the angle afforded her Naomi could see brown *and* white scurf in the parting of his lank black hair. She also noticed with a shock of recognition – it was a fact that she had registered before but only with her hands – that the back of Alan's head really did have little or no projection to it. There was an almost perpendicular line running from the apex of his scalp to where the hair flopped across his collar.

Naomi shivered. The translation of one sense into another left her feeling still more nauseous. The Doctor rattled his newspaper. 'Mmm . . . mmmm,' he grunted, a private assent to something he was reading, in that awful, affected, self-consciously absent-minded way that Naomi had come very quickly to despise. Naomi meditated on the peculiar quality of her husband's gaucherie. It was so poignant and total: as if he had just returned from a naff finishing school in Switzerland. Better to sit down opposite him at the far end of the table, and move the baby's high chair. Anything but sustain the aerial view. This Naomi did.

At eye level Alan Margoulies was much easier on the eye – pretty even. He had a long slim nose; flat dark brows; slightly protuberant but very, very brown eyes; and the mouth of a woman. His skin had the tinge of marble, and everything about him tapered: fingers, ear lobes, chin. He was slim and vigorous, and he wore his hair unfashionably long, hooked back behind his ears. He was never, ever still, not even now. Naomi could hear his crêpe sole slapping against the red tiles of the kitchen floor, and fingers of one of his hands were performing a drum solo on the underside of the table.

Alan sensed her looking at him. He glanced up into her eyes and smiled at her quite beautifully. He said, 'Why don't we get a sitter tonight? We could go out to dinner and catch a film. Whaddya say?'

Oh, he does still love me! Waves of pleasure beat up in Naomi's chest. It takes so little, she thought, and quite rightly despised herself for it.

Alan pulled the heavy front door shut firmly enough for the little panes of coloured glass set into it to rattle. He flexed his shoulders and set off on the one-hundred-and-fifty-yard walk to the Grove Health Centre.

Alan Margoulies was what is known as a 'conscientious man'. This is at least a third of the way up the career path to being a saint. Conscientious men (and women for that matter) often hear a sort of susurration in their ears when they achieve this prebendary status. If they concentrate hard on this susurration they can just about hear the words 'Ooh, he's a saint', repeated over and over again.

Alan Margoulies was a general practitioner who actually cared about his patients. His professional rise had been sufficiently speedy to hold at bay the cynicism and alienation that dance attendance on the healing art. Only thirty-two and already in line to become the practice head when old Dr Fortis retired; no wonder he had so much love for his patients, they were working so hard on his behalf. Lobbying all and sundry with their chance declarations: 'Ooh, that *nice* Dr Margoulies,' they said, in that very emphatic way that invariably makes one think that this Dr Margoulies must be a veritable 'Doctor of Niceness'.

And let us not forget that great moral and emotional template: home life. We've seen Alan Margoulies at home already. Not very nice perhaps. In fact not nice at all – egotistic, domineering, aggressive and duplicitous. But conscientious – blindingly, achingly conscientious, as Naomi could no doubt testify. After all, who else but Alan would have read her passages from Leach and Jolly whilst she was actually eggy-puking, lost in the great fastness of her first morning-sick session?

Alan walked briskly. His tapering body, clad in what he imagined was tan-fashionable suit bagginess, flexed and rippled in the sharp light that fell from between the clouds scudding over Archway Hill. If Alan looked upward from the petrified trench of the street he could see the steel bridge that crossed the sharp cutting of Archway Road. Alan knew that a lot of unhappy people committed suicide by jumping off that bridge. The impact on the road below, according to a doctor Alan knew who worked in Casualty at the Whittington, sent their femurs shooting up into their stomachs like cross-bow bolts. If, that was, they were lucky enough to avoid being hit by a speeding vehicle on the way down. While contemplating these people's action-packed demise his fine face became overcast with sadness and back-lit by sympathy. In two words: genuine caring. That is, until a little voice whispered in his ear: 'He's a saint.'

Alan stopped, and scratched back a long strand of hair that had become unhooked from his ear. I mustn't keep thinking like that. He rapped the thought out as type-punched words in his mind's eye. In some ways I do try to be really caring and selfless, but in others I am utterly selfish, utterly egotistic and very much a typical man. He continued: I have foibles and real failings. All too often I over-compensate in terms of the freedoms I allow myself, on account of my overwhelmingly committed, caring and conscientious programme.

What Margoulies was referring to in the above was his proclivity for extra-marital fucking. Most recently two couplings had been effected in the shared flats of student nurses who had done temporary placements at the Grove. But before that Alan had had a more protracted dalliance (in fact throughout Naomi's pregnancy) with a moody sculptress from Maida Vale. Sybil created pseudo-Easter Island heads out of building materials – breezeblocks and the like – and fellated Alan vigorously, which was something that Naomi could bring herself to do only occasionally.

Of course Alan was thinking magically, attempting

proleptically to influence the question of his canonisation. By admitting to his faults he wished to avoid the accusation of hypocrisy or egotism. Even to himself he couldn't make a flat statement about the adultery, because he found it too exciting. Sybil and the student nurses lay in the past, and recently sex with Naomi had started to get smelly. Smelly in Alan's mind if not actually in Naomi's body.

Levering his thin form off her torso, which was pancaked by his prodding on to the posturepedic mattress, Alan didn't so much smell her, as smell a nuance of her, an ugly nuance.

One of Alan's patients was the licensee of the local, a concrete pillbox called the Greyhound, which was stuck on a traffic island. The pub was accessible only through subterranean corridors that dripped with urine. His broad knuckles were tattooed: 'hate' on one hand, 'indifference' on the other. When the cynical publican's wife was pregnant, which she often was, he referred to her as creatin'. 'She's creatin' again,' he would report to Alan in flat tones, taking his heavy ease on the three-legged blond wood chair that Alan provided for his patients.

It was this expression that now linked itself to the eggy-smelling nuance in Alan's memory and put a stop to his moral inventory. Oh Christ, he thought, surely not, surely she isn't?

And then he substituted scented muffs like downy lavender cushions for the smell. Vaginas that hummed internally with a wet electric caress; the underside of breasts as smooth as warm pebbles, nipples so erect that each touch brought forth an 'aaah!'; and great flouncing, billowing, parachuting swathes of underwear.

For Alan had become thus: addicted to the pornographic whimsy of his own silly imagination. A dedicated truffler, up through lips of velvet, into lips of satin, through them to lips of silk and then finally on to warm lips, live lips, wet lips. After all he couldn't help it, now could he? He was old enough and married enough to know that people's bodies expand and contract; that they take on and let off ballast; that they are dry-docked and de-barnacled; that they even become infested – especially after an Arctic winter – trapped in the frigid pack ice.

It was this maturity, rather than his professional status which made his fantasies seem so absurd to him. And yet here he was – now within twenty yards of work – lost in the ravenous contemplation of a warm young snatch. A snatch that had yet to be punched from within by a baby's head. A scented snatch, softly encased in pure linen filigreed with girly embroidery. The whole framed by flat tummy, handlebar hips, suspender belt and dark stocking tops.

'Ooh-ooh!' Margoulies let out an involuntary moan and bashed through the swing doors into the main reception of the Grove Health Centre.

Bull was already there, waiting for him.

★   ★   ★

Bull had bettered his promised journey time to the health centre by more than four minutes. To begin with he had sidled down through East Finchley, driving like an invalid. But when he stopped at the confluence of the High Road and the Great North Road, by the pelican crossing which is level with the Elite Cattery, Bull touched *it* again and almost fainted clean away.

Copping this particular feel perhaps wasn't as disturbing as Bull's explorations after waking. After all, he knew that *it* was there. But in each new context the vagina seemed to take on a different guise, project itself as an alternative blight.

On this occasion the sensation of pulling up trouser leg and smoothing hand up calf almost gave the game away. Bull, although no Lothario, had been known to pull and push and gather material on his way to digital exploration and entry. This being so the vagina was able to insinuate itself as being more 'familiar', more acceptable, when encountered underneath clothing by touch alone. But this 'familiarity' was of course wholly inadmissible to Bull's mind. To acknowledge that one has a cunt on the back of one's leg at 9.10 am whilst paused alongside one of London's most desirable pet hostelries would be to go too far towards disturbing the natural order of things.

So instead Bull felt *labia majora* and *mons veneris* as fluid-filled sacs. Christ, it's a burn, he immediately concluded. A whopping great burn, already infected. With this new hypothesis Bull started searching for a cause. He racked his addled mind for information about the night before. After finishing work at his office Bull had gone to meet some of his rugby mates at Brixton Sports Centre. They had regular games of five-a-side football there on Tuesday evenings, in order to get fit before matches.

Bull had played vigorously and worked up a good sweat on his white and blocky body. Had he perhaps leant back against a hot-water pipe in the changing room? Sometimes when one is exhausted by exercise, one's lobes awash with additional endorphins and encephalins, one doesn't notice even quite severe injuries. But not *this* severe. Bull winced with the realisation, feeling the vagina prink once again on the stiff fabric of his trouser leg. And after the game? What then? They had gone on to the Atlantic in Coldharbour Lane where old West Indian men in nylon hats slammed down dominos. Bull had had two or three pints and jawed for a while. Had there been anything untoward? Bull couldn't remember anything.

And then on. It had been a working evening. Bull had the profound misfortune to be the cabaret editor for a listings magazine called *Get Out!* It was a job he cordially loathed. He had joined the magazine after a spell in the USA, at a time when American football and baseball were beginning to take off in London. Bull had written extensively on these and other sports. He was taken on as *Get Out!* sports correspondent.

But after a week there had been an office crisis. The

cabaret editor died on the job, in an incident involving a French funambulist and seven live eels (one of which was in flames). The magazine's publisher-cum-editor, an aesthete by nature, loathed what he called 'hearties'. One of his earlier ventures had been launching the hugely successful Harold Acton range of men's personal fragrance products. He cut back the sports section of *Get Out!* to half a page and shoved poor Bull on to cabaret.

So it was, that on the preceding night, for the nth time, Bull had found himself in a grotty suburban bar contemplating the sub-Escher pattern on the carpet, while a mortgage broker from Grays Thurrock clad only in a leopardskin jockstrap told jokes about . . . vaginas.

'Wickedly funny', 'saucy, irreverent and unsuspected', 'not for prudes or soap-box moralists'. These had been some of the press notices that had greeted this new star in the comic firmament. Through the sheer weight of the opposition's coverage Bull had been forced to go and check out Razza Rob, as he had been forced to check out so many like him before.

'Doncha wanna kno-ow! Doncha wanna kno-ow!' Razza Rob was working his audience. He fluted out the words in an exaggerated nasal singsong, twisting on the spot all the while, with an undulant shimmy that rendered his hairy little body quite, quite obscene. 'Doncha wanna know what happened to the gynie that operated on the world's largest cunt? Doncha . . .'

'Yes! Yes! Yes!' There was a scattering of drunken and bellicose shouts from the pub audience.

'She gave him knighthood when she left office!' A ragged peal of laughter greeted this. Razza Rob was encouraged and emboldened to push back still further the performance envelope of his satire. 'And what about the army gynie who got his hand stuck up the cunt of the commanding officer's wife? Doncha wanna know what happened to him? Doncha?'

There were more ragged cries. For some reason this foray into vaginal gags seemed to have grabbed the audience's attention in a way that Razza Rob's earlier badinage – ranging as it had across matters as diverse as shit, piss and puke – had not. 'Don-cha wan-na know-ow!?' He was drawing out the tedious catchphrase for all it was worth, beating out the syllables with leaden pulsings of his shopping trolley pelvis. The little pouch of spotted fabric that had the misfortune to contain his genitals oscillated furiously.

'Well I'll tell ya. He was dis-charged!' The audience erupted. Bull made his way to the bar for another Pils.

And then Bull made his way to the bar for another Pils, and another Pils, and yet *another* Pils. Until, after a while, he ceased to notice that Razza Rob just wouldn't let vaginas lie. The audience kept on lapping it up (they would have appreciated the pun). Wan clerks and their girlfriends from Accounts somehow found this cuntal humour sweet inspiration. They egged Razza Rob on until they were weeping with laughter, and their nylon chemises were half-mooned at the armpit with the heady sweat of release.

Although Bull preferred light comedy, he was as susceptible to peer pressure as anyone. Given the right circumstances Bull could appreciate a good joke at the expense of women's genitals just as much as the next man. Nor was it the particular atmosphere of the place, with its four square feet of spangle-sprayed stage and Woolworth's disco lights, that made the 'act' seem so depressing. No, Bull could have coped with that perfectly well – in a leisure context.

Bull was not averse to the occasional game of rugby union. An alumnus of an exceedingly minor public school, Bull was a competent prop forward who excelled in stolid, rhythmic pushing, both in the scrum and the lineout. After matches he was also well used to adopting similar tactics in crowded pubs, to secure foaming beakers of pilsner lager, the alcohol shimmering in the liquid with a crystalline brilliance borrowed from the sugar it had so recently been.

Bull could cope with the cunt jokes in his spare time, but at work it was a chore. Bull was glad he hadn't asked Juniper, a *Get Out!* freelance he was interested in, to accompany him. He felt certain that she wouldn't have approved of Razza Rob.

Eventually Bull had had to leave. The tiny bar-room was by now charged with a mad, cackling impotence. Razza Rob hated people getting away before the end of his cunt act. And anyway, he couldn't fail to recognise

Bull, whose constipated and unfeeling reviews, freighted as they were with unnecessary sporting analogies, were an easy source of resentment for *des artistes* to lock on to. Bull had never met Razza Rob but a description of him was in ready circulation. There just weren't that many cabaret reviewers on the London scene with Bull's big frame, tuft of ginger hair and frank, white features.

'Oi! You!' screeched Razza Rob, his voice lifting to Nuremberg pitch. Bull resolutely did not turn. 'Yeah, you!' Razza was stabbing a finger at Bull's broad retreating back. Some of the quisling audience were already measuring Bull for the 'participation potential' he might represent. 'Whaddya call a man with a cunt in the back of his leg?' A tatter of 'wots?' spattered from the audience. Bull felt the ridges of his ears harden with shame. There were only two bald boys in matching, short-sleeved shirts with tartan pocket-facings to part – and Bull would be free, into the suburban night.

'Fucked if I know, but any port in a storm, eh old chep?' Razza's imitation of Bull's slightly clipped, Pathé News accent was accompanied by him dropping to his knees and shimmying delightedly. He worked his raggy bouffant hair-do into a fizz whilst he simulated intercourse for all it was worth. A trainee auditor from Godstone fainted clean away with the excitement of it. Her Cinzano made an awful stain. Bull was in the car park, almost running.

Now Bull sketched over these events, the Pils had smudged the neural imprints and the detail wasn't forthcoming. Who can say whether Razza Rob, like some obscene magus, had inflicted the vagina on Bull. A magical curse pointing up the involuted redundancy of their common sexuality. Who can say? It does seem fitting however, apt. There would be no point in implanting a vagina in the back of just any man's knee. You might get some scion of raised consciousness; some almost-Iron John; some acquaintance of Dorothy longing to become a friend. No. Much better that this be just a *congruence* understood by us. And much better that it should be Bull, the dubious Bull, the shy Bull, the *conditioned* Bull, who had to bear the weight of this unacceptable transmogrification.

Horns roared right inside Bull's head. He was staring sightlessly at the cracked concrete that formed the parking space in front of the Elite Cattery. He let out the clutch with a lurch and the car promptly stalled. Bull sweated violently for the seconds it took to grind the engine back on, but his mind would not clear. He lurched past the garden centre, still trying to pick out from his record of the previous night the moment when it became reasonable to assume that he had been so drunk that he hadn't noticed his leg being burnt.

Could it have been some resentful artiste? This thought seriously occurred to Bull, a measure of just how the false burn's vast flap of fleshly corruption had disturbed the balance of his reason. Sitting at the Ton of Shale watching that bloody Razza man, someone could have probed my calf and the back of my knee with a heated poker, or one of those portable mini-elements used for boiling water in a cup . . .

But even as he analysed this, and checked also for any recollection of leaning up against some other unseasonably hot radiator or overheated exhaust, Bull knew that he could not supply a rational explanation for what had happened to his leg. As he pushed down the clutch he could feel once again that the burn's epicentre was scored deep into his leg. The point of weird sensation was at least eight inches obliquely upward from Bull's kneepit, knocking strangely behind Bull's ringing patella.

Bull depressed the clutch, feeling again all the burn's strange internality. His ancient Mini Cooper flipped over the crest of the hill and started down through the cutting towards Archway Roundabout. Moss shone like verdigris on all the rubber runnels of the car. Overhead Suicide Bridge ignored the sky and clamped itself to London's lagging land. Bull could make out the complicated pyramidal roof of the health centre, rising up from a tangle of Victorian terracing that lay both below and ahead of him.

2

First Impressions

'MORNING,' said Margoulies to Bull and the receptionist.

'Morning,' they chorused back. Margoulies paused, searching their faces to see if they had heard his little ejaculation. But all he could detect was Bull's anxiety and the receptionist's boredom.

'You aren't my 9.30 are you?' said Margoulies to Bull, whom he knew well enough to be off-hand with.

'There's been a cancellation, Doctor . . .' the receptionist broke in. 'Mr Gaston says he's now in too much pain to make it into surgery. Will you make a housecall?'

'Oh all right, all right. Tell him that if Helen Meyer can't fit him in I'll come by this evening.' Margoulies shook his head from side to side. The mock weariness of this gesture was clearly compounded of both caring and irritation. But only the kind of irritation a busy man assumes to show that underneath it there is still more caring. Margoulies smiled at Bull and said, 'Please come along when you're ready, you know where I am.' With another smile at the receptionist he swept on through another pair of swing doors.

Bull sat for a moment longer on the foam-upholstered bench. He was enjoying the relief that came with knowing that he was about to be treated. That the 'thing' on his leg was soon to be dealt with: extirpated, cauterised, sewn up, or otherwise disposed of.

Then he rose, plonked down the coverless *Country Life* he had been searching in for a good convalescent home, and with a nod to the receptionist followed on. Whilst the roof of the Grove Health Centre was roughly pyramidal, the bulk of the building was essentially circular. The administrative department, reception area, treatment rooms and nurses' clinic were in the centre of the building, the offices of the various general practitioners who worked for the Health Centre's two practices were located around the periphery. Small signs projected from the top of each office door, giving the name of its occupant. Bull passed by Doctors Hurst, Mukherjee, Fortis, Ambrose and Kowlakowski, before stopping at Margoulies. He knocked. 'Come,' called Margoulies from within. Bull entered.

The Doctor was sitting behind his blond wood desk, which was canted across the corner of the office. Behind him there was a pie-slice-shaped projection of glass which served the office as a window. The whole room was pie-slice-shaped: the exterior wall conforming to the outside circle of the building, the interior wall to the circularity of the corridor. An examination couch stood opposite Margoulies's desk, with a swishy plastic curtain mounted on the wall beside it. The impedimenta in

Margoulies's office was the usual GP's mixture of personal and medical artefacts.

As Bull settled himself in the three-legged chair, Margoulies was leafing through his case-notes. Bull found himself fixedly contemplating a selection of children's clay sculptures, blobbed about on the surface of the desk like miniature menhirs. Bull looked at them with his eyes alone, his mind concentrated, fixated even, on the back of his leg.

'Is it another ENT thing then, John?' asked Margoulies, peering up from the notes. Bull was a healthy young man, save for regular sinus infections, caused not by any innate quirk of Bull's physique but by the fat fist of an Old Malthusian mashing Bull's septum during a charity match.

'Oh no, Doctor,' replied Bull. 'It's something else. Some kind of wound or burn on the back of my leg.'

'If it's a wound or a burn one of the nurses could take a look at it.'

'But that's just it, Doctor.' Bull felt once more the nameless exasperation that had visited him talking to the receptionist. 'I can't tell which it is, a wound or a burn.'

Margoulies raised his eyebrows and looked up at Bull for the first time. Alan liked Bull. Bull had been one of his first patients at the Grove when Alan had started there some four years ago. Bull was seldom ill, but whenever he was he didn't whine or carp. He listened dutifully to whatever Alan's diagnosis was, and then followed to the letter his instructions. Alan thought of Bull as an essentially hearty, uncomplicated, rugby-playing type of fellow, in direct contrast to his own neurotic self-absorption and intellectual pretension. He had never had to append to Bull's case-notes the damning word 'psychosomatic'. But then there was always a first time for everything.

'OK then, old fellow, pop yourself up on the examining table and we'll take a look.' Bull did as he was told. He sat sideways on the examination table, slipping off his loafers. Then he swung his legs up and laid his large ginger head down on the crêpy white disposable antimacassar. 'Oh, I think we better have those trousers off, don't you?' Margoulies was extracting two-dimensional rubber gloves of a synthetic fleshy colour from a boxed dispenser. Bull fiddled with his elasticated belt and pulled his neatly-creased trousers down, over his knees and off.

As he did this Bull had to cant himself up, on to the curve of his buttocks, coincidentally adopting the same posture as he had when he first became aware of the vagina. Oh God, thought Bull, I hope it's nothing serious. Although another craven little part of him secretly hoped that it was serious *enough*. He was very well insured and anything . . . yes anything to get out of writing cabaret reviews for a few weeks.

Margoulies loomed in the periphery of Bull's vision, hooking his hair back behind his ears with a characteristic two-index-fingers gesture. Then Bull felt Margoulies's hands beginning to toy with his upper left thigh, moving slowly, palping the flesh with careful, detached fingers.

Bull stiffened and began to experience, for the first time in his thirty-something years, acute anxiety. This was different to the fear that he usually felt when he was touched by people in non-intimate situations, or had to undress in front of them. On these occasions Bull's secret horror was that his penis would be primed, limbered and rolled out for target practice. Bull could conceive of nothing more embarrassing than an involuntary erection – especially if a man, such as Margoulies, was touching him.

But this dread was something different. It was a fear of intrusion *into* himself, rather than of expansion into the World's gaze. Bull felt his leg as a soft, shrinking and vulnerable thing. He longed to cry out to Margoulies and warn him to examine his leg in a particular way, with specific firm, yet calm, movements. But his tongue was dried out and glued to the floor of his mouth.

Margoulies meanwhile was making small observations, aloud but ostensibly to himself, about Bull's leg. This was the way Margoulies liked to proceed. It didn't matter what the examination was for, cancer or the common cold, gangrene or gonorrhoea, Margoulies liked to do what he called 'putting it in the right context'. Margoulies couldn't quite go so far as to call himself a holistic Doctor, but he did believe that the injury or malaise should at least be treated within the context of the *section* of the body within which it was manifested, if not within the body as a whole.

'Turn over now, please. . . . Mmmm. Very pronounced *gluteus maximus*,' he murmured, sticking a rubber fingertip into the white softness of Bull's buttock, his other hand gripping the thick snake of muscle that curved around Bull's thigh. And then, suddenly, silence. Margoulies's mutterings were cut off as abruptly as if he had had a pad soaked with ether clamped across his face, and his hands fell away from Bull's leg.

Bull waited. And waited. All he could hear was Margoulies's breathing, which seemed to have become heavy, laboured and slightly intermittent. Bull lay still, holding himself in readiness for the Doctor's pronouncement, and, of course, willing himself not to get an erection. He stared fixedly at the way the plaster had been teased up into little fronds on the wall, like miniature stalactites.

Margoulies had of course seen the vagina. That was the explanation for his abrupt silence. His eyes rounded the horizon of Bull's broad, firm, ginger-fuzzed thigh, and saw it, tucked into the pit behind the knee.

Two observations struck Margoulies with equal force the very second that he clapped eyes on Bull's cunt: first that it lacked pubic hair, apart from a thickening and tufty teasing of Bull's leg hair over the *mons veneris*; and second that the cunt had not simply appeared in the pit of Bull's knee like an alien interloper, but rather that Bull's basic physique had been customised, within a very localised area, to accommodate the new orifice.

The two thick tendons on either side of the pit had been pushed out by what surely must be a ridge of new pubic bone. The muscle at the top of Bull's calf was clearly bifurcated underneath the skin to allow space for the entrance to the vagina, whilst the kneepit itself bulged out to house the projection of the mons, and the clitoris that already peaked from beneath its edge.

It was an astonishing sight for someone like Margoulies, who understood the anatomy of the human body from both within and without. And that was a relief, because it meant that the first few seconds of utter disbelief became centred not on the 'how?' or 'why?' of the vagina's presence in Bull's body; but instead on the technicalities of whether the vagina was a well-constructed thing, or merely an odd simulacrum, more akin to a penis-shaped potato than a functioning genital.

Margoulies did feel faint. That's true. He breathed deeply, and visions of all the medical literature on genital abnormalities that he had ever read began to flit in front of his eyes. But within seconds he steadied himself. Steadied himself by making two simultaneous and far-reaching decisions, decisions that, in Alan's mind at least, marked him out from all other GPs who might have been placed in this very peculiar situation. Decisions that reflected the justness of this particular phenomenon coming to his attention and his alone.

The first of these was to retain control of Bull as his patient, rather than referring him automatically to a gynaecological specialist. The second was, for the meantime, to withhold the truth about the vagina from Bull himself. Margoulies didn't doubt that the vagina could be explained. He was a scientist to the core, an absolute believer in the total discoverability and explanation of cause. But until he could divine the aetiology of Bull's vagina, Margoulies knew intuitively that the awareness of it would severely disturb his patient. To act otherwise would have been less than conscientious.

'What is it, Doctor?' Bull's voice sounded odd and phlegmy in his deep chest.

'Well . . . er . . . John. Well, you were really right on both counts . . .' Margoulies spoke the words with gratitude, as if he had been corpsing and had them thrown to him by the prompter.

'Whaddya mean?'

'Well, it's a very nasty wound, that's true, but it's also quite badly burnt.'

'I thought so! I knew it. And what's worse I can feel that it's pushed all the insides of my leg about. It's . . . It's as if I've mutated in some way.'

'Does it hurt very badly?' Margoulies's voice was laden with concern. He was by now standing over Bull, looking down into the freak's broad and freckled back.

'Hurt? Why yes . . . of course it hurts . . .' Bull's voice trailed away into nothing and a perplexed expression took up residence on his face. Hurt? How can the man be so stupid as to even ask, he thought. But now that Bull was called on actually to analyse the sensations he had experienced when becoming aware of the wound, he couldn't really, in all conscience, describe them as pains. Rather they seemed on reflection to be feelings of extreme sensitivity; neurological messages remarkable for a shocking newness that combined at once both the visceral and the voluntary; the feelings of being touched and of wanting to touch.

'Now, John, can you describe the pain for me?' said Margoulies. His voice came once again from the south of Bull. His dark head had disappeared once again beneath the hair-flecked dome of Bull's knee. But Margoulies couldn't concentrate on Bull's incoherent answer, struggling as he was to come to terms with this *thing*. He had only thrown out the question as a reflex, doctorly thing to do.

Margoulies used the balls of his thumbs gently to prise apart the outer lips of the vagina. The inner lips parted slightly as well. The skin of the vagina's interior was pearly pink and glistening; the clitoris poked up perkily from underneath the cowl of flesh at the top of the orifice. Margoulies peered closer and deployed his fine-beam flash. He braced his shoulder against Bull's thigh to steady himself. Interesting. There was no urethra . . . and . . . Well, he supposed it stood to reason. Margoulies struggled to apply an internal rationale; Bull was *virgo intacta*, surprising in a man of his age. The fleshy trapdoor filled the mouth of the true vagina in a most cosy and apt manner.

'. . . Sort of exposed, raw, and very sensitive.'

'Whossat?' Margoulies started guiltily.

'When my trouser leg rubs against it, Doc-tor.' The querulousness was creeping back into Bull's voice. But Margoulies didn't hear it. He was back, truffling around the vagina again. It really was the cutest little snatch he'd ever clapped eyes on . . . Whossat! Margoulies smacked himself internally for this abandonment of professionalism. Damn it all, he'd seen more than enough of these in his work, and he had never, ever made the mistake of confusing them with their leisure-time sisteren. Why this one now? It couldn't really be more inappropriate.

But then Bull's vagina really *was* cute. A dear little box. Its lips were just so, flanged just so. The pearly pink of the vagina's internal skin faded into the white, freckled skin of Bull's leg, just so. And the lips weren't too crinkled, the clitoris wasn't too long . . . Margoulies was testing the neural equipment of the orifice at this point. Touching the inside of both sets of lips, the clitoris, what ought to be Bull's second perineum (it was defined by a strip of brownish, crinkly flesh, running up and over the swell of Bull's calf), with a tongue depressor. From the tiny twitches and convulsions he felt running through Bull's leg with the flat of his palm; and the other, deeper tremors Margoulies could sense in Bull's abdomen, he could tell that Bull's equipment was functioning just as it should be.

'Just so!' Margoulies punctuated the thought with an innocent tweak of Bull's clitoris. Or at any rate that's how he tried to pass it off to himself, but in that very attempt lay the core of his duplicity. And this thin wedge of irony was the start. From here on in everything that the good doctor did was tantamount to taking a chain-saw to his Tree of Knowledge. For Margoulies had abandoned his professional perspectives, he had allowed his own likes and dislikes to affect his judgment. He was no longer acting in the best interests of his patient.

Naturally Margoulies had ample reserves of denial to damp down this awareness. He flotched off his rubber gloves with his usual insouciance and took a turn over to his desk. Bull remained prone and turned his round head on the scratchy paper.

'Well, Doc?'

'Well, John, it's not as bad as you might think.' (The inside surface of the patella must correspond to the mouth of the cervix; even as he mouthed the practised reassurances, Margoulies's professional faculties were constructing an internal map of Bull's new sex organ.) 'It is, as you say, both a burn and a wound. And frankly I simply cannot guess at what may have caused it.'

Margoulies sat down behind the blond wood desk and began to write something on the uppermost sheet of Bull's notes. Bull, still contemplating the abrasive wall, felt more reassured by this than by anything Margoulies had done so far. This was the way doctors were meant to behave: leaving their patients weirdly exposed while they senselessly plied the biro.

But what Margoulies wrote would have made Bull doubt the good doctor's sanity. The Papermate titivated the narrow feint with Margoulies's characteristic spyro-gyra of a hand. 'Cunt, cunt, cunt, cunt, cunt, cunt, cunt,

cunt, cunt . . .' he wrote. And his fine brown eyes stared sightlessly into the aquamarine sheen of a Monet reproduction that had been clumsily blu-tacked on to the wall above the examination couch.

'Well, we better get this wound or burn of yours dressed, hadn't we?' Margoulies snapped out of it and began to move about the office collecting crêpe bandage, adhesive tape, swabs, scissors and a bottle of distilled water. Bull began to feel better and better as Margoulies's tapering fingers softly palped the vagina's surround.

Margoulies wasn't quite sure what he was doing. He wanted to cover the vagina up so that Bull wouldn't discover what it was. He swabbed it with distilled water to give Bull the impression that he was disinfecting it. He then applied a translucent layer of Vaseline to the whole kneepit area. After that, he used thin strips of adhesive to butterfly stitch Bull's vaginal lips together. Finally he covered the whole thing with a sturdy but flexible covering of crêpe bandage.

Margoulies stood upright to finish the task. Looking towards Bull he applied loop after loop of bandage with strategic skill. After each loop he asked Bull to move the leg, and to tell him if the dressing was comfortable. Bull, increasingly at ease, felt the marvellous lightness that comes with knowing that one has had the *appropriate treatment*. When at last he popped off the couch and pulled on his trousers, he felt almost normal again. He took a couple of turns around the consulting room. He could still feel deep, internal rubbings and partings within his leg, but the immediate, surface sensation that had so horrified him was muted and cushioned.

'Now listen, John.' Margoulies was back at his desk, this time writing on a prescription pad. 'I've dressed this myself because I wouldn't trust the nurses either here or at the Whittington to do it properly. I want you to fill this prescription . . .'

'Should I take some bed rest, Doctor?' Bull sounded enthusiastic about the prospect. Sickly belly burn and ringing head of hangover told him to get horizontal with an insistence that now easily eclipsed the vagina's insidious effect.

'Oh no, I wouldn't say that was necessary. I should cut your day short, but in a way, with something like this, it's better if you keep moving.'

Bull was puzzled by this, but he trusted Margoulies implicitly. After all, why wouldn't he? How could he know that a parallel universe of perverse calculation was establishing itself in Margoulies's mind? How could Bull know that Margoulies's concern was first and foremost to stop Bull discovering the vagina before he, Margoulies, could . . . could . . . what? Aye, there's the rub. Margoulies was setting something up already. He was 'treating' Bull with all the cynicism of von Ribbentrop treatying away with Molotov. Margoulies had become a silent signatory of the hypocritic oath.

★   ★   ★

Bull stood in the pharmacy, his prescription clutched in his plump hand. Ahead of him in the queue two junkies were receiving their daily methadone script. They moved away from the counter, but only so far as a circular wire display rack of spongiform products, where they paused to drink the sweet linctus lustily. To one side of the shop a schizophrenic argued with a nylon-coated assistant about the 'cleanliness' of an emery board; whilst on the other two skinny kids with the shaven, blue-sheened heads of habitual ringworm hosts, riffled the lipsticks annoyingly in their acrylic trays.

The pharmacist plonked Bull's valium down on the ledge of the serving hatch. He stared at Bull with mild curiosity. Bull didn't look like the sort who needed sedation. He looked more like a hail-fellow-well-met type, full of bone-crushing bonhomie and stupid drinking games.

Bull took the pills from the assistant without troubling to read the label. He took his change and his receipt. The pharmacist, feeling the obscure power of the apothecary who alters moods at a distance through the use of such philtres and preparations, noted his bemused expression. And he would have been right about this, for Bull didn't have a clue what Diazepam was. He thought Margoulies had prescribed him an antibiotic.

Bull faffed around the precincts of Lincoln's Inn, looking for a parking space, and in the process twice tangling with the same bald and belligerent cabbie. Eventually he found a temporary resting place and struck out up the Grays Inn Road towards the offices of *Get Out!* The spring day had cleared and the clouds had scudded off to Sveningen, leaving London bald and bright under a high, blue sky.

Bull took the stairs gently, feeling the tug of the adhesive strips on his soon-to-be-pubic leg hairs. In the open-plan offices of *Get Out!* he moved among the tatty desks, each with its paper toupee, muttering 'hellos' to his various colleagues. They were either drinking plastic beakers of coffee, with their feet up on their desks, or else they were humped in the green wash of their VDUs, tapping away.

Bull settled himself at his desk, snapped on his word processor, and while the machine chatted itself up and into life he began mentally to compose his review of Razza Rob.

Now, as has been said, Bull was a sportswriter by inclination. And in fact (although it has no relevance to our story) he wasn't a bad sportswriter at all. He came to the business of describing sport not with the facile vision of a would-be novelist, but with the clear-eyed probity of a would-be sporting professional. Bull had become a journalist in order to be with the people he admired: sportsmen. He was a good rugby player but he had never kidded himself that he could be a professional. Because of this he brought to his sports-writing a practical knowledge and fluidity of expression that coincidentally rendered his prose quite excellent. Thus:

> Guggenheim received the ball with a coiled muscularity
> that then effortlessly exploded into a looping, feinting
> run which culminated in a drop goal of rare brilliance

was Bull's empathetic and vivid description of the high-point of a match between Wigan and Filey RFC 'B' teams.

While, on the other hand – as we have already remarked – Bull's cabaret reviewing suffered terribly from a leaden injection of sporting metaphor and analogy. Thus:

> Les Jongleurs Diaboliques never quite get off the starting
> blocks with their new 'theatrical experience' at the
> Diorama. The inexpert blocking that characterises Les
> Jongleurs' movements around the stage leads this re-
> viewer to suspect that they were directed by the late
> lamented Bobby Robson, in a belated attempt to re-
> introduce the discredited 4-3-3 formation to English
> soccer.

Bull's copy would regularly come back from the editor with all but the most straightforward of statements ruthlessly excised. Bull felt something like a prisoner on a chain gang, forced to dig holes and then fill them in again, without purpose, without reason. As his inability to write about it increased, so did Bull's loathing for all forms of cabaret, stand-up comedy, fringe theatre and other small audience entertainments.

Sport on the other hand continued to grip Bull with a passion. The only thing he would hate to miss through injury or illness was a forthcoming mini-tour of South Coast resorts by his Sunday League team the Wallingford Wanderers.

Bull had been playing for the Wallingford Wanderers almost since leaving school (except for the hiatus while he was in the USA). The team was loosely connected with his old school, but in practice drew on the friends and acquaintances of team members to find useful players. Most of Bull's mates were Wanderers. They were solid young men, quantity surveyors, actuaries, the odd dentist or retail services manager adding a hint of cosmopolitanism.

What Bull liked about the team most of all was that the Wanderers represented the acceptable face of small-club rugby. There was beeriness but not too much leeriness; and huggery but not too much buggery. In essence for all of them it represented a continuation of their minor public schooldays. And once a year the team went to play the old school's first fifteen. This was the high point of the season.

Trying to concentrate on a pithy demolition job on Razza Rob was difficult for Bull. He tapped out characters on the screen and then let the pulsing cursor eat them backwards, again and again. Images of clean green turf slid in front of his eyes. He felt the surge of sheer adrenalin-fuelled joy that he always experienced, lined up with his team mates, clean, pressed and raring for the kickoff. He felt the delightful shock through his leg that comes when you chonk the back of your boot into the greensward and hack out just the right divot to support the ball for a placekick.

The shock-in-the-leg sensation reminded Bull of his wound. He had been lost in a daydream. He felt woozy and relaxed. The valium did its job. Bull continued to function for the rest of the day while the sedative kept him calm.

At lunchtime Bull went out for a drink with a couple of his colleagues. One of them noticed him limping. 'What's up, John,' he said, 'pulled a muscle playing five-a-side?'

'No,' Bull replied, suddenly self-conscious. 'It's nothing, really.'

Margoulies took the smelly lift down into the sub-basement of the hospital. It smelt of the dead forefathers of old school dinners. The sub-basement had an oppressively low ceiling, and immediately outside the door of the lift the linoleum on the floor had started to decompose, breaking up into ragged, isolated island shapes, as if the surface had been subject to some tectonic shift. A porter with the face of a medieval villein – all warty wattle and Cyrano nose – directed Margoulies to where the closed stacks were housed, and opened the wire cage for him with a Yale key.

Margoulies snapped on the Anglepoise that stood on the small metal reading desk and went ranging along the shelves, peering at the spines of the thick medical reference works and bound journals, occasionally pulling one out.

It was Margoulies's lunch hour. The rest of the morning, after Bull's visitation at his surgery, had been an odd one for Margoulies. Alan had palpably felt his ethics and his restraint draining out of his mind like bath water. Round and round in his tortured brow went the arguments and considerations, until they disappeared with a ferocious gurgle. Only to be replaced by still more arguments and more considerations.

Alan's conscience told him that he was doing something wrong. Something very, very wrong. Something, in fact, that might seriously undermine his candidacy for canonisation.

Alan's reason also told him that when a man walks into your office with a vagina tucked behind his knee, the first thing you *must* do in order to preserve both your sanity, and his, is *tell someone else*. The abnormal becomes normal through its inclusion in the worlds of others. Exclude it and it begins to take on a penumbra of sinister otherness.

But the problem was this: Alan was already functioning within the dramatic irony of betrayal. His adulterous liaisons had opened up a gulf between what he knew and what others knew about him. Into this gulf came Bull . . . and his cunt. And worse luck for Bull, quite filled it.

Alan couldn't understand the why, but the more he tried to think about what he should do to help Bull, the more images of Bull that were strictly non-scientific started to flood him.

Bull was so vulnerable, so trusting. There was something rather pathetically sweet about his lumpy features and expression of huge and baffled sincerity. And he wasn't unattractive . . . Lots of women like men who are well built; especially with a rugby player's flabby solidity.

And the vagina. What an orifice! So seldom is it aesthetically appreciated. Men shy away from its very fleshly reality. They'll lick it and prod it, but they'll seldom take a really long, loving look. They prefer to regard it with children's eyes as the secret trap door leading to a room full of sweeties.

Perhaps it's because babies come out of it, Alan had mused, toying with his clay blobs while waiting for another tortured arthritic to crawl in from the reception area. Alan, for all his vaunted intellect, had a rather nauseous and jejune style of internal monologue. Is it another twist in the male psyche of the virgin/whore complex? We cannot bear to acknowledge the cunt's visual reality because to do so would be to acknowledge pissing, periods and the bloody, pushing heads of babies?

Of course Alan wasn't so sheltered as not to know that there are heaps of porno mags absolutely groaning with crotch shots. Full of cunts delineated with forensic precision; plastered on to the page, their silk thread slash and surrounding furze flattened like a river valley photographed from the air . . . But he was also perceptive enough to realise that these aren't intended to beautify the women who pose for them . . . they are intended to humiliate them, to expose them.

Alan was subjected to these reveries mercilessly. And even when they seemed to be taking an honestly reflective turn, as above – a direction that might lead him out of the psychological labyrinth into which he had descended at ten minutes to ten – he would be brought up sharply by another surge of lust. A surge that pushed Bull's anatomy before Alan's eyes bathed in an entirely different light: roseate, pulsing, undulant, sweetly erotic . . .

. . . Alan saw Bull posing naked in the striped shadow of a venetian blind – rather like Richard Gere in *American Gigolo*. He was swivelled prettily on one thick leg, like a discus thrower, pushing the back of his knee towards the silent voyeur. His pubis *nouveau* was sheathed tightly in a little pouch, a sort of mono-knicker. Wisps of hair poked out of the edges. Alan could just make out . . . those lips, delineated by the soft sheen of the silk.

It was in order to shake these images out of his mind – the awful cross-fertilisation between his fantasy life and Bull's genital abnormality – that Alan had repaired to the library of the local teaching hospital at lunchtime.

The receptionists, seeing Alan leaving the Grove looking harassed and preoccupied, tut-tutted to each other. 'Shee . . .' said the black and conical Gloria who had just come on shift '. . . the man done wo-ork 'imself down t' the bone y'know. Shee! 'N he's saint, ain't that the truth.'

The Saint's mind was full of chimeras as he walked towards the centre of town. Images of the marriage of organ and organ grinder into the most surreal and frenzied of combinations. But down in the sub-basement the closed stack of the library brought him some relief. Here the mind's eye changed to eyes on page, as Alan flicked over leaf after leaf of the *Journal of Abnormal Physiology*.

The faded half-tones, and worse, chromatically distorted colour plates, showed the most fantastic profusion of physical confusion: a man posed shyly – naked white belly billowing – his hand on the back of a kitchen chair, his chest a veritable palimpsest of nipples, some half-cancelling others, some saucer-large; another man screwed up the side of his head towards the camera, the Dürer whorls of his inner-ear containing a scrap of a penis; a woman, pear-shaped and otherwise chillingly ordinary, lay back to give the ultimate crotch shot: double-decker vaginas.

There was more. Much, much more. Alan flipped over page after page. He pulled down Nicholson's classic *Distortions of the Sex*, a book that had been rented out by those who could get their hands on it when Alan was at medical school. He laid it alongside the *Journal* and compared weird with weirder. In Nicholson, Siamese twins lay cunt-to-mouth, trapped by a webbing of flesh

174

into a life-long act of cunnilingus; a perfectly ordinary man's penis had another perfectly ordinary man's penis, growing out of it at right angles; a young woman, not unattractive in a pinched and mean English provincial way, had a clitoris the size of a parsnip.

But however many pages he turned, however much of this fleshly phantasmagoria Alan took on board, he could not find anything that even approximated to Bull's condition. Sure, there were plenty of hermaphrodites, but their vaginas were invariably distorted simulacra, tucked in alongside their penises. There was no one like Bull, with a vagina perfectly and beautifully formed, albeit in an entirely unexpected place. And furthermore, as Alan read Nicholson's text, although he came across some utterly bizarre stories of genital abnormality, none of them were remotely similar to Bull's genital nativity.

Plenty of little girls had, according to Nicholson, reached puberty only to have a wash of testosterone push their clitorises into penises and pull out balls from their crotches. But the same could not be said of little boys. If they weren't given a vagina from the off they never subsequently acquired one. And indeed this conforms to what we know intuitively. For the male physiology is a static and lifeless thing, a metabolic Empty Quarter, unaffected by the tremendous lunar pulls and washes of hormonal gunk that stream through its sister form.

Alan closed up the books with grim finality. He called

for the porter to lock the stack, and ascended via the stinking lift to ground-floor London.

So, instead of the trip to the library acting as a catharsis, it ultimately only served to exacerbate Alan's condition. Images of Bull began to flood into him like some sort of meditational illness. Alan found he could hardly concentrate on what his patients were saying during afternoon surgery. (Poor Dr Margoulies, they thought to themselves, the man works far too hard, he's *so* conscientious).

At the end of the day Alan took his house-call bag and went back home. Naomi was feeding the baby in the kitchen, just as she had been when Alan left that morning.

Alan cupped Naomi's cheek with one of his fine tapering hands and the baby's cheek with the other. He kissed them both and told them he loved them. Suddenly, the contrast between the grotesque images that had been projected into his mind for most of the day and the utter wholesomeness of this domestic scene struck him like a rabbit punch in the gut. It was all he could manage not to hang on the chestnut pelt of his wife's lovely hair and sob the whole story out into her neat ear. But manage he did. Alan knew that the first aid he had done on Bull that morning would only serve as a temporary measure. Alan felt devoid of ideas of how to help Bull, but he knew that he had to see him and do something.

'I've booked a sitter,' said Naomi. 'She's coming around eight.'

'Fine, fine,' said Alan. Not at all in a distracted manner, but with genuine emphasis. He had that ability: turning on immediacy, seeming intimacy, for Naomi; so that she felt that he was with her and her alone. And then he remembered the cancellation that had furnished him with Bull that morning. It was the perfect opportunity and it prompted him to say: 'I have to pop up to Archway and see a patient.' Naomi was surprised and a little put out.

'I didn't know that you had a patient in Archway.'

'Yeah. An old guy called Gaston. Strictly speaking he shouldn't be registered with me, but for some reason I'm the only doctor that he'll see.'

'Will you be long?' asked Naomi. Alan looked at his watch, it was six-thirty.

'If I hurry I can make it back by eight. I may have to drain his cyst.'

'You know Alan, you haven't put Cecile to bed for a week now . . .'

'I know, I know. I'm sorry, darling. I'll make it up to you both at the weekend.'

And he was gone. Out the door before another exchange with Naomi, lawfully wedded Naomi, could challenge the forgetfulness of habit.

Alan hung on to the image of his daughter a little bit

longer. For as long, in fact, as it took him to find and start his car. He used the image the way that so many duplicitous and driven men do: to produce guilt in lieu of conscience.

As Alan wheeled the car out of the terraced street where he lived and on to the High Road he felt the urgency of his house call, but underlying that was a deeper urgency, an urgency Alan could barely acknowledge. The road north to Mr Gaston's house followed on to where Alan knew that Bull lived.

3

Seduction

B ULL SAT IN the stuffy dusk of his bedroom. The occasional artic soughed down East Finchley High Road, its double bogeys clacking hard against the rubber strip of the pelican crossing.

Bull felt tired and woozy. Towards the end of the working day he had considered going back to the Grove to see Margoulies again. Perhaps he was allergic to the antibiotic? But he thought better of it. It wouldn't do to be a trouble to the Good Doctor. He would get a good night's sleep, and if he still felt the same in the morning he would make another appointment. Alan had told Bull to come in and see the nurse in another couple of days anyway, so that she could change Bull's dressing.

The truth was that the dressing had started to trouble Bull already. Because of the awkward location of the wound Margoulies had been unable to place flat coils of crêpe across it. Instead he had tried to brace the wound with a series of bandage buttresses running up and over the knee. Even when wounded and drugged Bull was a vigorous creature. The constant movements of his meaty leg throughout the day had partially displaced the bandage; and the delightful, cool sensation Bull had had at the surgery, as the wound was swabbed with distilled water and coated with Vaseline, had faded, first into no sensation at all, and now into irritation.

Bull knew he should take another pill but somehow he couldn't rouse himself from where he sat, leg outstretched, in front of the window, looking down towards the statue of the bald-faced stag that surmounted the portico of the Bald-Faced Stag. Perhaps I should go for a drink? mused Bull to himself. He felt a little lonely this evening, washed up. He was still young enough to associate illness with people being nice to him. He wished his mother were there to re-dress the wound and make him some supper.

But even the thought of drinking alcohol was sick-making. And going into a pub, how could he? Bull visualised the interior of the Bald-Faced Stag. It was dark and thick with acrid smoke. Big-pig men stood about in suits, leaning against things. As the swing door swung open to reveal Bull, their dead brown eyes tracked him across the carpet tiles, stripping away his clothes . . .

. . . That was it! I feel really vulnerable, realised Bull with a shock. I've lost some element of my basic bottle. Perhaps it's this injury? Or that terrible night last night, that really did depress me . . .

Actually it wasn't so much the Razza Rob act that had depressed Bull. As long as he felt confident of publishing a coruscating review of it – an utterly comprehensive panning, in the next issue of *Get Out!* – Bull didn't pay any mind to Razza's ribbing. But as he had struggled to compose the review that day, preoccupied by his leg and partially stupefied by the valium, Bull's editor had appeared at his shoulder.

The first Bull had been aware of it was the strong smell of *Cellini Per L'Uomo*, one of the Harold Acton range of male toiletries and fragrances. The Editor believed strongly in self-promotion. After the waft of aftershave, which was not dissimilar to an olfactory version of Fernet Branca, the Editor's blue spectacle frames had appeared in the periphery of Bull's vision. He scanned the twenty lines of green copy on the screen of Bull's word processor.

'Ah, um, John,' he managed to say at last. 'This Razza Rob review . . . Ahh we um, won't really need to run it.' Bull was uncharacteristically snappy.

'Whyzzat?'

' 'Cos um, er . . . Y'know Juniper has written up a little feature about Razza Rob and that will, like, include a review of his act.'

'What!' Bull was incredulous. 'The man doesn't warrant fifty words, let alone a feature. He's stupid, obscene, boorish and utterly unfunny.' Bull rocked back in his swivel chair and turned to face the Editor, who dissembled frantically.

'That's as may be, John, but he's getting a real following. This particular kind of comedy is really taking off at the moment. You know, we're not here to prescribe for our readers, John, we're here to describe what *they're* into. We should never tell them what to do.'

Bull groaned. This was the Editor's catchphrase. He'd even had it incorporated into a 'Mission Statement' for *Get Out!* which, in the form of a plastic encapsulated card with five bullet points, had been distributed to the uninspired and uninspiring hacks. The catchphrase formed point 3: 'Never Prescribe – Describe. Art is the mirror of life.' The Editor also had pretensions to being a Stendhalian. He had called his son 'Julien' and his son's pony 'Sorel'.

As soon as the Editor had gone Bull called Juniper. Juniper wrote regular freelance features for *Get Out!* She had also slept with Bull on a number of significant occasions. Significant for Bull that is – not for Juniper. Juniper had sexual intercourse the way that some people eat dry-roasted peanuts: compulsively, in large quantities and with progressively less pleasure.

Dialling her number Bull remembered a drunken evening three weeks previously when Juniper had consented to come back to Bull's flat. She had eschewed the sagging bed in favour of the kitchenette floor. She had gone on top. Bull had found himself contemplating a thick yellow rheum of grease and crumbs that formed an actual ledge under the edge of the gas cooker, while Juniper's hard chassis of crotch 'n' bum 'n' thighs had hammered down on to him. Her vagina had gripped Bull's poor penis with the riffling handclasp of an aspirant mason. Her chinless face had zoomed over Bull with Vorticist foreshortening.

'Hello?'

'Juniper, it's John,' said Bull.

'John?'

'John Bull.'

'John Bull? Is this some kind of a joke?'

Bull became flustered. 'No, it isn't. You know me, I do the cabaret listings and reviews for *Get Out!*'

'Oh, *John*. Of course, I am sorry, I must have been miles away. You know, dreaming and stuff.'

'What stuff?'

'Well . . . er you know, stuff.'

Bull pictured Juniper, with her bum, hips, U-bend crotch and flat tummy sheathed in mannequin-tight Lycra bicycling shorts. Her hairless ankles were as brown and symmetrically columnar as thick fifties chairlegs and her hard little chest was begirt with synthetic knobbled belts and bandoliers. All around her on the artfully stained floorboards of her studio flat, there was her stuff – the stuff in question. What stuff it was! Platform-soled shoes and lamé dresses; ostrich feathers and film posters; patchouli bottles and chillums; lapel badges and album covers; guitars and goatskin drums; hula-hoops and Ouija boards; compact discs and concert posters; head-bands and armbands; drumsticks and frisbees. All the detritus of forty years of popular youth culture . . . Juniper's stuff.

That's how Bull pictured it at any rate. The truth was that Juniper's studio flat was relentlessly minimalist. In keeping with contemporary ideas of style. For Juniper was one of those people, lost in their late thirties, who have gone on troubling to assume each little style and youth cult, even as it has been stillborn.

For people like Juniper have a sense of cultural history as radically foreshortened as the bonnet of a bubble car. And for them, each new wave of teeny trippers and boppers seems as significant as the decline of Ancient Sumer, or the expansion of the Russian empire under Peter the Great.

Although Bull had only ever seen her in her fourteen-hole Reeboks and cod-filleted Mercx bike shorts, he understood intuitively that this was just the latest form of the primordial loons and the Peruvian blanket chic.

When naked Juniper retained the imprint of so many decadences in the peculiar glacé quality of her flesh – it was as if she were basting herself from within. And her hair, currently worn in Pre-Raph pelt, had been so bleached, dyed and thoroughly teased over the years, that to touch it was like handling swarf with the consistency of spun sugar. Bull had refrained from running his fingers through her hair when they made what passed for love. He feared cutting himself.

It wasn't that Bull thought himself unattractive, although let's face it he was no oil painting (leastways not a Titian or a David – perhaps a Dutch burgher shitting in the corner of a Breughel), but he had a fundamental diffidence when it came to sex. Came in particular to the raw elasticity of any bond that might connect him to a woman, bind him in to the bouncy push-me pull-you of attraction (and repulsion). It was this diffidence that made him seek out the Junipers of this world. Those individuals whose sexuality was already fatally compromised and detached from the gender specific. By what? Neurosis? Social pressure? Who can say.

So, the tactile memory of sharp swarf hair, snagging at the soft webbing of his fingers, summoned up an access of warm feeling in Bull's big chest. How sad that I should mean so little to her, he thought, whereas to me she is all women . . . And why, the question nagged at him, did she betray me over this Razza Rob piece? She must realise that it's within my remit. Even if an article were to be written, it should, in the natural course of things, be commissioned by me.

'Juniper.' She was once more kabuki on the lacquered boards. Her stuff had vanished into some Narnia-sized closet of the retro. 'Have you actually written this Razza Rob piece yet?'

'Um, well, I've done the review bit but I'm going to interview him on Thursday evening, then I should have enough copy and stuff.'

'You know I went to see him last night . . .' Bull tailed off. He sensed a conflict. On the one hand he felt he ought to speak his mind about Razza Rob; after all it was a question of his critical integrity. But Bull stood accused, he was tainted with the universal smear of wanting-to-be-liked. The very fact that Juniper was doing the piece was probably a sign that she had already developed some overarching aesthetic architectonic, into which a taste for

Razza Rob's cunt humour could be neatly fitted, like the keystone into a building. Bull didn't want to alienate Juniper. He wished for more linoleum swishing experiences, more oblique sightings of crumbs, fluff, *confiture* and the like, rendered geologic by their unexpectedness.

'. . . Did you?' Juniper sounded pleased. She was either feeling especially damning, or especially enthusiastic, Bull couldn't tell which. She went on, 'I saw him . . . let me see . . . was it last Monday? I think it was. Let me see, I went to a crystallography workshop on the *Tuesday* . . .' She seemed on the verge of a digression into the tree spirit mumbo-jumbo that currently formed her credo, but to Bull's surprise she mastered the urge to sound off. '. . . It *was* a Monday,' she concluded. 'Because he was on at the Sheaf of Rape and they only have comedy gigs there on a Monday evening. Isn't he fantastic!' She trilled the explosive judgment.

'Well he's certainly popular,' Bull demurred, hoping he hadn't heard her correctly.

'And rightly so.' He had heard her correctly. She ran on again, 'He's pushing back comic frontiers with his act. He's digging up the road in the quiet cul-de-sac of British comedy.' Now, Bull realised she was quoting from her half-written article.

'But Juniper.' He tried to sound conciliatory, possessed of an opinion but willing to be swayed by sound argument. 'The act is nothing but obscenity after obscenity.'

'Get it right!' Juniper guffawed with golf-club merriment. 'It's cunt joke after cunt joke. Each more defiantly vaginal than the last.'

'But Juniper, isn't that just shoring up a set of obsolete attitudes, women-hating attitudes? Isn't he appealing to the basest fears and preoccupations of his audience?'

'Well, what *about* the audience?'

'What about them?'

'Weren't they enjoying it?'

'I suppose so.' Bull was deflated. In his heart of hearts he didn't want to be argued round.

'And what about the composition of the audience? Were there women there as well as men?'

'Yes there were.'

'And they were laughing, weren't they?'

'Yes, I suppose so. But maybe they were laughing just because they've been conditioned to have the same vile attitudes as the men?'

'Don't be stupid, Bull. You're so ten-years-after. People are a lot more sophisticated than you give them credit for. Razza is an *ironist*. You probably didn't notice' – but naturally, Bull gritted mentally, you did – 'but all these cunt jokes are just that: cunt jokes. They aren't jokes about women at all. They have nothing to do with women. Razza is cutting the *archetypal* cunt out of the woman – and displaying it for the world to see, and appreciate, that it's just a cipher – an empty category on to which people project their own distorted attitudes. After all, what's a hole once one removes it from the ground?' She was quoting the article again, Bull realised.

And indeed he was right, those very words still gleamed wetly on the LCD of the lap-top, which was perched on the corner of Juniper's futon platform in the next room.

'Well, I suppose it's . . . it's . . .' Bull floundered, angry at himself for failing to come up with a rejoinder to the facile riddle.

'Nothing at all. Bang on, mate. Nothing at all. Mmmn . . . No, I think he's brilliant, sexy too . . .' (Sexy? thought Bull. With that shopping-trolley pelvis? And those injection-moulded thighs, as thin as his calves? Disgusting, leaving the knobbly knees free-floating like fungi borne on a sapling's trunk. He was appalled) '. . . I think he's going to be very big indeed. In fact I'll stake *my* reputation on it.' Irony? The woman didn't know the meaning of the word.

Bull, to his credit, came back at her. 'I don't think you're reading him right, Juniper. Wait until you interview him. I think you'll find that he's just another funny-faced man with an inferiority complex, who made kids laugh at school to save himself from bullying and humiliation. Now he thinks he's got a crack at the big time. Go and talk to him. I'll be very surprised if he's able to give you any objective justification for his act at all. My theory is that he thinks that if he talks about women's genitals for long enough, he'll manage to get his grubby little hands on some live examples.'

The instant he had said this, Bull regretted it.

'That's probably *your* attitude,' snapped Juniper, 'you're projecting.' 'Projecting' was one of her buzzwords. During her protracted sojourn on the wilder shores of psychotherapy, she had somehow acquired the idea that all potentially laden and upholstered comments were necessarily subjective and self-revelatory pronouncements. All except her own that was. At parties Juniper had been known to mutter caustically, 'He's projecting,' when a man said something as apparently void of the psychopathology of everyday life as 'The old Soviet Union's in a hell of a mess, you know.'

'Maybe, maybe I am.' Hating himself, Bull became abject. Juniper's sexuality may have been completely circumscribed by neurosis, but for him the inside-outedness of her *mons*, defined as it was by the artful filleting of her Mercx cycling shorts, was more than he could bear. In that moment he contrasted her feral impatience yanking at his cock as if it were an oryx she had managed to down on the veldt, with his own dreamy inexactitude of touch. 'I'm not as sophisticated as you are, you know that. I'm always impressed by the rigour you bring to these things.' This shameless brown-nosing seemed to work. Either she was purring or he had a bad connection. As he finished speaking the purr seemed on the verge of turning into a giggle, so he went on. 'You have to teach me. You know how ignorant I am about all aspects of the theatre – and therefore about life.'

She giggled again. 'What are you saying, Bull?'

'I just thought . . . I just thought we might have dinner together. After you've interviewed Razza. I want you to put your analysis of his act in a wider context for me.'

'Well, it couldn't possibly be this week, I've got far too much on. I'm up against a deadline.'

'How about the weekend?' And once again, the instant he launched the fragile paper words on to the telephonic pond, Bull regretted them. The Wanderers' mini-tour was this coming weekend. They were to play four matches, Friday through to Monday. All Sunday League teams based along the South Coast. The fixtures were at Bexhill-on-Sea; Rottingdean; Brighton and Shoreham. Bull wouldn't miss it for the world. The freshness of spring, the animal joy of unfettered movement, and the whole package salt 'n' shaken by a sea breeze. What could be finer?

'We-ell, I don't know.' She clearly had a prospective invitation, thought Bull, but it hadn't been firmed up yet. 'Call me Saturday morning and we'll see how the land lies.'

'See how the land lies'. That was the phrase from the phone-call that now came back to Bull as he stared into the suburban night. But it was only as much of a euphemism as Bull's 'dinner', so did he really deserve any better? And anyway, why was he so intent upon Juniper? She was, quite frankly, silly. What with her fanatical modishness and fifth-hand hackery masquerading as philosophy. Bull knew she had other men, many other men, and probably women as well. He could feel it in the way the self-basting quality of her skin turned into grittiness, as she worked her way up to another utilitarian climax. It felt like the porous facing-stone of a London monument. A monument that had been recreationally scaled by a multitude.

But Bull feared rejection by Juniper far more. He feared that his thrustings were not firm and follow-through enough to satisfy her. He worried that his circumnavigations of her breasts were not emphatically solo – that his hands were all too obviously carrying the pilots of his sex-manual study. Bull wanted to graduate from Juniper's dry-roasted academy. And, added to that, on this particular evening there was this extra, nagging vulnerability. This extra sense of being put upon by injury, by his own inadvertent actions.

Bull's broad hand rubbed over the bandaged mound as a junior thuggee let off a roman candle in the car park of the modern Congregationalist Church two streets away from the flat. The flash of yellow-white light sheened the window pane into opacity. When it cleared a figure emerged from the tatters of Bull's retinal after-image. He stood across the road, in front of the Budgen Freezer Food Centre, looking quizzically up at Bull's flat, as if he had seen it before but could no longer remember where or when. It was Alan Margoulies.

Alan had driven North, up from the Archway Tower, past the Whittington Hospital and towards Highgate

Village. He absolutely intended to go and drain Mr Gaston's cyst. Gaston, a retired French teacher, lived in a shoebox cottage in the village. He lay all day, every day, stinking on a divan, his bilious, tweed-clad form surrounded by a drift of the yellowed and yellowing paper covers of *Éditions Gallimard*.

Gaston had a huge cyst in the very pit of his back. It was a cyst with a life cycle of its own – seemingly unconnected to Gaston's metabolism. No matter how many times Alan, or Gaston's health visitor Helen Meyer, drained the thing, it swelled back up again within thirty-six hours. It was, Alan often thought, as if the disgusting sac was parasitic upon its host's enormous reserves of vitriol and bile.

Alan fully intended to drain the cyst. And then, if there was time, drive the two miles on to East Finchley and see if Bull's dressing needed changing. It was the least he could do, considering . . . considering that he was going away tomorrow to the Health Authority's Learning Jamboree at Wincanton!

'Shit, fuck, damn!' Alan cursed and pounded the wheel of the car. It juddered and hummed like a giant tuning fork. 'Bull will go to the nurse while I'm away and then the game will be up!'

Alan drove straight past Mr Gaston's cottage. He flicked through the chicane and headed on down towards East Finchley. A little devil sat on Alan's left shoulder, a little angel on his right. On the right-hand shoulder of the little devil sat a littler angel; and on the left-hand shoulder a littler devil. It was the same for the first angel, and so on, and so on. This was the *reductio ad infinitum* of Alan's moral sense: a great Renaissance canvas depicting diminishing tiers of cherubim and seraphim, imps, satyrs and familiars. All towering up into an impossible void.

You see, Alan had all the equipment in place already. He had done his deal with the diabolic Russian Doll of dramatic irony. He had had his little peccadilloes and consigned his wife and child to the status of emotional also-rans. He was dutiful, yes. Conscientious, yes. I would never do anything that was disrespectful to my wife; he had thought this many times, whilst examining Sybil's round parting, as the sculptress's lips blubbered up and over his fine and tapering cock. I love my wife, he had said to himself with practised ease as his thighs were slapping against Sybil's buttocks. On more than one occasion, looking up, matching the trope to his stroke, he had caught the eyepits of one of Sybil's Easter Island statues regarding him from the dark garden with a face full of baleful and ancient amorality.

So that's how it was. Alan had effectively substituted his love for his wife for the floor of Euston Station buffet as a good mental tag with which to counter *ejaculatio praecox*.

But would he be able to feel the same way as he thrust with skilful, sinuous angularity into the pit of Bull's knee? Into Bull's cunt, not Sybil's?

There! It was out in the open. He'd yanked it from

under the rug. It was damp, compacted, putrescent, like an ancient meat pie folded into a dirty sock. Could he possibly sweep it back under again?

Alan swooped under the railway bridge and looked up at the statue of the stylised Red Indian that was set on top of East Finchley Tube Station. It was eternally frozen, this statue, in the act of firing an arrow towards Highgate Tube Station. What if the arrow were to be fired? Alan mused. Shot off, unleashed. What if the Achilles tendon-seeking missile were to be allowed to seek the tendon-edged pit?

It is necessary to understand at this juncture that Alan was guilty of hubris, pure and simple. In assuming voyeurism, bondage, sodomy and other really quite harmless kinks, to be nothing more (or less) than the evidence of their practitioners' arrested sense of irony, Alan had lost control. His own Schwarzenegger-sized sensibility had leapfrogged the poppers, the peep-shows, the crotchless panties and uterine fag-puffing sessions. Leap-frogged them and run off towards this *coup de foudre*, this Bull-thing.

Alan was unmanned by it. Thrown back into pubescent homoeroticism. He shivered on the touchline, his thighs wavering in the wide legs of his rugby shorts. Out near the thirty-yard line Bull was practising place kicks. Alan wanted so much to be like Bull – hearty, popular, accepted. He'd do anything to be like Bull.

Alan hooked his lank hair back behind his ears. He hadn't felt cold when he left the house, but he did now.

Along with his bag for housecalls, he pulled a herring-bone tweed overcoat from the back of the car and buttoned himself into it. He went and stood on the pavement and looked up towards the window of Bull's flat opposite, waiting for it all to begin.

'You'd better come in,' said Bull, once Alan had waved to him from across the road and then made his way around the parade to the flat's entrance. Standing in the doorway Bull noticed for the first time that he was at least a head taller than Margoulies.

Alan thought different things, whilst looking at Bull, lowering in the vestibule. He thought: I fancy him, it's true. But damn it all, I'm not queer, I'm just not.

Bull was looking uncharacteristically shabby. On arriving home he had stripped off jacket, shoes and socks; and since then he had been slopping around the gloomy flat in carpet-slippers, his shirt-tails escaping from his thick waist to form elephant's ears.

The sitting-room, when they arrived there, was already fully occupied by an extravagant coffee table. It was square-bordered, but cratered by a circle of glass six feet in diameter. Cubic, wheeled pouffes, which clearly matched it, stood about in awful caramel vinyl suitings.

They stood awkwardly at the edge of the room, as if the coffee table had usurped them. After too long a pause Margoulies said, 'I thought I'd better come by and take a look at that dressing, John.' He was hyper-solicitous. Bull, despite himself, was suspicious.

'You should have rung, I might not have been here.'

'Well I thought you probably would be . . .' Margoulies had a thought. 'Have you been taking those pills?' Bull sank down heavily on a tufty armchair. A big hand went to a ginger brow.

'I took some this morning but they made me feel woozy, so I didn't take any more.'

There was such pathos in Bull's posture. Such innocence in the way that he hunched his knees together, as if trying to hide his treasure still further from view. Alan knew he would have to tell him now, right away.

'John, I gave you those pills for a reason.'

'I know you did.'

'No, not that reason. I gave them to you because I felt that you needed sedating.'

'Sedating, why?'

'Because that thing in the pit of your knee isn't a wound or a burn, John.' Bull's eyes went round with understanding. His well-shaped features drew themselves together into an ugly knot of revelation. His clipped voice sprang back at Margoulies.

'It's cancer, isn't it?'

Alan felt so powerful and protective of Bull. So in control now of this odd seduction that he couldn't stop himself from laughing. The guffaw propelled him out of his chair, and he stood jiggling and chuckling with sinister solicitude over the hapless cabaret editor. Eventually he recovered himself enough to say, 'No, John, it's not cancer, nothing like that at all. Where have you got a full-length mirror? I want to show you something.'

Bull led Alan next door to the bedroom. He was so excited, so exalted. This would have to be the ultimate striptease. This was why the *Playboy* dynamics of Alan's sexual fantasies had seemed so silly and banal to him. For this was the Real Thing. Now the clashing colours and faded forms of Nicholson's tome came back to Alan, but decked in familiar, lacy filigree. This was true excitement!

At home Naomi Margoulies ushered in the babysitter – a foreign-language student whose face, under the hall light, shone with crusted acne.

'He went out to drain Mr Gaston's cyst,' said Naomi. She was so pissed off that she couldn't be bothered to contextualise the statement. 'I've no idea where he's got to.'

Alan and Bull had got to the bedroom. Bull snagged on the overhead light. It glared down at them from its chintzy shade like a disapproving landlady. On Bull's 'occasional' bed were scattered clothes. A rugby ball lay on the floor together with a tangle of other sporting kit.

There was a small bookcase in the underdeveloped bay window, stacked with old editions of *Wisden* and sporting magazines. Alan said, 'You'd better slip out of your things, John.' Christ! How he was enjoying this.

Bull unfastened his elasticated belt and slid his trousers off his rounded hips. Kicking off his carpet slippers, he teetered out of the trousers, shifting from one foot to the other, until he stood before Alan, Y-fronted and blinking.

Alan positioned him with his back to the full-length mirror, just as Bull had positioned himself at the very start of this strange day. Alan's touch may have been light and professional, but Bull sensed it lingering a half-beat too long. Alan undid the safety pins and began to demolish the flying buttresses of bandage. Loop after loop, skein after skein came away. And, as he undressed Bull, Alan felt that at last he was doing something truly sexy, something with real edge.

He hadn't felt like this since he was eleven and he and a school friend called Solomons had frolicked, naughtily naked, around the miniature cedars of Solomons' parents' formal garden. Together they had collapsed in a tangle of limbs as white as new shoots, and Solomons had touched Alan's trembling little cock, making him come for the first shivering time. Alan had ejaculated gouts of fluid, still devoid of spermatozoa and as clear as battery water.

Alan's homosexual phase had been brief. But Solomons went on to manage a ninety-bed 'travellers' hotel in Sydney, and Alan had heard rumours that he was mixed up in the drugs trade. It all seemed such a long way from Hendon.

But tonight even East Finchley seemed a long way away from Hendon. The last crêpe loop fell away and there it was, even prettier than Alan remembered it. Even more perfect. It had all the symmetry of a mandala, but it was vivified, animated, moving in more ways than one. Alan steadied Bull's thick leg, holding it in place, and stood up.

'Now look over your shoulder, John. Can you see it?' Bull could see it all right.

'What is it, Doctor?'

'It's a vagina, John. You've grown a vagina.' Bull's reaction was far more extreme, far more intense than even the conscientious, the caring Alan Margoulies could have imagined.

The big, ginger man knelt moaning on the carpet. A bubbling, keening sound came unbidden from the corners of his not unsensual mouth. Then he straightened the fateful limb towards the mirror, adopting a sort of half-squat thrust position. Alan felt detached enough to observe how satisfactorily Bull's leg muscles stood out, once his leg was tensed, displaying the invasive feminine biology to full effect. The vaginal surround, perineum, mons and pubic bone were so neatly implanted into the limb that the overall effect was surreal – straightforwardly in the manner of Dali, or Man Ray.

Bull craned his neck around and stared transfixed. In

the mirror he too could now see the errant orifice standing out, almost in relief, despite its recessed position. Alan goggled as well. The keening coming from Bull was gaining in volume. Alan started to mutter inanities in a prayerful undertone: reassurances; forecasts of possible treatments based on garbled excerpts of spuriously successful case histories, garnered from Nicholson, the *British Journal of Abnormal Physiology* and the like. The muttering and the keening did battle with one another in the polystyrene space of the room, while both men's eyes remained fixed on the by now parted lips of Bull's vagina.

Together they observed the stratifications of the orifice. The way the dry smoothness of the kneepit flowed up and over, into the mucal membranous strias of the vulva. Bull made a grunting 'Hhn, hhn' noise from somewhere deep inside his beefy chest. He sprang to his feet, fell across the bed, sprang up again. He swept the thick volumes of cricket statistics from the bookshelf on to the floor. He pirouetted, caromed off a wall, off Alan, off a doorjamb, and was gone into the corridor, roaring.

Bull saw it all. Bull understood it all. Understood the feelings of vulnerability that had been troubling him all day; understood the difficulties he had had in analysing the sensations that the wound, or burn, had provoked in him; understood Alan's behaviour in the health centre. But worse, far worse, Bull understood certain deep and painful things about himself that had always shamed him.

Poor, poor Bull. He stood, now hugging the humming fridge, and now butting the broken thermostat. He cantered whinnying up and down the corridor, kicking to bits the telephone and its fake Chippendale stoolette. He stood in the orange living-room and railed at the bald-faced stag, as if it were some ancient Nordic idol, a forest god with a tree for a cock, capable of re-manning him once more.

And as Bull joined the dots of memory and saw the sketchy picture of his latent femininity emerge from a myriad of locker-room blushes and missed emotional connections, Alan was with him – at his side – understanding, empathising, as Bull's wheezing intellect, like the little engine that couldn't, struggled to make sense of its own identity.

At home Naomi Margoulies stood on the half landing. The baby's mouth, gummy with sleep, applied itself to the racing pulse in her neck. Naomi had sent the babysitter home. As soon as she could put Cecile back down again, she was going to phone Helen Meyer. Perhaps the health visitor would know what had happened to her husband? He had never behaved like this before.

Bull stood hunched in the asymmetric space formed by the stairway leading to the flat above. Alan stood by him. Bull squatted in the gap beneath the formica kitchen surface, left vacant for the washing machine he had never troubled to purchase. Alan squatted by him. Bull sandwiched himself into the narrow declivity between the wardrobe and the wall, in the semen-stained darkness of the spare bedroom. Alan was sand-wiched alongside.

Both began to understand that in occupying these quirky sites in Bull's flat together, they were in fact encountering the mysterious and special character of their new relationship. And in the cadence of Bull's slowly subsiding hysteria there was an anticipation of a new loss of self, a new *petit mort*.

The first touch came when Bull was lying full-length along the skirting board in the little six-foot vestibule that connected the bathroom to the kitchenette and the front door. He was the picture of powerlessness. His sensible, striped M&S shirt was rucked up around his back, his white, cotton Y-fronts dewlapped over the flat surfaces of his buttocks. Alan's fine and tapering hand described an arc over him. He knelt as if stroking a cat. At the zenith of the arc Alan's palm made contact with the small of Bull's back. Bull stiffened but did not cry out or resist . . . Oh, cruel deceiver! For how could Margoulies not have known that in this moment of breakdown, of cracking distress, the thing that Bull, of course, still desired most ardently, was the dry, sensible touch of a doctor.

But very soon Alan was lying with Bull. Full-length as

well. His lips sought the firm warmth of Bull's neck, his hands reached forwards, around Bull, and ran over his chest, down to the top of his thighs. Alan's fine and tapering nostrils, their flanges as sharp as paper edges, dilated, taking in Bull's strong, meaty and reassuringly masculine odours. There was a tang of sweat as pungent as urine, and a deeper, almost farmyard aroma of digestion and decomposition. However, alongside these safe whiffs, Alan could detect something else, strained, fishy and yet flannelly. Like a lavender bag left in the sheets of the sea. This was the olfactory suggestion of Bull-as-woman; Bull as inside, rather than outside.

When Alan actually entered Bull his face was buried between the prop forward's well-upholstered shoulder blades. Bull's leg was bent back at the knee and tucked comfortably up, and under Alan's crotch. Even lying as he was – awkwardly on the floor – Alan's left hand was still free to wander. Free to stroke Bull's surprisingly slim cock, his massive belly, his gnat bite nipples.

Alan was transported. Bull *was* all woman to him. Bull's hysteria and now this tremulous capitulation. What could be more feminine? For Alan, they were like two crash survivors copulating amidst burning wreckage, deliriously affirming the very fact of living. And Bull's leg, how beautifully it rubbed up against Alan, rounding off each one of his own thrusts!

Alan had never screwed a virgin before; certainly not a virgin who was *intacta*. He had worried that there would be a lot of pain for Bull, and a lot of blood that might stain their discarded clothing, which lay wadded beneath the two thrashing bodies. Alan wanted the first time to be extra specially good for Bull. Alan sensed that it might be make or break. With a sexuality as potentially power-ful and omnivorous as Bull's now was, he might take his pick of partners.

Alan moistened the tips of his fingers with his own saliva, and rubbed it into Bull's parted lips. He nudged a finger tip into Bull's vagina, seeking out his hymen. Whilst another finger tip traced the slippery pod of Bull's clitoris. Alan was reassured. Bull's breathing had become deep and rhythmic, each breath coming from the very pit of his abdomen. Alan took the head of his own penis and pushed its head just inside Bull. Bull sighed. Alan held it there, tensing it and un-tensing it, letting Bull become accustomed to the sensation, before he thrust home in one long, fateful stroke.

It's like that, isn't it? Just as Raymond Chandler says, 'The first kiss is dynamite, the second is routine and then you take her clothes off.' It had been like that for Alan in his previous affairs, even the extended one he had had with Sybil while Naomi was pregnant. Sure, Alan went on enjoying the sex with Sybil, but at a fundamental level his lust for her had died the very first time he felt the shock of her pubic bone against his, and knew that they were now truly welded into one another. Alan was a one-thrust man. Not that he'd ever been exactly pro-miscuous. Perhaps it would have been better for all concerned if he had been. Rather, his sentimental self-absorption had managed to gild each of these terminal thrusts with enough self-regarding burnish for him to sustain the 'relationships' that legitimised them for months; and in at least two instances, for years.

While each thrust had, therefore, gone in, it had turned back on Alan, at some deep level *penetrating him* with the morbid realisation that his sexual being was a dull thing, a lifeless thing, a mass-produced marionette with chipped paint and fraying strings.

And, of course, it was the same as it ever was. Now Alan's rocks had hardened, swelled and gushed – in the immediate aftermath of climax Alan sensed Bull as liability, pure liability, triple liability. Alan was now having an affair with a man who had a cunt in the back of his leg. Worse still, the man was his patient. At the very least he would be struck off . . . No, Alan couldn't really conceive of the appropriate official sanction for this kind of behaviour, although possibly public castration by the Minister of Health might get close. Still lying, his fine features pressed into Bull's freckled spine, Alan saw in his mind's eyes the bright cuirasses of the Household Cavalry flashing in the Whitehall sunlight. In his mind's nose he smelt a waft of Givenchy from the Minister's fragrant cheek as she approached the quivering, half-naked Alan, who was lashed to the Cenotaph. The Minister's wedding ring glowed dully against the green, plastic handle of the garden secateurs she held in her outstretched hand; whilst in Alan's mind's ear the 'Sshk, sshk' noise the secateurs made as the Minister flexed them sounded horribly loud and ominous.

Bull stirred beneath Alan. And Alan felt his limp penis slide out of Bull's kneepit with lubricated ease. Bull struggled round in the fluff-encrusted runnel of the vestibule and brought his pale, frank eyes, with their horrible weight of understanding into the brown, trustworthy gaze of his seducer. They tried very hard to stare affectionately at one another.

And what did Bull feel throughout this? How was it for him? Shame on you for even *daring* to ask. Some things must, after all, be sacred. Some things mustn't be picked apart and subjected to such close scrutiny. But still, it is only fair to say that the experience was shattering. Bull felt violated, traduced, seduced, bamboozled, subjugated, entrapped and enfolded. He felt his capacity for action surgically removed. He felt, for the first time in his life, that his sense of himself as a purposeful automaton, striding on the world's stage, had been completely vitiated by a warm wash of transcendence. This must be like a religious experience, thought Bull, his veal cheek pressed against the double plug socket. And had he been better versed in such things he might immediately have given his vagina the status of stigmata. In which case the outcome of this strange tale might have been considerably different.

The two orgasms had beaten up on him from either

side. One came with each thrust of Alan into Bull, and the other derived from Alan's expert and emphatic tugs at Bull's cock. Though of such different natures and provenances they had somehow managed to merge together, like the Skaggerack and the Kattegat off Bull's Jutland.

Sad to say, although Bull thought that this feeling might just be a new love, he knew in his heart of hearts that this was just dependency wearing an ornate garb. For Alan was only a representative, he was not the whole organisation.

After they had made love the two men righted and tidied both themselves and the flat with studious workmanlike efficiency. Alan put the phone back together and crouched holding the fractured dial in two hands while he made the connection to Helen Meyer. It was by now almost 10.00 pm. The health visitor relayed that Alan's wife was worried about him. Alan explained that he had had an emergency bleep to visit another patient – he didn't mention Bull's name. Bull the patient no longer existed. The subterfuge was a safe one, Meyer was close-mouthed in the extreme. Alan asked her to call Naomi, apologise on his behalf, and say that he would be home shortly.

When Alan hung up Bull was standing over him in the corridor. The overhead light that dangled above and behind his head transformed his ginger hair into a fiery aureole.

'Will I see you again?' Bull was shy, almost blushing.

'John, I have to go to this damn Learning Jamboree thing tomorrow.'

'I know, your receptionist told me on the phone this morning.'

'It's down in Somerset. It runs over the long weekend. Still, I might be able to get away to London one evening, say Friday?' Alan was already calculating his duplicitous angles with the adulterer's practised ease.

'I won't be in London on Friday evening, I'll be in Bexhill-on-Sea. I'm going on a mini-rugby tour.' Bull said this tersely. His voice already had the hurt huffiness of a subordinate partner whose personal interests are held to be of no account.

'A rugby tour. That's interesting. That'll be a good idea, John, it'll keep your mind off things . . .' Alan's voice died away and they both stood, contemplating the 'things' in question. 'Look, anyway,' Alan resumed brightly, 'I can make it to Bexhill from Wincanton and be back within the evening. Where can I meet you?' Bull thought for a second. 'There's a big bar in the De La Warr Pavilion. Meet me there. It's on the seafront, everyone knows it. Meet me there at eight o'clock.'

They stood, clotted with shyness, their rendezvous made.

'Well, 'til Friday evening then,' said Alan.

''Til Friday,' replied Bull. They shook hands and Alan left, shutting the door with exaggerated care, as if frightened of waking a baby.

By morning Mr Gaston's cyst was so large that it could quite reasonably have claimed that *it* had a better quality of life than Gaston himself. And that perhaps it was *he*, rather than *it*, that should be drained on a regular basis.

4

Pursuit

T HE FIRST THING that occurred to Alan on waking the following morning was that he had managed to square things away with Naomi pretty convincingly, all things considered. But deep down he knew that regularity, and regularity alone, was the key to a successful adulterous deception. The night before had constituted an irregularity, therefore the seed of doubt – no matter how achingly legitimate Alan's excuse might have been in a multitude of other contexts – had been sown in Naomi's fine chest.

In those two hours of lost contact – of parting from the Mother Ship – Alan had entered the twilight zone.

Naomi left before him. She wheeled Cecile down the neat street of terraced Victorian villas on her way to the Ten O'Clock Club at the Grove Health Centre. Each house had its respective campaign sticker in its respective window, but on this particular morning Naomi paid them no mind. On any other morning she would have probably hailed them thus: 'Ah, the healthy evidence of a genuinely pluralist society,' for Naomi was nothing if not committed.

It's just that commitment had fucked off on this dark,

damp, leafy London morning. London had this ability, Naomi now knew, to take spring and turn it in to autumn, just by tweaking the air quality, raising its contrast. The privet hedges tossed like tethered donkeys at the knackers, and sprays of dirty rain fell across her cheek, and across the plastic rain cover of Cecile's pushchair.

Naomi felt sick. She felt sick, she realised, because she was unquestionably pregnant. Or could there be another explanation? Could there . . . please?

At the Ten O'Clock Club all the toddlers and babies were glued together by Marmite hands into a pullulating swarm that circled the brown, disinfected floor with a Doppler wail of need and recrimination. Naomi threw Cecile to the multi-cellular creature that sported amongst the finger paintings and joined the other mothers, and a father.

The other mothers, and a father, were sitting on miniature chairs drinking tea out of plastic paint-beakers. The mothers talked about their children; their children's ailments; their own ailments. It was as if their very presence within the perimeter of the health centre made them more acutely aware of the fits and starts of their malfunctioning bodies. The father sat with them but kept his own counsel. His pipecleaner body was tubed in worn denim. His gasmask bag lay on the lino next to his booted feet. Every so often he touched the scrappy end of a roll-up to his brown, bearded lips and leaked a piddle of smoke. He was, Naomi observed, reading the *Guar-*

dian 'Society' section as if he didn't in any way belong to it.

Naomi knew him slightly. She knew that he was a child psychologist at the Gruton Clinic, who specialised in difficult toddlers. Naomi and Cecile had once passed him in the street when he was with his little boy, Hector. The two-year-old had been bemusedly leaning against the plate-glass window of the bank, while his father treated the passers-by to a full-scale tantrum. 'I won't have it!' shouted the Child Psychologist. 'I can't take it!' he wailed. He had emptied the contents of the baby's changing bag on to the pavement and was tossing around nappies, Wet Ones, Calendula cream and changing bags, all with whirling-dervish abandon. Naomi was happy to scrape by without being noticed.

Normally Naomi would have talked with the other mothers, and father, about any one of the numerous local self-help groups that they were severally and variously involved with. But this morning the talk was all of legs ivied by varicose veins; bowels that tortured their respective anuses into pastry-cutter shapes; heads that were tintinnabulated by the air-pressure changes occasioned by the rise and fall of catflaps; and endless, runny colds. The tea slopped in the paint beaker. Naomi slurped it down and felt it slopping in her stomach. 'Four times a night,' said Gail Hutchinson, somewhere off to Naomi's left, 'each one bigger and stickier than the last.' There was a small rash of 'Nos!' Naomi rose and made her way unsteadily through the kitchenette. In the miniature stalls, with their doors – just the right height for a calf's neck – Naomi knelt and gratefully voided egg, waffle, Special K and tea into the titchy toilet.

She stayed there for a while, staring down into the terminal soup, as if, before being consigned to the recently privatised sewer, its tummy globs and salival strands might form and re-form into a prescient tableau of her future. Her future with Alan.

Alan was sitting at the lights next to Regent's Park tube station. He was in his black Citroën XM 3.0SEi. Too much car for a conscientious GP, but too little for the *Übermensch* he had so recently become.

A trio of dildo aerials, thick and rubberised, sprouted from above the dreamboat's tinted rear window. Across the fascia of the car various pin-point lights glowed with machine vigour. On the black velour of the seat-cover lay Alan's black attaché case. On the black rubber floormat lay his black medical bag. Clipped to the dash was his wafer-thin black cellular phone, with its enviable console of green buttons. The information pack for the Health Authority's Learning Jamboree lay open on Alan's black-clad knees. The papers the folder contained had been ruffed out invitingly. But Alan wasn't reading them; he was concentrating on the traffic lights. He was assessing the weight, volume and potential velocity of the vehicles that coughed around him. His incisive mind flicked indiscriminately between the contorted penetration of the night before and calculations of the now. All this was to the rhythm of the black music that thudded from the car's eight black, rhomboid speakers.

The light changed and Alan hit the accelerator, savouring the almost neural response of the powerful engine. He went barrelling off through the traffic; lane-switching; accelerating; braking; forging on in a seamless, solo strip-the-willow that took him flying through the exhausted trough of the Marylebone Road, hitting five green lights in succession, and up on to the cold heights of the Westway flyover.

Alan exalted as the black wedge of car lifted him above the wrinkled skin of the city. Ahead of him the flyover described a sinuous curve as it stretched to the West. Squalls of spring rain lashed the window, but the gusts that bore them didn't displace the car's track by even a millimetre. Rock hard and rock steady, plunging on to her, Alan saw for the first time that the line of the flyover formed the stick shape of an enormous woman. The head was the elevated roundabout at White City. From there one extended arm was formed by the motorway spur that ended in Shepherd's Bush round-about. The other arm was flung over the woman-figure's head. It arced into a three-lane elbow, and then placed its hand in Acton. The woman-figure's long back curved this way and that over Notting Hill, before rising to a concrete runnelled rump, that split; one thin leg dangled down to kick petulantly at Paddington, whilst the other was loosely crossed over it, foot firmly on the Marylebone Road.

Right now Alan's car was charging like a runaway vibrator, towards the very crotch of the flyover. Alan appreciated that he was about to penetrate the woman-figure with 170 brake horsepower. He felt just fine. The floating digital display of the Citroën's speedometer teetered to a hundred as Alan plunged through the macadamised maw.

He revelled in it! He felt that now, at last, he understood the matrix that encapsulated his life. He had scaled the heights of medicine – and with them the heights of morality. He had married a beautiful and committed woman, together they had an adorable, dark-eyed child with a fashionable French name. He had lasciviously pronged bohemian sculptresses and sturdy health workers. Now came his greatest coup! His great synthesis of the experiential: Bull. Bull the man; Bull the woman; Bull the cunt . . . But what if he's fickle? The sudden uncertainty jerked Alan's foot from the accelerator. The car wavered and nearly side-swiped a panel truck.

The rest of Alan's drive to Wincanton was marked by a see-saw between this exultation and this remorseful fear. Somehow the realisation that his affair with Bull might fail activated Alan's guilt about Naomi and Cecile. For a while they ceased to be ciphers, ironic columns for his public theatre and his private cinema. Instead they were damnably separate centres of self. With feelings. Tedious, shitty little feelings for which he had some milksop's sense of responsibility.

Now everything had to be focused on the next rendezvous with Bull. All emotional roads led to Bexhill-on-Sea.

Bull slept the sleep of the justly shagged. He slept hunkered deep down into the tortured springs of his mattress. In sleep, Bull's heavy corpse assumed stylised poses, embedded in the bed's surround like a bas-relief. One arm was thrown back, the other out, just like the Westway flyover. At certain times Bull's eyelids flickered with the Noh play of the unconscious, then Bull whimpered, clutching a rugby-ball-shaped space to his pudding pectorals. At other times, in deep repose, the bug legs bicycled and canted themselves just-*so*. Just so that his two sets of genitals were neatly juxtaposed within the same tight frame.

The time-switched spotlight that by night lit the antlers on the bald-faced stag that stood on the pediment of the Bald-Faced Stag had long since been extinguished, and the thin beige dawn was draining through the net curtains, when Bull was woken by the rattling and ringing of the phone in the hall. He cursed and fought off the duvet aggressively, as if it had broken into the flat and attacked him while he slept.

Bull batted along the corridor from wall to wall and crouched by the noisome thing.

'Hello? John? I hope I didn't wake you?' It was his boss, the effete aesthete who published *Get Out!*, and, worse, pretended to edit it.

'Er . . . no. Well . . . yes. Actually I was getting up anyway.' Bull felt more assured by his habitual diffidence than by the fact of his being alive. And it acted as a bulwark while, the Bakelite still cabbaging his ear, the memories of the previous evening began to flood in.

'I was only calling to see how you were. Some of the chaps said that you were injured in some way the night before last; and that you went home yesterday looking rather green. You didn't say anything to me . . .' This was a reproach. '. . . I hope it's nothing serious?'

'No, no, nothing at all.' (I have a cunt in the back of my knee.) 'I feel fine.' (I feel mad. Mad.) 'I'm on my way in.' What else can a man do but go to work?)

'Oh good. I'm so pleased to hear it. I wanted to have a little word with you. Nothing important, just a little word.'

How little a word? mused Bull, making his way to the damp certainties of the bathroom. 'A', or perhaps 'the'? If it was really *that* little, he could have safely let it scuttle down the phone line. He snapped the cord and the light over the sink sprang on. Bull opened the leathern flap of his Gentleman's Travelling Dressing Kit (a present from Mummy four Christmases ago), and extracted a pocket mirror. Then he bent down and wedged his head right between his knees. Frozen like that Bull seemed to be on the verge of nutting the bath mat. He wielded the pocket mirror and confronted his vagina. It had grown during the night!

Whereas yesterday the fine ginger hairs on the back of Bull's calf had teased themselves into a vague whorl over his *mons veneris*, now they had regrouped and increased in both length and thickness to produce a definite tuft, and even a nascent triangle. And below the vagina, the wrinkled zip of brown flesh that Alan had correctly identified as Bull's perineum was now choked with hairs like an overgrown railway cutting.

Bull drew the right conclusion: whether or not the sex session with Alan was the cause, the vagina was noticeably maturing.

Straightening up, *he* felt maturer. More grown-up. After all, simply because a chap has a gash, a beaver, a fanny, the old bearded clam embedded in his poor peg-leg – that's no reason to write him off. Plenty of the boys Bull had been at Markhams College with had gone on to peculiar destinies. Only last week Bull had read in the paper an item about a boy who had been two years above him. A man now of course, although apparently still a boy at heart, in terms of his vicious amorality and his relentless definition of his sexuality through aggression and violence. This boy then, risen in a provincial bureaucracy, a social services director or some such, had danced around a fire (gas, with imitation logs), ululating, prancing, buggering, and ultimately garotting, a number of pubescents whom he had stupefied with Mogadon-spiked scrumpy. It had been a *cause célèbre*. Worthy of 'comment'.

And even Tittymus, Bull's friend and contemporary, had slid into the Lanes at Brighton. Where he and his black boyfriend, Duvalier, camped and distressed both themselves and their stock of furniture. Tittymus still dared to attend the regular Markhams reunions on the Isle of Grain. And he was accepted! He *and* Duvalier, in matching brass-buttoned blazers, their breast pockets emblazoned with the Sussex County Cricket Club badge. It was absurd, but it was true. Surely there was some way in which Bull could gain acceptance for his 'peculiarity', in this world in which social and sexual characteristics were already being tossed and dressed like salad?

Musing mind, as ever with Bull, went with musing hand. He found himself in the middle of his Tittymus reverie gently exploring the slick softness of his clitoris, a tiny bead of excruciating erogeneity, that Margoulies had dealt with cursorily and coarsely during their coming-together in the vestibule. Bull taught himself rapidly that what his clitoris required was not a staccato pressing – like an ulcerated middle manager banging on a lift-call button – but a teasing, suggestive stroke. A touch that existed more in *his* anticipation than in *its* execution.

Bull squatted, and then slumped against the clacking Melamine of the ill-secured bath siding. His masturbation was intense, intercrural as well as penetrative. His fingers arced, dipped and dived, his broad brow fogged up, his eyes glazed.

Bull came this time with shattering high-pitched timpani of feeling. It was wholly different to the percussive bashing of the night before. Shattered, he lay panting on the crocheted oval mat while a new epiphany visited him. Masturbation brought self-determination. Bull felt somehow more subtly, but more certainly, connected to the world, than he had of late. As if, within the lineaments of this admittedly unfathomable new sexuality, he could yet discern deeper, more concrete verities than he had ever been subjected to before.

But entering his car, as it stood on the moss-lined concrete pan in back of the Parade, Bull collapsed. He was dressed for the office, in a sports jacket, clean shirt, well-pressed trousers and penny loafers. His only concession to his vagina had been to wipe it clean and sheath it in a knee-high sock. Now the concavity, the internality, the very *ingressability* of the car, yawned at him. He felt sick and pitched headlong across the front seats. Eugh! The vinyl seat covers were ribbed with raised strips, forming a gullet-like impression. Bull repeated and swallowed.

It didn't help that Bull drove a VW Beetle. The rounded form of the car, with its buttock bumpers and mammary bonnet, now defined him sexually far more than it ever had socially.

Even when he recovered himself and assumed the automatism of London driving, in which the brain is rendered hypothalmic and intentionality takes on the status of breathing, Bull was not delivered.

Doors, windows, garage forecourts, railway tunnels, even bus shelters. All struck at him with forceful, imagistic resonance. It's all cunts! Bull exclaimed to himself, his eyes flicking from the cowled hollow of the car's fascia to the numerous portals that studded his route. It's all openings, entrances and doorways . . . London itself, Bull now realised, was essentially a network of tunnels. It was patently absurd to describe the city's architecture, as Bull had heard the art critic at *Get Out!* do, as 'phallic'. The church spires, the war memorials, the clock towers, the skyscrapers – Brutalist, Purist, Constructivist, it was of no account – even poor old Nelson; they were all terminally irrelevant, ultimately spare pricks. The real lifeblood of the city, Bull now saw, was transported in and out of quintillions of vaginas. The city was a giant Emmenthal cheese, and the experience of entering it was both greedy and erotic.

The shaken man could barely haul the steering wheel around hard enough when it came to parking at Lincolns Inn. He staggered, rather than walked, into the offices of *Get Out!* The nondescript, open–plan office, which spread across the first floor of an undistinguished block on the Grays Inn Road, had acquired a ghastly aura for Bull. But he couldn't decide whether this was a function of his new awareness of vagocentricity, or whether there was something else, some tense expectation about the place that heralded change.

It was the latter. Encountering the Publisher in his glassed-in tank of an office, Bull was cordially, but summarily, fired. 'I just can't see that we're ever going to re-start the sports section,' said the Publisher. He was mopping his brow with a cambric hanky soaked with one of his own colognes, although the temperature hardly warranted it. 'And as you've often said yourself, cabaret wasn't what you were hired to write about.' Bull was speechless. He stared at the leather-flanged oxbow of his instep and tried desperately to resist the sexual lode of the image. The Publisher thought he was being difficult.

'I shall of course give you a generous settlement in lieu of notice . . .' Bull continued to keep his own counsel – observing, instead, the incongruity between the boudoir smell of the office and the work-in-progress impression the Publisher had tried to convey with dummied-up covers and galleys lying in a raffia work pile on the broad desk. '. . . So that's two months' wages . . .' Bull didn't stir. 'Oh all right, call it three. Frankly I think I'm being damn decent, considering that you've been here less than a year.'

Bull found himself speaking, saying, 'I don't know how you can write off sport like that. Tens of thousands of people are interested in sport. All the cities, parks and open spaces are packed, at every hour of the day and night, with people dribbling here and there, and playing both by themselves and with each other . . .' The Publisher stared at Bull with an odd expression on his face. 'Look, John.' A new tone had entered his voice.

'Let's just go and clear your desk, shall we? None of us wants a scene, now do we?'

Bull allowed himself, passive and yielding, to be hustled out of the offices of *Get Out!* His office belongings – more *Wisdens*, some papers, a gonk mascot, computer discs – all were tumbled into a cardboard box. He managed to affect nonchalance with his ex-colleagues, who murmured, 'Bloody hard luck, John,' whilst secretly thanking the great Recruitment God in the sky that it wasn't them who were going down the tubes.

The Publisher himself held the swing doors open for Bull, and his fluting tones followed Bull up the crowded street. 'Of course we'll be happy to consider any free-lance projects you have in mind, John.' Bull heard this but faintly. The musky tickle of the box rim was jammed against his nostrils. He was lost in a deeper, earthier consciousness. A reality in which the concerns and petty justifications of the Publisher were so much puerile time spent wanking. Bull was so far gone that he didn't even trouble to ask the Publisher who was to replace him as *Get Out!* cabaret editor.

In a field somewhere near Wincanton Alan Margoulies was kneeling in a tent. It was one of those very old hundred-pound army tents. Big brown awnings of saturated canvas swayed over the heads of the thirty-or-so general practitioners who were huddled inside it.

There were three other tents in the field, all exactly the same. Each one had its complement of medics, and from the centre-pole of each there flew the Health Authority's pennant.

On arriving at the field Alan had been issued with a clipboard, a map, a badge, an orienteering compass and a regulation Health Authority orange cagoule, with PARAMEDIC in big, black lettering across the back.

Alan felt damp and bored. He had thought that the Learning Jamboree was going to be a free-form exercise in which the GPs themselves would devise strategies for getting to grips with the new legislation in an open-air context. He had neglected to read the information pack, and it transpired that there were 'Facilitators', tedious bureaucrats who all looked horribly at home in this scout-camp ambience. This particular one was calling his complement of doctors to order.

'Ladies and gentlemen, can I have your attention please.' He rapped on the whiteboard behind him with the edge of his compass. The listless chatter in the tent subsided, reading material and cups were downed, thirty non-standard hair-dos swivelled to the front. 'We're here for a long weekend of learning. I know that you're all busy people, people with demanding jobs. So I'm not going to ask you to concentrate too hard on the whys and wherefores of what we're going to be doing. I would ask you to trust me and my fellow facilitators to look after that side of things. What I can guarantee is that if you throw yourselves into the learning exercises that we have devised, I can assure you that you will get results when it comes to grappling with the complexities of the new system.' The Facilitator uncapped a magic marker at this point, with an audible 'plop', and turned to face the whiteboard. Alan noted that, with weary predictability, the back of his orange cagoule bore the legend FACIL-ITATOR.

The Facilitator began, with great crudeness of technique, to draw a plan on the whiteboard, referring constantly to the relevant section of the OS map.

It was somehow appropriate, Alan felt, that the Facilitator should prove so miserably inept with the whiteboard. No matter how hard he tried he simply couldn't get the legends for the map he was drawing, to fit on the board. If he wanted to write 'Spring Copse', the 'copse' ended up vertical, the spidery letters climbing down the edge of the board on spastic feet. The Facilitator started to grunt with the effort, and in time his grunts began to synchronise with the squeaks of his Magic Marker. The doctors began to grow restive. Alan had already seen quite a few he knew, including Hurst and Mukherjee from his own practice. But he was more amused to see Krishna Naipaul, who had been at medical school with him. Krishna was what Alan called a 'naughty doctor'. He was prone to writing slightly dodgy prescriptions for his friends, and making love (at least when he was an intern) on the slippery surfaces of operating tables that had only recently been hosed down.

Alan ran into Krishna Naipaul every year or so at some

GPs' beano or other. He rather guiltily enjoyed Krishna's company – for Naipaul was nothing if not *not* conscientious. He *was* nothing. Alan envied his ironic detachment and had often wished he could muster such easy cynicism. He couldn't for a moment imagine that Naipaul had ever been afflicted by the Tolstoyan, moral self-obsession that had so scarred Alan's early life. His life B.B. (before Bull).

But now? Well, Naipaul would be surprised if he knew the exciting new departure that Alan had so recently made. In the past Alan had slightly haughtily declined Naipaul's invitations for them to 'have fun together'. But now, kneeling, wet corduroy grating on his knees and wafting in his fine, tapering nostrils, Alan thought, why not, confident that even in a dump like Wincanton Krishna would have some angle.

Bull wandered London, jobless and equipped with his new insight into the cityscape. He wandered all day, dazed, depressed and disconnected, unaware that his mental state was so underpinned by strange chemistry that he had not a sorbet's hope in hell of coming to terms with what had happened.

In Bull's liver the micro-refinery of pulsing tubes shuddered with the unexpected order to manufacture unsuitable hormones in staggering quantities. The nodes and strings of genetic information formed weird shapes, like cancerous pretzels, which oscillated out into the racing red water of Bull's bloodstream.

From time to time Bull would enter a hotel or a fast food joint and politely request to use the toilet. As the fire door slid shut behind him on its pneumatic, intercourse arm, Bull would bend double, progesterone and oestrogen nauseas competing with one another to make him vomit. As soon as he had wiped another cravat of bile from his chin, Bull would repair to a cubicle. Here, moving his big body around in its confines, he adopted a position that looked as if it were part of some particularly unsuccessful martial art, and scrutinised his vagina.

Every time he did this it had changed. It had grown. To be more precise: it had grown up. It had acquired a tousled coif of hair. In lop-sided set and ginger fuzz, not dissimilar to Bull's head hair. In the aftermath of his sex session with Alan, Bull had not been dismayed by blood, spunk and mucal discharge . . . that was the trouble, not 'eurgh' but acceptance.

And in his leg, so cruelly and scientifically delineated by flat striplight against the Formica cubicle siding, Bull sensed internal changes as well: shiftings, muscular growth, sinister accommodations.

Wending o'er the paved lea, in the forenoon, rain still flicking at his pink cheeks, Bull felt (oddly enough) depressed for no good reason. He couldn't understand why he was so unhappy. Alan was known by one and all to be the most kind and conscientious of men – what more could Bull want in a lover? It was a little too early in their affair for Bull to put pressure on Alan to leave his wife but that would come in its own time, albeit with acrimony and tears . . . And so what about the job? It was true that he hated it and hated cabaret. It would have been mendacious of him to protest too much. He had made a reasonable living as a freelance in the past, he could do so again. So why these pricking tears? This strange humming tension? His ankles seemed full of water; if he pressed the flesh it went white with a pink surround. And each time he looked at them the lips of Bull's vagina were parted like an analogy.

Places of ingress still fixated Bull. Seeing a broken window along his aimless route, Bull felt that that was what had happened to him. His vitrified hymen had been broken into shards by Alan's thick dick. A bizarre inversion of *Kristallnacht* indeed.

Behind the Swiss Centre Bull found himself staring up at the St John's Hospital for Skin Diseases. The building was empty and derelict, its windows boarded. But it was the moulded mortar curlicues surmounting the tiered façade of the old Hospital which grabbed at Bull. What a sick irony, he thought, to beckon in the skin-diseased with these obvious rollmops of epidermal corruption. They were like his vagina; the simile appalled him. He leant, struggling to retain his equilibrium, against the window of Poons Restaurant, but recoiled instantly. Several brace of the restaurant's speciality, wind-dried duck, dangled in the window. Their orange flesh and flattened, angled limbs reminded him of Juniper. Their headlessness and prone position made him think of himself. He could not resist going in and asking to use the toilet.

The Vent-Axia moaned, and outside in the crepuscular, ancient light Cantonese voices yelped, zinc pannikins clattered, huge duck tenderisers smacked down – thwock! Bull considered the chipped aspect of the toilet; the 'Not Drinking Water' sticker over the sagging sink; the verdigris in the grout runnels of the tiling; the plaited but now frayed nylon twine that comprised the commode chain; and finally the rust that erupted in red ramparts all over the toilet's metalwork: the pipes, the cistern, and even the hinges of the ill-fitting door.

Bull's leg was becoming alien to him. He stripped it and held it away from himself, positioning it this way and that. Bull may have been disturbed, riven, confused, but he still had the strength of character (damn it all! This was a man who had gone to gold on the Duke of Edinburgh scheme; a man who had backpacked in the Catskills; a man who had finished first in an assault-course event organised as part of a press conference by a major DIY retailer) coolly and clinically to observe the progress of his own mutation.

There was a fundamental decency about Bull that lingered in the imperfection of his features, a fundamental decency that would have made him a good person to be kidnapped with in Beirut. One could imagine Bull's parents being very correct on their lawn, when interviewed. But latterly one could also imagine them becoming rather strident and bolshy, denouncing Government policy and launching their own campaign to free their son from the breakfast room of their detached house.

Their son meanwhile would be keeping his fellow-hostages' spirits up by telling them stories of the kind of high-jinks the Wanderers got up to on their tours. They would be the sort of stories that would revolt these men (American academics, Italian photojournalists, diplomatic envoys and the like) in any other context. But here, South of the Green Line, with thin plaster trickle and water drip underlining the utter horror of their predicament, these men would laugh, laugh, laugh. After release they would blink into the lights. 'It was Bull,' they would cry to a man, 'Bull kept us alive, with his solidity, his strength of character and most of all with his sense of humour.'

Thus it was that Bull rallied. Looked his new genitals in the eye, considered their deepening, their reddening, and saw his womanhood beckon.

But standing an hour later in Piccadilly poor Bull was seized and shaken by another epiphany. The window of Lillywhites directly abutted that of Boots. Behind one plate-glass sheet was a sales display for tights and other feminine impedimenta. Behind the other there was a display of rugby equipment. The Boots' display featured a beautiful plastic leg, all caramel and sheer in slick sheeny stuff that would be bliss to feel. Around it, scattered as if discarded in passionate haste, were other stockings and tights, their seductive hues forming a sensual collage on the ruched velvet that lined the window.

Whereas the display next door was poised and virile. It too featured a disembodied plastic leg, but whereas the female leg's truncation drew the eye inexorably to the point where its precisely chopped groin should be joined to a soft and scented pudenda, the male leg was all solid and impulsive, kicking out on its invisible spindrift of acrylic, a rugby ball frozen, glued, to the very tip of its shiny boot. It was as if this leg had been amputated in the very act of punting the ball over the row of office buildings and shop units opposite and into Clubland. Positioned around this leg were trusses, jockstraps, socks, workmanlike garters, headbands, shirts, shorts and more socks, all of them lined up neatly on the Astroturf.

But which one is mine, thought Bull, ranging from one display to the other, his gaze running up the female leg and then down the male. Who am I? the former cabaret editor moaned, and American tourists poised behind him in brand new Burberry wondering whether he was exclaiming at some exceptional bargain.

At length he tore himself away and made some purchases: press-on panty-liners, Feminax and vitamins in Boots; a truss and two headbands in Lillywhites.

But despite this decisive and seemingly mature acknowledgment of his dual nature, in the bleak mid-afternoon Bull found himself crying once more, this time outside King's Cross Station.

He leant up against the window of Wendy Burgers and watched the human mess circulate the station parade. Dossers and junkies formed companionable knots that broke up the streams of commuters and working folk. The spring rain still spat out of a dirty sky. Bull heaved and spluttered. He was alone in the world, he realised. Cut off, unable to confess his true nature. Oh, why had he allowed Alan to seduce him? If it hadn't happened he could've gone to the Proper Authorities. Bull felt certain that he could not be entirely alone in his predicament. Somewhere in this great pluralist society there had to be a self-help group for people like him, some sort of Vaginas Anonymous.

Bull was oblivious to the tarts, but they weren't of him. Standing in their stretchy pink microskirts and PVC stilettoes, they felt the cold and assessed all male passers-by for commercial value. Bull looked like a possible John. After all, his tears could be a premature access of remorse, guilt before the event.

From a long way off Ramona had been watching Bull. He/She sensed that Bull was his/her kind of client. He/she went on talking to Gail and Leroy, but his/her heart wasn't in the conversation.

'Sherri's got some stones. Yairs I know she has, 'anna cunt owes me 'n stuff.' Gail said this and took a suck on her Special Brew, fronds of vari-coloured hair floating in the breeze around her scuffed brow.

'You'll never get 'em out of her, girl. Pick up a punter. When you've earned I'll sort you. Don't I always see you right, girl?' Leroy puffed himself up, as conscious of his status as a pimp as another man might be of his as an alderman. Ramona wearied of it. He/She broke from them and sauntered across the road towards Bull.

'Are you lookin', dear?' said Ramona in his/her best bed–and–breakfast voice.

'I'm sorry?' Bull looked up, his broad brow surprised.

'Lookin' fer coompany like?' Normally Ramona would have abandoned ship on the basis of Bull's bewildered tone. The last thing he/she needed was a fuss of any kind. But he/she persisted. There was some-thing so pathetically vulnerable about this big man in blazer and grey flannels. And as for Bull, his grief and isolation had temporarily robbed him of what little street wisdom he possessed.

'Company? I'm sorry I'm not sure I understand you.'

'I've a little room, darling, not far off, jus' a few steps from here. We could get acquainted.' Giving the familiar sales pitch came more easily than Ramona had expected. He/she anticipated instant rejection from so many potential punters. They only had to look into his/her angular face with its too–strong features, and blue sha-dow, already by this time of the day, gathering substance underneath the slick of his/her foundation, to recoil.

But for some reason Bull didn't recoil. He saw Ramona for what he/she was and sensed immediately the possibility of an ally.

'You say it's not far?'

'Jus' round t'corner, love. Come on, let's walk, it's

bitter standin' here.' Ramona drew the folds of her once-fashionable black velour coat-robe around her high shoulders and ostentatiously shivered.

'You know . . . I'm not really interested in . . . you know . . . it's just some . . .'

'. . . Some coompany you're after. I understand, love, no need t'be embarrassed like.'

Leaving the parade in front of the station Bull and Ramona looked as companionable as an old married couple. They disappeared towards the Caledonian Road.

Alan felt a lot better after a hot shower. He had got atrociously wet and cold during the afternoon's learning exercises. He half suspected he might be coming down with a cold, for if there is anywhere worse for contagion than a hospital ward it has to be a gathering of GPs.

Alan, naturally enough, had taken control of the orienteering group he had been placed in by the bland and inefficient facilitator. Leadership came easily to Alan. Indeed, if he wasn't given the opportunity to lead he became apathetic very quickly. The other GPs sensed this and gave in rather than face his irritation.

Today's exercise had centred around the need to avoid bureaucratic entanglements when it came to implementing the new NHS reforms. The GPs split into groups, each of whom had an objective, to reach a given depot point where they would acquire symbolic 'patients'. These 'patients' (really little loops of coloured string) then had to be transported to the right 'hospital' (really a copse) for treatment. Along the way there were various opportunities either to increase the group's budget for hospital treatment, or for the patients' waiting-list time to be increased by falling foul of bureaucratic mire (really *actual* mire).

In their orange cagoules the GPs grappled with their maps and orienteering compasses. It was lucky they had Alan. At least under his leadership they managed to get all their 'patients' into their requisite 'hospitals' before dark. Other groups were less fortunate and were still wandering the Somerset countryside far into the night. Facilitators armed with high-powered torches had to be sent out to look for them. One of the older GPs even had a touch of exposure and had to miss out on the paint-gun event the following day.

The shower may have been hot, but it was still the same depressing trickle of water Alan had come to expect of provincial bed and breakfasts. Still, he had been pleased to discover that Krishna was putting up at Mrs Critchley's as well. All he needed to do now was make a quick call to Naomi, and then he and Krishna would be free for the evening.

Alan ran into Krishna in the humped corridor of the establishment. The wily medic was looking burnished and venal. Earlier in the day the chilly conditions on the orienteering course had nearly turned him as blue as his namesake. But now, warm and properly dressed,

Naipaul was looking forward to an evening of sordid encounters. As far as he was concerned the more sordid the better.

The two doctors left Mrs Critchley's B&B on East Street at ten minutes past eight. She had armed them with a Yale key looped on to a bit of gardening twine, should they find themselves carried away by the bright lights of Wincanton and wish to return after ten, when she locked up for the night. But even by half past eight they seemed to have exhausted the entertainment possibilities of the town.

The pubs were all so segregated that, for Alan and Krishna, entering them was like being displayed a series of *tableau vivantes* in a museum of local history. In the White Hart there were genteel alcoholics, drinking sweet wines and gin with flat tonic; in the Unicorn there were rural headbangers – chicken sexers with their dirty girlfriends, all plump but rendered piscine by the startlingly tight fit of their stonewashed jeans. Alan and Krishna stayed long enough for a half in both these places, weathering the hostility that emanated from both groups. They then crossed the broad High Street and passed by the clock tower, around which a small knot of aspiring underage drinkers cursed on the handlebars of their mopeds.

'The *jeunesse dorée*,' Krishna quipped in mock-Oxford tones.

'Whossat, youse darky cunt?' came back from the middle of the knot as quick as a thrown knife. The two minority group medics hurried on, all snobbery temporarily eaten up by fear.

In the Piebald Plover the Wincanton branch of MENSA was having its monthly meeting. Alan and Krishna poised moodily by the bar and eavesdropped on conversations of staggering autodidactic pretension. They supped moodily on Scotch.

'I thought you would have some angle on Wincanton,' said Alan at length. To his left a tiny woman in tweed was banging on about Etruscan wall painting. 'This place is dead, dead, dead.' Krishna snorted with laughter.

'Yeah, not exactly Bangkok is it? Still, if we want a little action, a guy I know called James Poole recommended we go and see somebody he knows here . . .'

'Well why didn't you say so before? You could have spared us all this tedious pub-crawling.'

'We-ell . . .' Krishna had gone into a debauched drawl. 'I did think you might find the scene a little bit *outré.*' He shifted against the bar, one slim brown hand went to his crotch where he lightly and lovingly arranged his slim brown genitals inside their slim brown tailored housing. Alan thought at once of fucking Bull, and couldn't prevent himself from laughing at the idea that anything Krishna Naipaul could come up with on a Thursday evening in Wincanton could be remotely *outré* in comparison.

'Oh, I think I can stand the pace, Krishna.' Alan turned the laughter into a dirty giggle for his benefit.

'OK. If you're up for it, then let's go.' He banged his whisky glass down on the bar and beckoned to the mutton-chopped landlord. 'Excuse me, do you know of anywhere that we might get something to eat around here?'

'Let me think . . .' said the landlord, although he hardly looked capable of it. 'There's bar food at the White Hart but they stop serving at 8.30. Otherwise you might be better off driving into Yeovil.'

'What about that new place?' This came from one of the MENSA crowd, a compliance clerk who had once translated a John Le Carré novel into Esperanto.

'Oh yairs.' This jogged the landlord's memory. 'If you like that sort of thing, there's a new sort of Greeky place on Bell Lane.'

'That sounds fine,' said Krishna. 'Where do we find Bell Lane?'

They got the directions and exited. Alan was intrigued.

'If this Poole bloke knows about this place, why did you go through all that rigmarole?'

'Cover, Alan, cover. We must mind our backs in a place like this.' They tromped off down the wet provincial streets.

The 'Greeky place' turned out to be the Tiresias Kebab Bar. A fat porky pole of kofta kebab twirled a greasy pirouette in the window. The place was undistinguished in the extreme. Things were pickled in big jars on the counter. Behind, and above the spluttering range, was a backlit cabinet that showed garish photo-graphs of indigestible meals. Through a fretworked archway Alan could see a few small tables covered with gingham-patterned oilcloth. No one was eating at them. In the takeaway section of the Kebab Bar there were only two customers, grub-white girls whom Alan thought he recognised from the crowd in the Unicorn. They were slobbering on saveloys when the two doctors came in.

Seated at the back Alan and Krishna ordered their meal from Tiresias himself. The *patron* was so buxom in his white singlet that Alan mentally diagnosed him as gynaecomastic. But the food was surprisingly good. Both Alan and Krishna had stuffed vine leaves and they downed two fine, lemony bottles of retsina. They declined the 'Tiresias Special Kebab', which, it was explained to them, was 'a mans on the bottom, a womans on the top, and a skewer through both of them'. And for the rest of the meal they managed to avoid catching their busty host's eye.

Tiresias brought them tiny cups of thick Greek coffee. Krishna sat back from the table with a contented sigh. 'Well, now we've eaten I suppose we ought to fuck,' he said, sipping his coffee.

'Fuck what exactly?' Alan's bemused gesture encom-passed the plump proprietor and the two ghastly girls who still lingered. Krishna huddled forward over the little table, gathering Alan into his conspiracy. His cultivated tones fluted with dirty enthusiasm.

'Poole told me that there's more to this chap Tiresias than meets the eye. This is a front, Alan.'

'A front? A front for what?'

'Only one of the biggest pornography and prostitution rings in the South West.'

'Golly!' Alan was incredulous. He waited for there to be a scene as Krishna beckoned Tiresias over.

'I'm a friend of "Mr Poole".' Krishna pronounced the name like a password.

'Oh, Meester Poole,' the Greek seemed to be playing his part as well, 'Meester Poole is very good friend of mine. And friends of Meester Poole are friends of mine. Would youse gentlemens like some raki?'

'We would love some raki.' Krishna was now puffed up with the success of his underworld contact. 'And we would also like some company for the night.'

'Some company? Offcourse. To be alone it is a bad thing I think. We wish always to be togethers, to live lifes to the full. That is how we do things in Greece you knows. We lives lifes to the full!' Tiresias was so emphatic and Zorba-ish about this that Alan half expected him to start dancing, his big tits bouncing in the yellow confines of the kebab bar. But instead the Greek pulled up a chair and bringing a bottle of raki from the back of the dusty bar cabinet joined them in their prurient conspiracy.

★   ★   ★

So it was that two hours later Alan found himself being vigorously but dispassionately fellated, in the covered dustbin area of Mrs Critchley's B&B, by one of the chicken-sexers' girlfriends who had been hanging around the kebab bar. Krishna, who was unmarried and seemed to have no fear of the Medical Council, had smuggled his tart up to his room, there to thrash on nylon sheets. But Alan, shaking with unnatural lust, had paid up front for this sad experience. Even the thought of the scorn he would pour on Naipaul the following morning failed to counteract the painful rasp of the flat back of his head against the pebbledash of the wall he was leaning on.

'Nyum, nyum, nyum,' gobbled the girl. And, looking down at the dark roots of her peroxided hair, Alan realised that, let alone remember her name, he couldn't even recall what her face looked like, so completely, since she had unzipped his fly and got to work, had his mind been filled with images of Bull.

5

Apotheosis

A FEW HOURS EARLIER Bull had been having a companionable cup of tea with Ramona the transexual prostitute. It wasn't a familiar story, and Bull hadn't heard it before: 'Me father, he were a welder in t'shipyards. The Swan Hunter yards on Wearside. All he ever wanted me t'do was follow him into it, like.' As he/she said this, Ramona squatted in the corner of the fusty bedsit, splashing boiling water from the electric jug into mismatched mugs. Bull couldn't help noticing the angular muscularity of Ramona's calves and thighs. The transexual, he reckoned, had just the right build to make a really first-class number eight rugby forward.

Ramona handed Bull his tea and sat by him on the squishy little bed. He/she went on with the tale. 'All I remember as a child is bein' taken down to t'yard by me mother. They wouldn't let us in, right. They said it were too dangerous fer kids like, so she would just point. And in the distance there would be this tiny figure, yer know, crawling like, on this huge hull, or keel or whatever. An' we would jus' look, an then suddenly there would be this shower of sparks, 'cos 'e were weldin'. An' me mother would say, "Thas yer father, lad. Wun day yu'll be welder jus' like him".'

'And were you?' asked Bull.

'Oh aye. I went to t' tech' an' got me City & Guilds. I started in t'shipyard on the very same day that they got their last ever order. It were for a dirty great oil tanker. The *Anubis* it were called. I worked on that wun. Did all the spotweldin' on t'afterdeck. An' I were up there wun day, way up in the sky, lookin' over t'estuary, when suddenly, like, I decided I wanted t'be a woman.'

'You mean it had never occurred to you before?' Bull was incredulous. He had read many many magazine articles on the subject.

'No, never. I know it's right unusual, but thas the truth. Oop until that day I'd just been a happy-go-lucky lad, fookin' and fightin', not a thought for the morrer'. An jus' like that I were visited wi' all these, like, *sensitive* feelin's. So I came t'London and pretty soon I were on t'game. You know it's the only way types like me can get t'munny together for the shots and the op.'

Ramona sighed wearily and took a great gulp of tea. Bull saw out of the corner of his eyes the ex-welder's crinkled Adam's apple rise and fall in his great gorge. For in truth, as is always the way, Ramona was the most unsuitable candidate for womanhood imaginable. More unsuitable than even me, Bull thought to himself. Ramona's face was overpoweringly masculine. He/she looked not unlike Desperate Dan with the addition of a strong Roman nose. The thick blond hair that had been teased into Dallas cascades on either side of the blue jaw only served to underwrite the impression that Ramona was a chimera, or a representative of some new, third sex.

But Ramona was friendly. And he/she hadn't troubled Bull for either money or justification. Perhaps he/she can accept *me* for what I am, Bull dared to hope. 'How far have you got with the . . . you know . . .'

'The sex change?' Ramona was unabashed. 'Oh, t'whole way, lad. I know it don't look it, but they say this is as far as I can go. Bit of a disaster reelly, 'nt it.'

'But, you're . . . I mean, I thought that . . .'

'Aye, so did I, lad. I thought t'hormone treatment would like give me a feminine body. But all iss' dun is like give me a feminine coating. I'll show you if you like. No charge.'

Ramona sprang up from the bed and began to disrobe. What he/she had said was revealed as the truth. Although he/she had breasts and a superficial coating of subcutaneous fat, which parodied the female form, underneath it, there all too clearly remained the firm musculature of the Wearside welder Ramona had been destined to become.

In his earlier incarnation Bull would have been horrified at viewing the transexual's parts. But now? Well, the dry penile pocket which Ramona displayed to him was nothing, absolutely nothing in comparison to his own new arrangement.

'Yer can tuch it if you like.' Ramona was thrusting

244

his/her fake vagina towards Bull. He recoiled. 'Is' no fun really, yer know. They like cut out all the blood vessels and stuff. And then they tuck the skin back inside. But I've no clit or nuthin' like that. Straight sex has been nuthin' t'me since the snip. And anyways the punters round here like it all up the bum, y'know. *My* bum, that is.'

'Oh really?' Bull felt vicarish.

'Oh aye. They're mostly papists of course. Italians and such. It must be somethin' t'do wi' their religious beliefs an' that. So all in all it's been a bit of a waste.' The giant pseudo-woman balefully regarded his/her vagina as if it were a vast marrow that had also-ran at a garden show. Bull sensed that now was his moment.

'You know, Ramona, I'm not exactly what I appear to be.' And as he said this Bull became once again horribly aware of his leg's radically independent gender; its strange metabolism; its awful vulnerable yearning.

'What d'ye mean, lad?'

'Well. It's difficult for me to say this . . . I'm worried that you might be shocked . . .'

'Let me tell you, lad, I've been on the game at the Cross for four years now, an' I reckon I've seen just about everything. There's nowt new in the fiddlin' department as far as I'm concerned.'

Bull took heart from this. He stood up, and feeling the old vulnerability, not the new, the vulnerability he used to feel slipping his things off in Alan Margoulies's surgery, he dropped his trousers and turned his back on Ramona.

For long seconds Bull heard nothing. And then Ramona screamed. Screamed like a giant foghorn on the Wear. Screamed with all the volume of his/her great chest. Screamed and screamed and screamed. Screamed so loud that Bull could still hear his/her screaming as he rounded the corner of the Caledonian Road, a good three hundred yards away from the prostitute's bedsit, running as fast as if he were about to score a match-winning try.

The Wanderers were all aboard their minibus. There was much good-natured badinage and some jolly singing as they bowled down the A22 towards Bexhill-on-Sea. It might surprise the gentle reader (and even the vicious and unprincipled reader) to know that Bull was among the loudest of the singers, and the readiest of the quippers. His fellow-players were astonished by his good humour, and most of them put it down to his being de-mob happy, having lost his awful job at *Get Out!*

But the truth, as we know, was far stranger. Bull had, he thought, reached a new equilibrium, a new acceptance of himself. He understood as soon as he got home why Ramona had screamed at the sight of his vagina. He understood also the strange and nameless tension and anxiety that had gripped him throughout the day. He was getting his period.

No wonder he had bought the panty-liners and the

Feminax in Boots, his feminine unconscious knew what was coming. Standing once more in the Council's orange light, he had dabbed away the brown stains on his calf and applied the panty-liner, using one of his jock-straps to create a parody of a mono-knicker. The very assemblage, the idea of which had so excited Alan Margoulies at the outset of their strange affair.

And despite stomach cramps in the night, Bull was still full of resolution the following morning. He would, he decided, break entirely with Margoulies. He would continue as he was. And so what if he had to conceal his vagina for the rest of his life? So what if he could never marry? These were things he could accept. This was the decent thing to do: keep one's personal and vile idiosyncrasies to one's self, not inflict them on a blameless world.

So Bull outsang and outjoshed the rest. The minibus bowled through the shocking green of a bright English spring day, and all aboard felt a gleeful anticipation of the match to come.

In the changing-rooms Bull was especially careful to mind his back. But he'd sussed out his *modus operandi* well in advance. An elasticated knee-protector, of the kind commonly worn by sportspeople, neatly encapsulated the jock-strap and panty-liner assemblage. And in case that wasn't sufficient, Bull also took the precaution of wearing particularly long socks, and on his left leg a very tight garter. None of his team mates suspected anything. They took his explanation of a 'troublesome gash' at face value.

The match was an overwhelming success. The visitors won with a remarkable try in the eighty-second minute of the game. The try was scored by Bull.

He had been in the scrum, locked into that strange, straining phalanx of heavy men, his shoulders grating against both those of the opposing prop forwards, and against the little bony collarbone of Mickey Minto, the Wanderers' Maltese hooker. The ball came in fast, straight across to where Bull heaved, his big ear Lego-locking into the big ear of the opposing left prop. One swift slash of Bull's boot immobilised his opponent (who howled at the unfairness), another took it back to the wing forward, Dougie MacBeath, who broke hard and fast down the left wing. He was brought down within ten yards by a gaggle of Bexhill Bears, but before he fell he managed to flick the ball back to Bull, who was following on at the head of the Wanderers' pack.

Bull hugged the warm ball to his chest. The score stood at forty-two points all. Seagulls swooped and screamed over the Bears' goalposts. Beyond them Bull could see the lambent play of sunlight on green sea. The Bears' ground was superbly situated on a chalk bluff, high above the Channel. What with the crispness of the day, and the firmness of his new resolution, Bull felt capable of flying, taking off and soaring over the defenders who, within seconds of Bull receiving the ball, had ranged themselves between him and the touchline.

Bull feinted, Bull dodged, Bull stuck his broad palm – hard and cold like a defrosting chicken – into the expectant faces of the defenders. Bull felt as if his boots had acquired turbochargers. He revved over the turf. Behind him there were cries: 'Over 'ere, John!', 'Man-on, John!', 'My ball, John!' Bull paid them no mind. This was clearly his moment. He could tell it by the way that the defenders seemed to be moving in slow motion – backwards. It was as if they ran away from him and then leapt up from the ground, gratefully pressing his palm to their bruised faces, scrofulously receiving the King's touch. It was that easy and sanctified a moment.

And then, when he actually crossed the touchline, Bull found that he had to make a decision. With this fantastic turn of speed perhaps he ought to make the leap? Over those two boy spectators, ano-racked by adolescence, and away. This was the Channel speaking. Speaking directly, imagistically, to that other *manche*. Bull felt deep, buried sensations, under sock and jock-strap and panty-liner. The two channels seemed to speak to one another, figuring the possibilities of an alignment, or alliance.

But Bull didn't jump. He swerved beautifully – dipping down like a yacht – kinked slightly to avoid his final challenger, and finally placed the ball precisely on the sward, bang between the posts.

Against precedent Towser Bridges, the Wanderers' captain, allowed Bull to do the conversion (for Bull was not known as the greatest of kickers). This was the 'chonk' of boot into turf Bull had so longingly antici-pated during those two, dark, cunt-riven, London days.

This was the free play of muscle and youthful vigour that Bull had set against the bogus credo of Juniper, and the pallid aestheticism of his ex-boss . . . Ach! But it didn't work. Even as the ball lifted, and converted as surely as Wesley, Bull knew in his heart of hearts that the joy of rugby might distract him, but it could not cancel out what had happened between him and Alan Margoulies. It could not fill in the gnawing genital gulf.

So it was that after the match, once Bull had allowed himself to be bought a few congratulatory pints, he slipped away from his mates. He was glad to do so; never before had he felt quite so oppressed by their self-assurance, their seemingly unquestioning masculinity.

Bull walked the streets of Bexhill, moving towards the De La Warr Pavilion on the seafront, and his rendezvous with his lover.

Alan had had another tiring day at the Learning Jamboree. At least the weather had held up. But if anything the exercises designed by the facilitators were even more asinine than they had been the day before. They involved roleplay. The various GPs had to adopt the perspective of their patients and act out their anxieties and frustrations.

Alan was honest enough to admit to himself that in the roleplay he found a sinister congruence with the doctor–patient charade he had so recently enacted with Bull. But as we have remarked before, Alan's sense of irony had long since become so rampant that anything was grist to its mill. Nonetheless the day was given over to images of Bull, just as the previous night's 'fun' had been so awfully compromised.

I've never behaved like that before, thought Alan. He had his pride, after all. There is a big difference between gaily porking some squeaking nurselet in a studio flat in Chiswick, and allowing the prostituting girlfriend of a retarded chicken-sexer to suck you off in the dustbin area of a provincial guesthouse. Clearly the Bull-thing was to blame. But maybe he is as anxious to get back into society as I am, thought Alan, and resurrected the first view he had taken of Bull's genital abnormality. Namely that it might make his clinical reputation, just as the Siamese perpetual-cunnilingus machine had done for Nicholson. 'And if not . . . perhaps . . . perhaps . . .' Perhaps what? Perhaps the kindest thing to do would be to *kill* Bull. Alan couldn't quite formulate the thought, but it lay in his mind nonetheless. Heavily, like a poorly digested meal.

But while all this was thought, action was something else. More dissembling to Naomi on the telephone; more carefully cultivated images of his sweet daughter's sweet burblings, as if they could somehow undercut all the weird shit he was bound up in. At the end of the day Alan gave Krishna Naipaul the slip. The dirty doctor hadn't been sated by his activities of the previous night and at fishpaste sandwich time he had suggested to Alan a return trip to Tiresias's establishment.

Alan drove back into Wincanton and hurriedly changed at Mrs Critchley's. If he put his foot down he could make Bexhill by eight-thirty.

Juniper and Razza Rob faced one another across the cool pool of highly-focused greenish light. Juniper pushed her plate to one side and sighed contentedly.

'Mmm,' she said. 'Razza, that was fantastic. You'll have to give me the recipe before I go. I never imagined that anybody could do so much with nuts and mushrooms.'

'Actually almonds, boletus and truffles. The topping was fresh ricotta, teased and shaped.' Razza's voice betrayed not irritation at this philistine's crude appreciation of his cuisine, but a wry love of bringing on the untutored, who he enjoyed precisely because of their lack of sophistication.

'I just didn't expect to be fed at all, let alone so magnificently. Usually someone I'm interviewing expects *me* to feed *them*. And anyway how did you know that I was a vegetarian?'

Razza gestured enigmatically. 'No one who appreciates the subtleties of my work as you do could possibly feed on carrion.'

Juniper looked at Razza Rob with frank admiration. It

had been just as she had suspected. Arriving at Razza Rob's unprepossessing council block in Grays Thurrock, Juniper had been beckoned into a Tardis of high culture. Behind the chipboard veneer of his front door this secretive, almost reclusive mortgage-broker had created a temple to the avant garde.

Naturally what struck Juniper most forcefully was the disjunction between Razza Rob's stage persona – all wiry aggression; gimcrack obscenity; dangerous, frustrated lust – and the quiet, almost refined man who ushered her in.

Shorn of his spangled jockstrap, clothed in autumnal beiges and browns, Razza Rob's face in repose was serious and thoughtful. As the tape recorder whirred he steepled his fingers and gave each of her questions deep and serious thought.

'I would say that since "outrage", or "repulsion" only really exists in the mind of the beholder, it is foolish to try and generally distinguish the things that provoke these feelings, from those that don't. Furthermore, the mind-set that observes and considers this "thing", is itself chronically relativised by a whole panoply of other factors. The analogy would be to ask someone to take an accurate reading with a theodolite when both they, and the object they wish to take the reading from, are both in constant motion.' This little *aperçu* came from Razza Rob in response to Juniper's slightly more basic question: 'Tell me, Razza, do you think your critics are right when they describe your cunt jokes as obscene?'

Despite the challenge presented to her by this doyen of the smutty, Juniper couldn't stop her attention from wandering from what Razza said to the magnificent decor of his flat. It was astonishing, but in this cramped and narrow space, with its front door opening directly on to the kitchen, and the other rooms leading off an abrupt corridor, Razza Rob had managed to create a sense of light airiness which engendered an atmosphere of aesthetic optimism. The walls, Juniper noted, were coated in steel-grey hessian, just the material she herself would have chosen . . .

No, not true. None of the above, that is. It would be nice if it were. It would, in fact, be a nicer world altogether.

'You fucking anybody regular then?' asked Razza Rob. But rather than answer the question Juniper found that she couldn't lift her eyes from the spectacle of his pullover cuffs, dabbling in the pool of tomato ketchup that occupied half of his oval platter.

'They do provide forks, you know,' said Juniper. She still couldn't decide which was worse; watching him eat, or averting her eyes but *knowing* what he was doing.

'Forks for forking. Issat what you mean? Her, her, her, her.' It was appropriate that the sound of the cunt comic's guffaws should be so gender-specific.

'Look, Razza, we're here to do an interview, so let's talk about your comedy, shall we, and not my sex-life.'

'Yeah, all right, but y'know, they're . . . they're sort of, umm. I mean . . . right, I make cunt jokes right? And, like, well, you've . . . you've got a . . .'

'A cunt, yes. So, what of it?' But then it dawned on Juniper what the runtish jester was aiming at. 'Oh, I see. You mean to say that there is an inextricable relationship between the very *fact* of my genitals, and the *fact* of your comedy. And that furthermore the telling of cunt jokes, whatever their nature or provenance, is a valid cultural pursuit because it helps to reify something that otherwise would be entirely vitiated by the phallocentric discourse? Is that it?'

'Well, er, yeah, sort of.' Razza Rob looked around the steak house balefully. No matter what kind of crudities he flung at this woman, they bounced off her. Then she grabbed them out of the air and incorporated them into this ghastly spiel. Parts of which she kept breaking off from eating in order to scribble down in her notebook.

Juniper had been disappointed by Razza Rob, but not half as disappointed as he had been by her. Felix Brownlow, Razza's agent, had told him, 'Just chuck more cunt jokes at 'em. Specially if they're women. Women, deep down, can't stand those cunt jokes. And women journalists hate them more than anything else. Remember that you're meant to be controversial. Remember that, Razza. The more people you upset the better.'

But Juniper wasn't about to be upset by a squitty little mortgage broker from Grays Thurrock, especially one who insisted on being interviewed in a steak house on the Mile End Road. Not now she was the cabaret editor of London's bestselling listings magazine, *Get Out!* No, she was going to take this dross and transmute it into gold. She'd even flatter the little jerk to do it. If she had to, that is.

Razza tried another conversational gambit. 'Doncha' wanna know why women have legs?'

Bull faced Alan across the Crystal of Nargon table. Beneath its glass surface little televisual pellets plunged in furious, colourful trajectories towards electronic oblivion. It was the only table the couple could find in the main bar of the De La Warr Pavilion. The others were all packed. There was a convention being held in the vast Modernist building, and the conventioneers thronged its flight-deck landings. They stood in staring lines, their faces turned to the sea, their gaze blank against the windscreen windows. Both Bull and Alan felt conspicuous without plastic name-bages. Both of them were drinking the indifferent local bitter. Both of them were in lust again.

'I'm not sure I can take much more of this.' Alan's hand (fine and tapering, as has been remarked before) shook something fierce. Beer sloshed on to the games table and temporarily provided the Crystal of Nargon with another not-so-special effect. 'I feel really guilty about it all. I'm deceiving my wife, I'm in breach of the medical ethics I'm sworn to uphold and most importantly I'm using you . . .'

'. . . Using me? Whaddya mean, using me?' Bull was querulous once more. He had had to wait half an hour before Alan turned up. Just enough time for him to put away a couple more pints to add to the couple he had downed with his team mates after the match. Bull was tipsy enough to feel assertive. Now he didn't even wait for Alan to reply. He upped and offed to the gents, guiding his big sportsman's body through the archipelago of tables as if it were an autonomous drunk person that he was escorting.

In the gents Bull took out his stubby cock and peed hard, peed like a fireman hosing a chemical incident with fuzzy foam. And as he peed he regarded his original genitals. Regarded them with the puzzled stare of a stranger. Why, I can't say I've really paid much attention to these recently. And he emphasised the 'these' by shaking himself dry and repocketing the limp assemblage. And it was true. Ever since his startling metamorphosis Bull had all but forgotten about his most obvious masculine attribute.

True, when he had made love with Alan there had been a cock-rubbing aspect to the whole thing, but it was purely secondary to the fact of penetration. It was as if his penis had gracefully stepped aside, like a retiring diva introducing her successor to the adoring audience at La Scala. Together they sang one final aria, before the older woman bowed out.

Oh Christ. What if my cock and balls were to wither up and drop off, thought Bull, splashing his anxious countenance with tepid water. He had seen something of the sort happen when sheep were castrated. A gadget put a tight rubber band around the base of the scrotal sac. In time the sac blackened and then simply fell off. I shouldn't want that . . . The beer in his brain kept him buoyant, able to contemplate the most horrible involutions of his gender with a certain archness. He returned to where Alan sat, and the tipsiness easily shifted gear back to a tingling lust.

Alan looked up, hooking his lank hair behind his ears. His face was tense with contemplating the awful truth that they had to, just *had* to deal with. Gone was the *Übermensch* who had so cheerfully powered his way to Wincanton; gone was Sybil's lover; gone was the Good Doctor, the prebendary saint. Alan was thinking of going to the head of his practice, old Dr Fortis, and confessing the lot. A GP as old as Fortis would have seen myriad odd things in his time. Bull's vagina and Alan's response to it. His breach of professional ethics. It couldn't be the oddest thing that he'd ever heard of . . . could it?

Perhaps he would then have to go with Fortis and see some higher authorities. Certainly the senior administrator and perhaps even the Minister herself. Alan accepted that he would be unable to practise at the

Grove any more, and that his chances of promotion were likely to be annihilated. But need it necessarily be the end of his career? For heaven's sake, these were the nineties, not the twenties. People were far more understanding nowadays of the weaknesses of the flesh. Perhaps he would be allowed to move away quietly. Naturally Naomi would have to be told everything, but she was an enlightened woman. She campaigned for homosexual rights . . . perhaps the revelation of his conduct with Bull would be just what was needed to revive their own flagging, emphatically marital sex-life?

But then Bull's freckled face appeared once more on the other side of the electronic games table. It was reddened by beer and had that underlying vascular dilation that comes either from exercise, or from its anticipation. Clapping eyes on him was just like clapping hands on him. And once again Alan felt the raw erotic edge of the forbidden. He remembered the stiff and complex sexiness of his last coupling with Bull. His resolution was abandoned. It bent, buckled, shrank and then melted, like a crisp packet chucked on a fire.

Within the half hour the two men were embracing in room five of the Ancaster Guest House, prop. Mrs Turvey. Mrs Turvey had been surprised by Bull's early return from the De La Warr Pavilion. She had tagged him, rightly, as a rugby player, and assumed that he would be out on the piss until the small hours. She was surprised, and a little suspicious as well, at the sight of Alan, who certainly *didn't* look like a rugby player. But she was reassured when the two men asked if she had a pack of cards that they could borrow. She did. And a cribbage board. They seemed very pleased – and so was she. In twenty years of keeping the guest house, Mrs Turvey had never known anybody who played cribbage to be involved in immoral goings on.

So it was that the long weekend passed. By day Bull played rugby. By night he made love with Alan. And in the small hours Alan drove his large black car back across the blackened countryside of southern England to Wincanton.

Alan's dark and handsome face became still darker. Violet shadows appeared under his fine eyes. The stress was getting to him, but he just couldn't stop.

On Saturday evening they met in the snug of the Old Ship on the seafront at Brighton. As Alan came in Bull was shamelessly blubbing into a schooner of sherry. It took twenty minutes for Alan to get the story out of him.

'The game was going brilliantly. Dave Gillis had scored twice straight from the line out and we'd picked up a couple of other tries by sheer hard rucking. I just wasn't thinking, I suppose. I'd been late into the dressing-room, I couldn't find the ground. All the rest of the team were there already. I suppose I didn't take enough care with my knee protector . . .'

They had scrummed down. Bull had felt the hard

head of Gillis the lock forward ram against his hip; he then heard an audible 'oomph' as Masher Morton, the Wanderers' number eight, plunged his head between the hard haunches of the two locks. Sixteen men strained together, sixteen pairs of eyes searched the turf, waiting for the scrum half to feed the ball in, thirty-two boots twitched with anticipation, waiting to delve and hack.

'It was awful, Alan. I'd never thought about it before. I'd never seen the scrum for what it was: a sexual thing. I mean all those men, hugging each other, straining together. And then the ball being shoved in, like a . . . like a . . .' Bull couldn't get the words out but Alan caught his drift. '. . . Anyway, when the ball came in it fell straight at my feet. I hooked hard for it with my right boot, and just then I felt my knee protector slipping . . .'

Bull had looked down horrified. His extra jock-strap was lying in the mud. His kneepit was completely exposed. Caught like that, in the scrum, he was utterly unable to move. He was, however, able to look back and catch sight of the appalled face of Masher Morton, the Wanderers' number eight. There was no need for Bull to even speculate as to what it was that Masher had seen.

'So what did you do?' Alan asked breathlessly. 'What could I do,' Bull snapped. It was clear to Alan that Bull felt a measure of the blame was his. 'I had to get the jock-strap and the knee protector back on and play out the rest of the game.'

'But what about Morton? Didn't he say anything?'

And there was the good fortune in the whole story.

Morton was a boozer. In fact he was the Wanderers' principal boozer. Prone to mixing his drinks into dreadful gut-curdling combinations: port and gin; bourbon and vermouth; beer and Polish spirit. Morton had seen Bull's vagina. Seen it as clearly as he saw the ball. But then he had also seen a werewolf stealing his underwear in the small hours of that morning. Morton was shaken. He retired to the dressing-room to contemplate abstinence.

When the rest of the Wanderers joined him in the plunge bath after the match, there was much good-natured badinage. 'Masher says he saw a cunt on the back of John's leg! Ha, ha, ha!' 'One over the eighty last night, eh Masher!' 'Show us yer oyster bed then, John me old darling!' And much other ribaldry as well. Bull had escaped, shaken, but his secret intact.

'I'm not sure that I'll be able to play tomorrow. They may remember. They've been asking me why I don't stick around in the evenings. It's not like me, you see. I'm normally really cheerful. I normally go out and socialise with them.'

But that wasn't all. And as Alan teased the rest of Bull's sorry story out of him, he was aware of how like his marriage his relationship with Bull was already becoming. For it was the same when something happened to upset Naomi. Alan would have to spend a long time getting her confidence, making the right sympathetic noises, before eventually she would tell him what little slight, what small contretemps during the day, had made her so weepy.

'It was a shitty day.' Bull was still blubbing; the snotty sheen on his upper lip was unattractive, as were his reddened, piggy little eyes. 'After you left this morning I called a girlfriend of mine in London. I'd made a tentative plan to go out with her this evening . . .'

'. . . And she wouldn't?' Alan couldn't help snapping. Bull came back hard. 'What are you saying? That a woman wouldn't find me attractive. Is that what you're saying?'

'Now calm down, John. Of course I'm saying nothing of the sort. But you have to get all of this in proportion, don't you.'

'Anyway. I suppose I may as well tell you. After all, I've nobody else . . .'

Bull went on and told Alan how Juniper had not only rejected him, but how she had also, far from inadvertently, let slip the fact that she had taken Bull's job. In fact she intimated to Bull that it was due to her intervention that Bull had been fired. Bull was gutted. But Alan wasn't paying attention to what Bull said about Juniper; about the job; about their frenzied floor-bound couplings; about Juniper's silly views, her patronage of Razza Rob. Alan had picked up on something else altogether. Something that Bull was wholly unaware of having said: 'After all, I've nobody else.'

This was what stuck with Alan. And stayed with him as, in the small hours, he headed fast along the coast road, en route for Southampton. For he knew it to be true. Bull had told him of parents who had moved out to

Portugal to spend their retirement golfing on the Algarve. And how his father had met his end climbing out of a golf buggy one day. He had tripped, rolled across the immaculate sward of a steeply raked green, and died, choleric and twitching, in a bunker. Bull had little contact with his mother, who had married the club chairman. There were no Bull siblings.

'It's my word against his.' That's what Alan kept thinking. He beat out the words in time with his fine finger-flicks against the black leatherette cover of the steering wheel. 'That's all there is to it: my word against his. If he says I did it I can simply deny it. Why need an *Übermensch* be destroyed by fate in this fashion? I must rise above it, master it.'

And although he lay once more with Bull the next night at the Crown Hotel in Shoreham, Alan's mind was elsewhere. And when they parted and headed back to London separately the following day, Alan had no intention of ever seeing Bull again. And even if he were to feel a poignant pang, no, a multitude of poignant pangs, each time he passed a sports shop, or a playing field, or saw a child on its way home from school, duffel bag bulging with soiled kit, he would not relent. Alan saw his lust for what it was: a closet queen, parading in the assumed pasteboard finery of love.

★　★　★

It's an everyday story, wouldn't you say? This sad tale of Bull. Poor, poor Bull. Used and abandoned. There's nothing new under this red dwarf emotional sun of ours. We grow up in sickly anticipation of love, romantic love. We sense with overweening joy that ours is but one amongst an infinity of unique sensibilities. What cruel irony that it is this very infinity that we later seem to find such a dreadful fag, and a bore to boot. We live out our lives with the studious, alienated politeness of big city dwellers: 'I know you're interesting,' we seem to beam telepathically at our fellow sufferers, 'and have hopes and fears of a unique quality, even views of some perspicacity. But none today please! Ting!'

So, in the light of the above, can we blame Alan? To be more precise, can we be bothered to blame Alan? Also can we be bothered to pity Krishna Naipaul, who, as Bull and Alan headed for London, was still trapped in the polymorphous perversities of the Tiresias Kebab Bar in Wincanton? In the neon wash from the freezer cabinet an odd triple-decker sexual sandwich twitched on the tiles. On the bottom was the flat white pudding of the chicken sexer's girlfriend who gobbled Alan. Above her the corn-fed corpse of Tiresias himself flowed over her like hot fudge on to a sundae. And above both of them, arching back in fear and frenzy, the naughty doctor wriggled and scampered on the Greek's big back, for all the world like the satyr that he so clearly was. Probably not. For in line with the disillusionment outlined above, we have jettisoned our capacity to judge the relationships of others. In this world where all are mad and none are bad, we all know that the finger points backwards.

So, no nausea please as Alan returns on a Monday evening to the terraced house he calls home. Of course he is still anxious, he has yet to tell Bull of his decision. He also knows that there will be tough times ahead, when Bull, who is, after all, some kind of journalist, starts shooting his big mouth off. But Alan knows he can weather it, because in essence he is a family man. See him now opening the door with his key, tucking his black attaché case behind the coat-rack in the hall. And here's Cecile, stomping towards him on chubby legs. Alan sweeps her up and kisses her sticky cheek. And here's Naomi, looking committed. Towelled from the bath, she smells good.

They all smell good as they cuddle in the hall. And Naomi figures this has to be the right time to tell Alan that she's pregnant again.

Bull had a farewell drink with the Wanderers in a roadhouse. Amidst plastic beams and hard against a fruit machine that had a microprocessor with a far larger and more efficient random access memory than the publican, Bull tried to salvage something of his relationship with his team mates.

'I'm really cut up about losing my job,' he told Dave Gillis for the umpteenth time. 'It's tough to find free-lance work in a recession.'

'Yeah, I know all that, John.' Gillis was tetchy. After Bull's performance during the mini-tour he, for one, would have liked to have seen him dropped from the team. After all, amateur rugby is as much to do with socialising with your mates as it is with playing the actual matches. Gillis had always rather suspected Bull. There was something too good to be true about his lack of side, his open and friendly features. Gillis wouldn't have been surprised if Bull was a poof. 'But where the hell have you been getting to the last few nights? We've been having a bloody good time. It's been the most successful tour any of us can remember, but you've been buggering off every evening after a couple of pints.'

'Yeah, well, Dave. I have got a bit of a confession to make. There's this bird I've been seeing.' (It was terribly easy for Bull mentally to change Alan's clothing and shave his legs. In Bull's mind's eye he made rather a fetching damsel.) 'And, well, she's married like.' Gillis surprised himself by being relieved. 'Well why didn't you say! For Christ's sake, we all would of understood. Oi! Lads. Johnnie boy here has a bit of the old forbidden on the side. That's why he's been sloping off all over the tour.'

There were guffaws from the assembled Wanderers. Big, certain men in blazers. Bull was much praised for his athleticism. For scoring so many tries when he must have been shagged out from the night before. There was much backslapping, and stiff punches to the upper arm. Bull felt enfolded once more by the smegmatic closeness of male camaraderie, and felt ghastly and fraudulent. He wasn't able to get away to London for another couple of hours.

The journey was exhausting. What with the booze, the rugby, and the contorted sex he had been having with Alan for the last three nights, Bull could barely make it up the stairs, once he had managed to crawl up the hill from the tube station. He staggered into his flat and footed down the corridor to his bedroom, where he slumped down. Too weary to undress. He waited for oblivion to come.

But it wouldn't. Bull felt the beer slop in his belly. Perhaps I need to go and drop some ballast before I sleep, he thought to himself, and rose from the bed. When he was on his feet, the tightness in his stomach changed to nausea. Bull hit the corridor at a run, and vomit was spurting from his mouth before he made it to the bathroom. Kneeling and wiping Bull pondered his nausea. He didn't have more than five or six pints in the pub, certainly not enough to make him puke. And then the realisation tiptoed in, leaving the door ajar on that other world, that other hidden nature of Bull's that he had done so well to deny for the past few hours.

For he knew by now that nausea danced attendance on those other parts of himself, those parts that lager simply could never reach.

Bull stripped, and stood once more before the full-length mirror where it had all begun, twisting himself to regard his vagina and its surround. Bull was aware now that his leg had developed a biology of its own. The period that had started in Ramona's bedsit had ended within twenty-four hours. The night Bull had met Alan at the De La Warr Pavilion, he had had the added embarrassment of explaining that it was his 'time of the month', when Alan and he came to disrobe in the cramped confines of room five. Alan had scoffed at the very idea of Bull having a period, even after he had seen the dried and stiffened clouts. He had explained to Bull at great length that his vagina was an independent thing, cut out from its natural surround. He had pointed out to Bull that he had no urethra, and that the vagina itself was stopped by the back of his patella, as surely as an engine cylinder is capped by its big end.

And indeed, since Thursday, Bull had felt none of the inexplicable tremulousness that had characterised the two preceding days. He had assumed that his biology had ceased to dance in a lunar light. And so it had. What hubris of Alan to take his pleasure and not deploy his expertise! It would have only taken him a superficial examination, the tiniest admixture of business with pleasure, for him to have rumbled. For the truth was that in the mini-feminine world of Bull's leg, everything was in perfect running order. It was all compressed, true enough, and distorted, not unlike the internal organs of a midget. But it was all in perfect running order. Bull's cervix that is; Bull's ovaries; Bull's tubes. Bull's womb, which, as it dawned on him that the calf muscle cramps he had been having that day might have an origin other than muscular stress, was pushing out in a slow act of biological attrition.

Bull found himself dressed and in his car. He knew there was an all-night chemist open in West Hampstead, a chemist where he could buy a Predictor pregnancy testing kit.

Bull crouched in the cramped confines of the cubicle, and his face distorted into a crazy mirror grimace as he watched the bluish solution in the plastic beaker turn a violent pink.

So that was that. Seduced, traduced and banged up to boot. Well now it was time for Alan Margoulies to show just how conscientious he really was. Now was the time for the Good Doctor to put his money (and it was bound to cost an awful lot of money, unless, that is, he was prepared to do it himself) where his mouth had so recently, so lickedly been. Bull, back in his car, gripped the wheel with ferocious strength. He felt that he might easily have torn it from the steering column and thrown it out the window, were it not that he needed it to guide him towards his deceiver.

Bull knew where Alan lived. The fool had mentioned it in passing, as they had lain together one night, entangled and idly discussing mortgage depreciation and the interest-rate crisis. Now Bull drove there fast, parked up, and concealed himself in the privet of the tiny front yard. Concealed himself in such a way that he could see in to the lighted kitchen without being seen. He peeked through the venetian blind slats and saw his lover, and with him his wife, Bull's rival.

They were drinking champagne. Alan always kept a bottle in the fridge for special surprise occasions, and this was one. He and Naomi had always said that they wanted to have a large family. They had an awareness that although the world might not need that many more children, it did need children that were brought up by overwhelmingly conscientious and committed people. Since that clearly meant them, there was something of an obligation on them to fulfil a better than average quota.

And in this new life, he could find himself a new beginning. Alan raised his glass, toasting himself as much as Naomi. (We have remarked before on Alan's awful soliloquies. And here was an excellent opportunity for one.) Shocking things still shot in front of the new father's eyes, but they were fading. He knew that in time, once he had weathered Bull's fury, that they would disappear altogether. He scrutinised the pretty features of his good wife. So that explained the eggy smell, she was creatin'. And Alan found that once he was actually aware of his wife's pregnancy his physical repulsion began to abate. He could even imagine them making love again. Perhaps even very soon. Maybe as soon as they finished the champagne.

Outside in the garden Bull saw everything. He shifted, feeling cramp in his right leg, and the swelling discomfort in his left. Hot tears rolled down his pudgy cheeks. A hot flush crept down from the roots of his ginger hair. He saw them smile together; he saw them hug one another; he saw them kiss; he saw them drink champagne. How the hell was he to know, as he watched the tragic dumb show, that this wasn't just any old ordinary evening for the Margoulieses. So Alan had lied to him about his marriage as well! He had said that it was all over, that he felt nothing for his wife, that he would up sticks and live with Bull, were it not for the possible career repercussions. And here he was carousing, with that very look in his eyes that Bull had seen before. The look that immediately preceded Alan adopting a pseudo-rural accent and saying to Bull, 'Why don't you roll over now, m'dear'.

Bull crouched and shuffled backwards out of the yard. He felt shamed and ashamed. And as he straightened up in the dark street he looked up, and over towards Archway. There it was, arching across the night. Its single span perhaps offering some sweet relief. Suicide Bridge.

He parked in a nearby street and walked out on to the bridge. Below him the lights of London spread away in a wash of low wattage. Their dimness gave the lie to the very vastness of the city. Bull heard its distant roar, its night-time sough, its terminal cough.

It was the betrayal he couldn't stand. Everything else he could have borne – even the ghastly thought of his coming, elephantiatic confinement – but not the betrayal. He no longer wanted to live in a world that harboured such duplicity. He clutched the thick, old bronze of the safety rail and made ready to hoist himself over in one, swift, practised bar vault (he was, after all, a fairly competent athlete). He was ready to meet him, or her. Whoever the sick joker was, whom he must perforce call his maker.

Epilogue

B UT BULL DIDN'T kill himself. Instead, hiding his pregnant leg inside a pair of hopelessly unfashionable loon trousers that he found in the bottom of his wardrobe, he fled to San Francisco.

There, by the Bay, where the light quality alone assists in the suspension of disbelief, and people are more accustomed to the bizarre, Bull had his and Alan's love child. It was a boy, and Bull, in some lurch of atavism, had it baptised an Episcopalian.

The clinic's exorbitant fees and even more exorbitant hush money were, surprisingly enough, paid in full under Bull's special rugby injury policy. Which just goes to show that actuaries really have their work cut out for them nowadays.

If you're ever passing Cardiff Arms Park – not that that many people do just that – drop in and visit the sports goods and memorabilia shop there. A large, gingerish man will welcome you. And even if you quite clearly aren't going to buy anything, he'll make you feel at home with his easy charm and his frank and open features.

Although not a Welshman, Bull has become entirely

accepted here. His enthusiasm for the great game is never in doubt. As a single parent he did arouse some comment amongst the sporting community when he came to live in Cardiff. But over the years his large and darkly handsome son Kenneth has become popular with the local kids, very much one of the boys.

THE QUANTITY THEORY OF INSANITY

'He writes like a devil'
MAIL ON SUNDAY

This is the sparkling debut with which Will Self burst onto the literary scene. In it, we discover a superhumanly dull tribe of Amazonians, the terrible, seductive secret of Ward 9 and why you are right to think that London is full of dead people. Full of his trademark jagged-edge satire and dark wit, this short-story collection is acerbic, hilarious and, most of all, utterly unique in its imaginative vision.

'Very funny and very good, with that unmistakable sign of the genuine comic writer's absurdity that unfurls logically from absurdity, but always as a mirror of what we are living in – and wish we didn't'
DORIS LESSING

THE BUTT

'Self writes here with an adroit impersonation of coarse exuberance that makes *The Butt* as readable as a blokeish airport novel ... Ingenious'
SUNDAY TELEGRAPH

When Tom Brodzinski finally decides to give up smoking during a family holiday in a weird, unnamed land, a moment's inattention becomes his undoing. Flipping the butt of his last cigarette off the balcony of the holiday apartment, it lands on the head of the elderly Reggie Lincoln, and burns him. Despite Brodzinski's liberal attitudes and good intentions, the local authorities treat his action as an assault. Soon the full weight of the courts and tribal custom is brought to bear. What follows is a journey through a fantastically distorted world, a country that is part Australia, part Iraq and entirely the heart of distinctively modern darkness.

'*The Butt* is Self's most gripping and disturbing novel in years'
HARPER'S BAZAAR

MY IDEA OF FUN

'This is a brilliant first novel, obscene, funny, opulently written, and, of course, agonisingly moral'
OBSERVER

Ian Wharton is having devilish and murderous thoughts, courtesy of the influence of Mr Broadhurst – companion, confidant and the manifestation of Ian's mental illness – who is now apparently being carried around in his wife's womb. How he got there isn't important (though Dr Gyggle, Ian's psychiatrist, might disagree), but what he wants from Ian certainly is...

'No one else I can think of writes about contemporary Britain with such élan, energy and witty intelligence. Rejoice'
NICHOLAS LEZARD, GUARDIAN

GREY AREA

'Brilliantly original, Will Self is one of those rare writers whose imaginations change for ever the way we see the world'
J.G. BALLARD

The stories in this bizarre and disturbing collection include the revelation of the eight people who control the whole of London life; a nightmare vision of Soho where every waiter is an unpublished novelist; a poetic tour of the British motorway; and a heady night in the home of a bickering couple. This is a truly inimitable showcase of short stories.

'A demon lover, a model village and office paraphernalia are springboards for Self's bizarre flights of fancy ... this collection explores strange worlds which have mutated out of our own'
TIBOR FISCHER, FINANCIAL TIMES

BLOOMSBURY

GREAT APES

'A brick dropped into the stagnant pond of contemporary English prose'
NEW STATESMAN

When Simon Dykes wakes one morning, he discovers that his girlfriend has turned into a chimpanzee. And, to his horror, so has the rest of humanity. His bizarre delusion that he is 'human' brings Simon to the attention of eminent psychologist (and chimp), Dr Zack Busner. For, with this fascinating case, Busner thinks he may finally make his reputation as a truly great ape.

'Exultantly hallucinogenic ... achieves the rare feat of temporarily altering the reader's perspective'
GUARDIAN

WALKING TO HOLLYWOOD

'Apocalyptic humour and fizzing contempt'
Guardian

Obsessive, satirical and elegiac, in *Walking to Hollywood* Will Self burrows through the intersections of time, place and psyche to explore some of our deepest fears and anxieties with characteristic fearlessness and jagged humour, pushing memoir to the limits of invention.

'Extremely funny ... quintessentially Selfish – dazzling'
Times Literary Supplement

BLOOMSBURY

THE SWEET SMELL OF PSYCHOSIS

'A tour de force'
TIME OUT

Thrust into the seedy underworld of hack reporters and Soho drinking dens, young Richard Hermes is skidding down a cocaine slope of self-destruction in pursuit of the impossibly beautiful socialite-cum-columnist Ursula Bentley. But between Richard and his object of desire stands his omnipresent nemesis, the lubricious Bell, doyen of late night radio shows, provider of drugs and gossip, and ringmaster of the Sealink Club. Erudite and witty as ever, this hilarious novella is vintage Self at his acerbic, incisive best, brilliantly illustrated by Martin Rowson's sharp, dark, satirical pen.

'Self is the master of the art of a telling sentence'
OBSERVER

JUNK MAIL

'An explosive collection'
J.G. BALLARD, GUARDIAN

Martin Amis, William Burroughs and Damien Hirst; East End crack dens, cocaine and hallucinogens; English culture, satanic abuse and severed heads in liquid nitrogen. Punctuated by his other-worldly cartoons, *Junk Mail* is a Self-selection of his most brilliant essays; an innovative and irreverent trawl through a landscape of drugs, literature, politics, art and motorways.

'Locking antlers with his personal gods of British fiction, we finally get the undivided Self in all his maddening brilliance'
SPECTATOR